THE RECKONING

BOOKS BY TEYLA BRANTON

Unbounded Series
The Change
The Cure
The Escape
The Reckoning

Under the Name Rachel Branton
Tell Me No Lies
Your Eyes Don't Lie

AN UNBOUNDED NOVEL

THE RECKONING

TEYLA BRANTON

*Daniel Boone
Regional Library*

White Star Press

This is a work of fiction, and the views expressed herein are the sole responsibility of the author. Likewise, certain characters, places, and incidents are the product of the author's imagination, and any resemblance to actual persons, living or dead, or actual events or locales, is entirely coincidental.

The Reckoning (Unbounded Series #4)

Published by White Star Press
P.O. Box 353
American Fork, Utah 84003

Printed in the United States of America
ISBN: 978-1-939203-47-2
Year of first printing: 2014

To my husband, TJ, who is my greatest help,
my biggest defender, the father of my seven children,
the source of all kinds of fascinating information, and
my partner in crime. I'm glad we share so many interests,
especially of the science fictional kind. You are my hero, my
fixer of all problems, and my best friend. I hope someday
soon we will finally get that no-kids vacation we always
talked about, but

if

we

don't,

just

remember . . .

I LOVE YOU!

CHAPTER 1

WE HUNKERED DOWN IN THE BUSHES AND WAITED UNTIL THE patrolling guards passed. My nerves tingled in anticipation, my Unbounded genes kicking in. We'd slipped over the massive stone fence surrounding the estate but were still far from our goal and the evidence we'd come to steal. Intel on a recovered thumb drive had led us here, but we didn't know for sure that our information was correct. Not one communication circuit in the world had made even a roundabout mention of it, which meant those responsible were being careful not to use any regular channels.

The large house didn't appear different from its neighbors, at least not visually. Aerial photographs taken of West Lake Hills, a suburb of Austin, Texas, showed only a sprawling mansion with manicured lawns, stables, a tennis court, an elaborate swimming pool, two connecting guesthouses, and a parking lot rivaling those found outside many shopping malls. It was rumored to have a second pool inside the house itself, along with a race track and two racquetball courts.

None of this was unusual for Mr. Desoto, a billionaire whose various companies held several important US defense contracts. Even the security of patrolling guards wasn't that far out of the ordinary. But the fact that I couldn't sense inside the house meant they had Emporium technology and were aware that someone like me existed.

"Ready?" Ritter Langton asked. Even in the dark and with my mind shield closed, his presence was tangible to me. Tangible and compelling. I had the ability to see all life forces, even if their thoughts were blocked, but I perceived him differently. Probably because I considered him mine.

I nodded, reaching for the hood I carried in my pocket to cover my pale skin and blond hair. Next to me, the dark-haired Mari Jorgenson did the same. The hood was made of metamaterials like the bodysuits we wore, or in other words, particles smaller than the wavelength of light. Cort had been working on them for the past century, and finally technology was catching up to his theories. Though these new prototypes didn't make the wearer truly invisible, they helped hide us in the dark.

Ritter glided to the edge of the bushes, his sharp eyes penetrating the darkness, searching for signs of danger. He wouldn't be going inside the house because Mari and I planned to shift out once the shield was down, and we couldn't take him along with us, but he'd be close in case something unexpected happened. Hopefully close enough for me to use his combat ability if we ran into problems. I was good, but next to his ability, I looked like a beginner.

"Check your suit's heat nullifiers." Stella Davis, the fourth member of our party, glanced up from a small tablet she held in her hand. "I can't guarantee they'll have infrared, but if this information is as important as I think it is, they'll have something in place to check heat sources for anything larger than a cat." She took out a device twice as thick as my cell phone. "Here it is."

I was supposed to plug the decoder into any computer attached to their network, and it would give Stella access to their computers so she could disable the house's shields.

"Be careful," Stella added. For all her two centuries of experience with ops, her slanted eyes radiated nervousness. That was because Mari was one of Stella's two descendants to survive our ongoing conflict with the Emporium, and Stella really didn't like her going inside the house. Being nearly immortal didn't mean as much as it might when your worst enemies were every bit as immortal and knew exactly how to permanently end your existence.

Stella put on a blinking headset that looked somewhat like a thin crown with tiny pieces of metal that worked their way past her sleek, dark hair to make contact with her scalp, providing a neural link to her computer. As a techno-path, she could use the device to compare and manipulate data at a rate several dozen times that of an average human. Even with the odd-looking headset, Stella was arrestingly beautiful, owing in part to her half-Japanese heritage, but mostly because of the nanites she controlled inside her body, enhancing her features faster than her Unbounded genes could put them back to normal.

"I'll let you know when it's in place," I said. I didn't tell Stella I'd take care of Mari; she already knew. We Renegades, self-appointed guardians to a mortal human world, who for the most part were unaware of our existence, took care of our own. We were closer than family.

"What if the shield isn't connected to their computer?" Mari asked, almost startling me with her closeness, though I could clearly sense her life force in my mind. The metamaterial suit did seem to help her with stealth. Not that she, a shifter, needed improvement in that area.

"The shield is generated by electricity." Stella pulled a knit hat over her headset to obscure the tiny blinking lights. "If the controls aren't linked to their network, I'll simply find their outside circuits and blow them up." She gave Mari a bland grin. "Don't worry. If you run into trouble, I'll sic Ritter on them. We'll make sure you can shift out."

Mari couldn't teleport past the invisible barrier any more than I could sense past it. But that was only an annoyance, not an insurmountable obstacle.

"Just don't blow up the house until we're out." This I said mostly for Ritter, who as a combat Unbounded sometimes got a bit too much into his work.

He looked my way, his eyes black and glittering in the dark, sending a delicious wave of heat through me. I put in my earbud, checked the attached mic, and pulled on my hood. "Ready."

Ritter led the way. Had he wanted, he could have left us far behind. Even without the new suit, he could move fast enough that he was difficult to see. If he dropped his mental barrier, I could channel his ability, but it wasn't necessary now, and doing so might alert a sensing Unbounded working for the Emporium, if any were near. It was always a possibility.

Two weeks ago, after my last encounter with an Emporium sensing Unbounded, I'd ended up with a shiny, black, snake-like thread in my head. I'd tried pushing it out, blasting it, and otherwise decimating it with my mental ability—all without result. It was still there, contained now, but I hadn't discovered its purpose. Doing so was on my short list of priorities.

Even through her mind shield, Mari's exuberance glimmered from her. So different from the accountant she'd been before her Change had made her one of us. I extended my own mental shield to cover her. She wouldn't even realize I was doing it, but it made me feel better. At the first hint of danger, she could shift back to the airfield where my brother, Chris, waited with our plane, so she was actually safer than the rest of us—well, provided we turned off their electric shields so she could use her ability. But because of her rare talent, the Emporium would pay a high price to get their hands on her and her ovaries, so I felt protective of her.

Ritter guided us unfailingly through the bushes, keeping to the shadows when we neared the house. The two-man patrol we'd dodged earlier came around again, triggering motion lights on the house. I could tell from looking at them that they were human, not Unbounded—a useful aspect of my gift—but their minds were blocked, if poorly. With only a little pushing, I saw from their thoughts that while they were familiar with the Emporium, they knew nothing about the file we sought. Not that it really mattered because we were almost certain where it was being kept. A part of me was relieved they were mortal, but another part was angry at the Emporium's penchant for using mortals. If something went wrong, mortal agents too often meant more deaths.

Deaths I wasn't willing to be responsible for.

We sat still beneath some trees as the patrol passed, but they didn't even look our way. The January night was a bit colder than it had been in San Diego, home to our new headquarters, but mild enough for our purpose, and the suits kept us comfortable. When the patrol was gone, Ritter gestured for us to wait while he took care of the motion lights. He sprinted forward across the grass toward the house. A light on the roof came belatedly to life, but he was already out of sight. If anyone was observing, they might assume some animal had tripped it. A few seconds later, the light winked out of existence.

Ritter signaled with a whistle, and Mari and I started forward. Even this close, I couldn't penetrate the shield around the house, so they had to be using a lot of electricity to maintain it. No doubt in response to what had happened in New York, when we'd gotten past their shields at a prison compound.

I removed the launcher from my back and shot a grappling hook onto the roof above a second-floor window of the spare room we were targeting. Pulling the grappling rope toward me until it caught one of the numerous chimneys, I activated the retraction feature and began walking up the side of the house as it towed me upward, my stomach clenching with revulsion.

Climbing wasn't the problem. It was only what happened once I got high enough for my acrophobia to kick in. I'd conquered it for the most part, but being someplace high always required effort. I was ever aware of the fear, knowing it would burst free and paralyze me if I allowed it any space in my mind.

"Five minutes," Ritter said in my earbud.

Five minutes during which Mari and I had to climb to the window and wait there until the patrol changed and the alarm was turned off so the guards could sign in and out for their shifts. That was when we'd force the window open with the crowbar I'd brought along for the job.

I reached the window ledge and balanced between it and my hold on the launcher. Mari was still rising with her own launcher and rope, painfully slow. Finally she shifted, disappearing from below and appearing next to me on the window ledge, grabbing her rope again just in time to stop herself from falling. Somehow she managed to prevent her abandoned launcher from banging into the side of the house as it dangled at the end of the rope.

"No way is this coming out of the eaves," she whispered, staring up at where her grappling hook had penetrated the siding instead of making it on top of the roof. "I didn't aim so well. I'll have to leave it behind."

"I'll take care of it once you're inside." Ritter's voice came to our ears. "In fact, I'll take care of Erin's, too, since I'll be up there."

I didn't doubt that he would. His ability gave him strength, speed, and agility I only guessed at even after experiencing it firsthand. Two hundred and seventy-three years of practice helped, I supposed. All of which was a good thing tonight. We hoped to be in and out with no one the wiser. It was good to steal information from our enemies at any time, but far better to do it without them knowing we were onto them. Especially when we were dealing with the Emporium and the people on their payroll.

"Car approaching," Stella said in our earbuds. "Get ready."

My free hand closed around the crowbar, sliding it from my belt. If the house hadn't been so protected, Stella would have used her technology to learn the house alarm codes, but whatever prevented me from probing the house also prevented any kind of signals from coming out. Our spybots were useless. If this house was attached to the Internet and the outside world, it was by cables buried deep in the earth.

"They're opening the door," Stella said. After several seconds, she added, "There, that should be enough time for them to have put in the code."

"You're clear to enter," Ritter added. "No one in sight on this side of the house."

My senses verified Ritter's observation, so unless there was a sensing Emporium Unbounded nearby who could mask his life force, we were good to go.

I jabbed in the crowbar, but the window didn't budge.

"Uh, any time soon, Erin," Ritter muttered.

"Why don't you come up here and do it yourself, Your Deathliness?" I put emphasis on the nickname I normally used only when he was irritating me.

"Maybe I will." His voice held a mixture of threat and promise.

I reached out, tapping on his shield. *Let me in.* He couldn't keep me out, not anymore, though he would be able to soon. All our Renegades were practicing shielding after I'd proven false the long-held belief that mind shields always worked. I'd learned that some sensing Unbounded—at least me and Delia Vesey, one of the Emporium Triad leaders— could break through normal mental shields. The discovery had come about partly because of desperation, but mostly because I was new and didn't know I wasn't supposed to be able to do it. Ava O'Hare, who was the leader of our group of Renegade Unbounded and also my ancestor, couldn't break through shields before I showed her how. Now she could break through the shields of our newest Renegades, who were mentally the weakest.

Ritter dropped his shield, and I channeled his ability, seeing immediately how to solve the problem. Mostly it was just brute force. The window slid open.

You owe me, Ritter thought.

He had no way of knowing if I'd picked up his thought, so I chose to ignore it. His Deathliness was arrogant enough without me egging him on. The fact that he was that good didn't help matters.

As I swung into the room, the shield over the house cut me off from Ritter, and I felt a yank of loss that was all out of proportion to a simple disconnect with any other person. I shouldn't feel that way, despite our relationship, but I did.

"They are *so* going to know we were here if they open this window," Mari said, sliding her hand along the frame before she closed it.

"The room's unused," I said. "It could be months."

"It's so dark." Mari flipped out a penlight and swung it around the room before snapping it off. Long enough to verify that no one lurked in the corners.

Too bad I hadn't been able to maintain contact with Ritter, whose ability gave his eyesight a boost in the dark. We were also cut off from communication until we disarmed the shield.

"Come on." I led the way to the door.

We'd both memorized the plans to the house and knew where the security room should be. Careful research on Stella's part had revealed that Mr. Desoto had installed a state-of-the-art surveillance system, complete with cameras and a dozen monitors. What we didn't know was if someone actually watched the monitors constantly. It was, after all, Mr. Desoto's residence, not one of his many businesses, though apparently our intel was correct about him storing important information here—the patrols were proof of that. Since it was his home, however, and patrols made regular circuits around the house, we were hopeful that instead of constantly monitoring their camera feed, the patrolmen would check the security room only if their computer programs alerted them to something suspicious.

We moved silently into the hallway and down a flight of stairs. The room we'd entered was far from the master suite, where I assumed Mr. Desoto was enjoying his evening, and that also meant we had a good way to go before we neared the security room where I had to plug in Stella's decoder.

After gliding through a long hallway and a sitting room, we started down the front stairs that were illuminated by a slice of moonlight shining through the huge window over the entryway. The crystals on an elaborate chandelier above the entryway glittered as they eerily reflected the moonlight. Next to me, there was a brief change in the air and a soft pop. I knew without looking that Mari had shifted. She reappeared down below and crouched behind a wall table, giving me the all-clear signal. I finished descending the stairs the usual way, and as my foot touched the bottom stair, a series of beeps came to us faintly. I froze for a few heartbeats until I realized it was the alarm being reactivated by the new patrol. Hopefully, that meant the security room was unmanned.

We continued farther into the house, nearing the kitchen. When noise of a lid settling on a pot came rather too loudly, I put my hand on Mari's arm and pressed us up against the wall of the hallway, sending out my thoughts to see who it was. I couldn't sense past the house's invisible barrier, but now that we were inside, everything in the house was available to me. The noise had come from the live-in cook, who was getting a jump on tomorrow's meal preparations.

No mental shield protected her thoughts. She was watching a television embedded in the wall, wearing headphones so the sound would have no chance of disturbing Mr. Desoto, though his suite was far enough away that it wouldn't be a problem. I saw in her mind that she planned meals only for one person the next day because Mrs. Desoto and her two teenagers were visiting her sister in Chicago for the weekend. There was, of course, no information about the security room or where Mr. Desoto might keep his top secret files.

When inside people's minds, I mostly remain an observer, careful not to touch their thought streams that appeared to me as rivers of sand cascading from some imaginary ceiling and then curving sideways and away out of sight before reaching the floor. All the scenes of their current thoughts or any memories they were pondering would fling by at tremendous speeds, showing me details about their lives. If I touched the thought stream at all, people who knew of Unbounded would immediately suspect someone was inside their minds, while regular mortals might suspect they were going insane. Permanent damage was possible inside anyone's mind, which was why I preferred to examine an unconscious person, since it was far easier to obtain information while the brain was sleeping.

But there were ways around my no-touch policy. I formed a thought of my own and set it adrift near the top of the cook's thought stream. It floated for several seconds, drifting closer to the stream, until all at once it was sucked inside.

Almost immediately, she began thinking about the security room and the nice young man who was on the night shift. I gently released another thought. A suggestion really. She should take him a tasty snack. Again, her mind took over.

Yes, some of those cookies she'd baked today and a hot cup of gourmet coffee with cream and two sugars the way he liked. The good kind of coffee and not the cheap stuff the patrol made themselves from a coffee pot inside the security room. The boy reminded her of her own son before he'd married and moved to Florida.

Keeping the link with the cook open, I refocused on Mari and the dark corridor where we hugged the wall. "Bad news," I whispered. "There's a guy in the security room, but the cook's planning to take him some coffee. Her thoughts say he's young enough that even if he's Emporium, he can't have Changed."

"If she's taking him coffee, we can use the magic powder instead of gassing him to sleep," Mari said with a grin.

The magic powder would put an average-sized man asleep within two minutes but was gentle enough that he'd think he'd just fallen asleep. It wouldn't be enough to keep him unconscious for more than a half hour, but that was plenty of time for us to play havoc with his security system, grab the information we sought, and get out. There was also a little something extra in the powder that would make the man traceable for up to a week within a certain range. It wasn't anything we'd probably need in this situation, but we never passed up an opportunity to learn more about our enemies. If he was an Emporium operative, that little addition might lead to his capture when all this was over.

I waited until the cook had the coffee brewing and had walked around to the far side of the large counter, her eyes fixed on her movie. Then I did a double check for life forms. Sensing no one in the immediate vicinity, I whispered to Mari to drop her shield. Mari couldn't shift to a place she'd never been or couldn't see—unless someone she was strongly connected to was in that location—but I could see the kitchen area quite clearly through the cook's mind, and I could channel Mari's ability.

Crouching, I shifted to the near side of the counter and reached up to drop the powder into the mug the cook had waiting near the coffee maker. Given the very small amount of powder and the reading glasses on the counter, I was positive she wouldn't notice when she filled the cup. Seconds later, I was back with Mari. *Let's move,* I said to her before severing our mental connection.

We continued down the hallway and cut through another sitting room that was near the security room. There, we waited in the dark by the door. Within minutes, we heard the flip-flop of the cook's house slippers as she moved down the hallway with her tray. I opened my senses and went along for the ride.

She knocked on the security room door. "Hey, Walker, it's me, Melissa. I've brought you some decent coffee instead of that black slop you guys brew in there."

The door was opened by a man who couldn't be older than mid-twenties. "Hey, thanks. I really appreciate it." He took a sip of the coffee, followed by a longer gulp. "Wow, this is amazing!"

"You're welcome. I know it's no fun working the night shift."

He laughed, pushing back blond hair that was, in Melissa's opinion, too long. "This job's actually ideal. I've gotten a ton of studying done in the month I've been here. If I finish my degree, I'm hoping Desoto will move me up. I'd like to work at his factory in security management."

"Which factory?"

"I'm not picky."

"You'll do it. He's good to work for. He rewards loyalty, and to take the night shift like this, you've definitely shown that."

Lovely to know they liked their boss. I felt a twinge of uncertainty. Maybe the information on the thumb drive was wrong about Desoto. After all, his business was to provide weapons to the US government. He should be one of the good guys. Yet the electronic shield around the house screamed that he was in bed with the Emporium or someone as equally dangerous. Anyone who worked for the Emporium was our enemy and an enemy of all mortals.

For all the information I was getting from Melissa's thoughts, I saw nothing from the security guard. *Walker,* I reminded myself. He might not be old enough to have Changed, but someone had taught him to close his mind. I needed to get inside his brain to see exactly what he knew. Was he an Emporium agent? If so, did Desoto know he had an agent inside his house? It made sense for the Emporium to keep an eye on him if he had dealings with them, but Desoto might not be aware that all his movements were being watched every bit as carefully as he watched anyone who might be approaching his house.

I pushed against the wall surrounding the guard's mind. It was gray like stone but was already crumbling under my touch, and I wasn't exerting much pressure. *It's the drug,* I thought.

Thankfully, Walker bid goodnight to the cook and went back to his chair behind the monitor. His thought stream was slowing. I caught images of his mother, a Styrofoam cup from his favorite coffee house, and a girl he'd gone out with the week before. Nothing about the Emporium or the information we'd come for.

He set down his coffee mug and blinked as the monitors blurred. Then he was out, the drug taking effect so fast his mind didn't even have time to register that he was tired. All at once, I was in the lake of his unconsciousness, dodging memory bubbles. More of his mother and of a woman with long blond hair. A computer in a cubical, newspaper clippings. So much information. If he worked for the Emporium, I wasn't seeing any sign of it. Not that it really mattered. Our job was to get the information, not waste time determining his loyalty.

"Well?" Mari whispered.

I swam up out of the lake and left his mind. "He's out."

The cook had long vanished back the way she'd come, so we crept into the hall and opened the door. It wasn't locked, and from the thoughts in Melissa's mind when she'd given the guard the coffee, locking it wasn't customary. Her knock had been for the sake of politeness.

"Watch the door," I told Mari as I sprinted to the computer the guard had been working on and pushed the decoder into the USB port. Codes started running across the screen. "Hopefully, it only takes out the shield and whatever is blocking communication. If the whole place goes dark, Desoto's going to know something's up."

Mari's laugh was a small explosion in the stillness. "This is Stella we're talking about. When has she ever been wrong about something to do with computers?"

She had a point, and I grinned under my hood. The thing was tight and uncomfortable, and even as I had the thought, Mari was pulling hers off and wiping beaded sweat from her forehead. Her long black hair was pinned tightly against her head, and the style made her brown eyes seem even larger in her heart-shaped face. Though she was less than a fourth

Japanese and looked more American than anything, she still resembled Stella, who was her fifth great-aunt. Mari had been a simple accountant before her Change, but now she added columns of numbers with barely a glance, folded space to teleport—or shift as we called it—and always knew exactly what time it was. She was a bit impulsive these days, and I liked her more for it. She'd come a long way from the catatonic state she'd fallen into after her husband's betrayal and subsequent murder by the Emporium.

Mari's attention transferred to the unconscious Walker, whose messy hair reminded me of my brother Jace's, except the guard's hair was shorter and had a bit of red highlighting. "He's good-looking, isn't he?" Mari asked.

I fingered the textbook next to the keyboard: *The Ethics of Journalism.* "Not my type. Or yours."

A frown creased Mari's face. She brought out a small knife from somewhere and twirled it in her hand. "You think he likes knives?"

"Not like you do. Looks like more of a pacifist to me. A bookworm."

"Well, he's cute anyway." Mari brought the hand holding the knife near her cheek and delicately scratched her cheek with her finger. "Speaking of men, did you and Stella work out that nanite thing? You've only got two weeks left before the big day."

My stomach both jumped and twisted at her words. Two weeks. Right. Not a lot of time. Before I could decide if I would answer Mari, Stella's voice sounded in my ear. "I'm in. Accessing the database now. Looks like I won't need you to enter anything from his keyboard. The decoder is enough. I still need it plugged in, though, so leave it and get going. I'll have the codes for you before you get to his office."

We left the security room, turned a corner, and continued down a hallway until we arrived at the office. As predicted, there was a lock, and Mari drew out her tools. She'd taken to picking locks almost as well as knife work.

By the time Mari had the door open, Stella was speaking into my ear with the information she'd found in Desoto's computer system. "The combination is forty-two, eighty-nine, fifty-eight, A, Q, R."

Inside the spacious office, I dodged a marble statue and hurried to the bookshelf. There, I flipped a hidden lever detailed in the house builder's plans that Stella had hacked days ago from his computer. The bookshelf swung open, revealing a panel on a door. "Repeat the code," I said to Stella.

"Here, let me." Mari moved past me. Of course, she'd remember the sequence. "This is so James Bond," Mari exulted as the door swung open.

Two easy chairs with a small table between them and a fancy wooden filing cabinet were the only furnishings in the tight space. I hurried to the cabinet and began searching for the file on Iran. I almost hoped it wouldn't be there, that our intel was wrong. Because if we were right, an unspeakable evil was about to be leashed upon the world.

The file was there. Mari helped me spread out the pages, which I carefully photographed and sent to Stella, who scanned them for readability. She directed a retake of only one page.

Mari and I were both quiet as we returned the file to the cabinet and made our way from the room, the flush of success having turned into a realization that our information was correct. Desoto really was planning to supply Iran with plutonium and help start a war.

"I'm erasing the record of the entry into the room," Stella told us. "Now get my decoder and get out of there."

"Be careful." Ritter's voice this time. "One of the patrol guys just went back into the house."

We hadn't heard any beeps from the alarm being deactivated by someone entering the house, but that wasn't unusual considering how large the place was. I linked to Mari's mind, and we shifted back to the sitting room near the security office.

A man with dark hair came down the hall. Not just any man, I saw, as he strode past the opening to the darkened sitting room, but an Unbounded. So Desoto did have Emporium agents working right here at his estate, and the Unbounded likely worked directly for the Emporium, whatever Mr. Desoto believed.

The man opened the door to the security room without knocking and didn't close it behind him. "Walker?" we heard, followed by a slap. "Hey, wake up! Those sheep can wait for counting another time. Good thing I needed coffee, or Desoto might have found you sleeping on the job. What were you thinking?"

"I don't know," came the groggy response. "I wasn't even tired when I got here." His mind shield wasn't yet in place, and I jumped inside to observe from his eyes.

"Here, I'll get you some more coffee."

"Wait, that's the good—"

Too late. The patrol guard poured the remains of the first cup of coffee into the drain of the narrow sink that was in the corner of the room, his quick, agile movements signaling his ability in combat. Even so, I was debating the wisdom of shifting in and out for Stella's device when Walker said, "Hmm, what's this? I don't remember that being here before."

"What's what?" the Unbounded turned toward him, holding a stained coffee pot from the brewer on the narrow counter.

"Oh, nothing. I think I'm still half asleep." Giving the patrol guard a sluggish grin, Walker slipped the device into his pants pocket.

Why had he done that? I was pretty sure I could make him take it out again, though controlling people wasn't easy, but I didn't want the decoder to be discovered by the Unbounded patrol guard any more than Walker seemed to want him to notice it, so I let it stay.

"You okay now?" asked the guard, setting a new mug of coffee in front of Walker.

"Yeah. Thanks for the coffee and for waking me. You saved my butt."

"Just don't let it happen again."

"I'll triple up on my caffeine. No worries."

I was about to ask Ritter and Stella if they wanted us to wait for the Unbounded to leave so we could distract Walker and grab the device when Ritter's voice came through our earbuds. "Scratch meeting us at the car. We've got company out here. We'll need your help."

CHAPTER 2

WE SHIFTED, FOLDING THE SPACE THAT SEPARATED US FROM THE others, reappearing outside in the bushes next to the ten-foot stone wall encircling the property. Stella had already packed her computer equipment in her bag, and Ritter I couldn't see, though I sensed him on top of the wall.

"What's up?" I asked Stella.

"Hunters. Apparently, they've found our car."

"You've got to be kidding." Hunters espoused a religion whose primary objective was to find and kill any Unbounded, regardless of their loyalties. To Hunters, Renegades who battled to save humanity were, by virtue of their near immortality, held in the same contempt as Emporium agents who sought to bring mortals into servitude. Many Hunter leaders themselves were descendants of rejected mortal offspring of the Emporium, and recently, they had begun tracking distant relatives to find those who had Changed. These relatives included some of our remote family members as well as those of the Emporium. The

Hunters watched them, sometimes insinuating themselves in their lives. Mari's husband had been a Hunter, and we'd barely saved her from a true and final death at their hands.

"I wouldn't kid about Hunters." Stella held out her hand. "Decoder?"

I grimaced. "We couldn't retrieve it without causing a commotion."

She reached for her bag. "Was it still plugged in?"

"No."

"Then don't worry about it. Even the fail-safe has a fail-safe. Hopefully, they'll just think it's some equipment they overlooked when everything was installed. The information will self-destruct after two hours or if they plug it back in."

That guard put it into his pocket. Why? The thought prevented me from feeling relief at Stella's words.

"I can shift back to the airport and rent a different car," Mari said. "You guys can just start hiking out to the main road. Go around the Hunters. I'll meet you there."

Ritter dropped silently from the wall behind Mari, causing her to startle. A hint of a smile touched his lips, but his voice was hard. "They aren't here because of us. They must have followed one of Desoto's employees."

"The patrol guy who came inside is Unbounded," I said.

He nodded. "I think the Hunters only chose the same place we did to park because it's the perfect location if you're planning an attack. Needless to say, they seem curious about why the car is out there."

"You think they plan to attack this place?" I asked. "How can they be so stupid? The cameras will catch them before they've disabled the alarm, and the police will arrive soon after."

Ritter scowled. "Agreed, but maybe they plan to abduct

the patrol. They have the means and the determination—and they don't care if the Emporium finds out. If they manage to take out the patrol and get inside, our advantage is shot. The Emporium will suspect that someone knows about their plutonium deal."

"So we get rid of the Hunters." I couldn't believe we had to protect Emporium agents from our joint enemy. Usually, we didn't mind leaving Hunters alone because in a strange way they were our allies against the Emporium—at least when they weren't trying to murder us. We still hadn't been able to convince many of them that Renegades worked for humanity instead of against it—or maybe they simply didn't care. All Unbounded were a scourge they had the responsibility, because of their linked heredity, to obliterate from the earth.

"Erin and Mari, you shift beyond them," Ritter said. "Stella and I'll take them from the front. Use the tranques as long as you have them." His gaze settled only on me. "Once you're there, channel my ability." His mind was already opened. *And don't get shot,* he thought.

I ignored that last bit. "How many are there?"

"Looks like fifteen, but you'd better verify. And they're packing big time."

We climbed over the wall into the unlandscaped region that still belonged to Desoto for a good couple acres until it joined his neighbor's land. The trees and other vegetation were sparse but enough to hide our approach.

As Ritter indicated, the Hunters were seriously armed, but Ritter had been right in his count, and four against fifteen was grossly unfair for the Hunters, especially since we had surprise on our side. Mari was a bit bouncy in her step, which told of an anticipation that I understood only too well. The Unbounded genes gave us a confidence that wasn't always realistic, but it sure felt good to act, especially after creeping around Desoto's trying not to be noticed.

Five of the Hunters stood in a loose circle chatting, while the others unloaded their van. *Was that a rocket launcher?* They were serious about whatever it was they had planned. One of the men was peering inside our car, obviously wondering what the vehicle was doing outside the wall.

I sent my thoughts out. The men in the circle had their minds shut tightly, which told me they had experience with Unbounded. I could have broken in, but enough thoughts radiated from the others that it wasn't necessary to expend the energy—I'd need all my strength for the battle at hand. It would be easier if we could simply kill them, but they were part of the humanity we'd vowed to protect.

"They know that guard from the security room," I told Ritter and the others as I picked up the information from their thoughts. "Walker's his name. He's been asking them questions regarding Unbounded." I focused on the older man peeking inside the car window, seeing in his mind that he was one of the Hunters who had talked with Walker. "There's not much more than that. Maybe Walker revealed the presence of Unbounded here, or the Hunters deduced what their conversation meant without him knowing about it. I can't really say."

I thought again how Walker had put Stella's device in his pocket and hadn't shared it with the Unbounded patrolman. What did that mean?

"Showtime," Ritter muttered. "On your call, Erin."

Mari grinned at me, silenced tranque pistol in hand, showing none of the reluctance that she had when using a weapon with real bullets. Her shield was gone, and I linked to her, sending a picture of the area on the other side of our car. *Let's get as many as we can before they see us,* I told her.

A brief disorientation and we were there. I reached for Ritter's mind, while still keeping track of Mari. I could only channel one ability at a time, but I could use my own talent to protect her if needed. She was the most inexperienced operative here and had shown repeatedly that she'd risk herself if she thought we were in danger. I could take out several Hunters with a mental blast, but it would leave me helpless so it was something I only used as a last resort.

Now, I sent to my friends.

I started firing. My third man fell and Mari's second before the group turned in our direction. Two men at the back dropped from Ritter and Stella's fire, followed by two more. Nine down. They opened fire. The *rat-a-tat-tat* of their automatic weapons sliced through the stillness of the night. We had to hurry.

Mari crouched behind the car, while I went over the top, using Ritter's speed. He was already there. I landed on one rotund Hunter while bringing my tranque gun down on another. I rolled as I fell. Another turned his gun in my direction, but I was already diving away, the bullets spraying the short grass. Twisting, I came around, my foot out, kicking the gun from his hand. He slammed his fist at me, but I deflected it with my left arm and jabbed my right hand into his gut. He grunted and leaned forward into my next punch. I looked around as he fell, but I already sensed everyone was down.

"Get them into their van," Stella said. "It won't be long before someone comes to investigate those shots." She grabbed a guy and started tugging him to the van.

I sent my thoughts out wider, finding two more life

forces slinking in our direction. They were dimmer than the average life forces, which meant they were shielded. Before I could warn the others, Desoto's two patrolman emerged from the trees only twenty feet away. I caught a glimpse of automatic rifles before a spotlight blinded me.

"Stop," said a voice I recognized as belonging to the Unbounded who'd found Walker asleep in the security room. "Put down those weapons."

Unbounded. Both of them, I told the others. *Mari, stay behind the car until I tell you.*

Ritter, Stella, and I dropped our tranques and raised our hands as the Unbounded moved closer. I could see a red dot on Ritter's forehead, and as there wasn't one on Stella's, I figured another must be on mine. Though the bullets wouldn't kill us, we'd be out of commission long enough to lose the information we'd obtained unless Stella had already uploaded it to our servers. Worse, we'd be back in Emporium hands.

I'd rather die a true death.

I pushed at their shields. Tight, but I could get in. Summoning a mental image of the ancient machete I'd picked up in Mexico, I jabbed it at one of the mental barriers. The real machete was back in my closet in San Diego, but visualizing its image sometimes gave me the extra force I needed to break into stronger mental barriers. The swirling black mass was tough enough that it told me the Emporium was beefing up their own mental shields. For an instant, I wondered if Delia Vesey had admitted to her people that shields could be breached by certain sensing Unbounded. I doubted it. But she could have told them we created a device to do the deed. That would protect her people without exposing her seventeen centuries of lies.

"Who are you?" demanded the second patrolman. Squinting, I could just make out that he had dark hair and a haughty manner that usually accompanied most Emporium agents. Unless they recognized us or were gifted with the rare sensing ability, they wouldn't be able to tell that we were also Unbounded. Maybe it was possible we could talk our way out of this.

Stella put on an innocent expression, apparently having reached the same conclusion. "Hey, we were just out here paintballing and ran across these weirdos. They were having some sort of disagreement. We just waited them out."

A snort from the first patrolman. "That might make sense if we hadn't seen you take out half of them. Now we'll ask you nicely one more time, who are you?"

Stella shrugged. "Well, it was worth a try. Anyway, they weren't here looking for us. They're Hunters. You know what that means."

The first Unbounded came forward to check the nearest Hunter for the telltale insignia: a hunter with a rifle. He bent over at the same time I finally penetrated his shield. His gun was still pointed at Ritter's forehead, though, and I had no doubt he could make the shot even with his momentary distraction. Just like Ritter, he wouldn't need to pause to aim.

I felt Ritter tense. *Now, Mari,* I put into her mind. She shifted, appearing behind the second Emporium patrolman, the one with his rifle aimed at me. Had she chosen him because she felt Ritter could take care of himself?

Mari's target turned, even as she appeared, his combat ability apparently warning him of a danger he couldn't yet see and hadn't planned for. On one level I was aware of her stepping close, slipping her knife almost gently up under his ribs. The guard I was linked to started to fire. I pushed hard, sending a flash of mental energy into his mind.

The shot left his rifle and I felt Ritter jerk. Yet in the next moment he took off from my side, launching himself at the guard. I sank to the ground, spent as Ritter reached his target. The man's gun went flying. Fists flew in a blur. If there had been any doubt about the patrolman's ability at combat, that was put to rest immediately. Even so, my confidence in Ritter was such that I might have enjoyed the battle, if not for the blood drenching his head and face. He looked gruesome, like something from a slasher nightmare, and his grim expression made me shudder. This was the man I hopelessly loved.

I tried to stand in order to help him, but my limbs wouldn't obey. Fortunately, even wounded Ritter was more than a match for his opponent.

"I got him, Ritter," Stella said.

I looked to see her pointing a rifle at the guard, who froze as he noticed the weapon. Ritter stepped forward and dealt him a crushing blow. The man crumpled.

Stella bent to check the pulse of the man Mari had knifed. "I was careful," Mari said. "He'll heal in no time."

"No one else has shown up." Ritter wiped blood from his face with a cloth Mari had found somewhere and then held it tight against the side of his skull. "But if we take these two with us, the Emporium will know something's up." His gaze slid to me and then skittered away.

I knew what he needed me to do. I tried again to rise, with as little success.

Stella came over and crouched beside me. "You okay? You made him miss Ritter, didn't you? It's natural you'd be drained. It always happens when you overexert yourself."

"Not like this. It wasn't as much effort as I've used before. I can still see. My head doesn't even really hurt."

Stella frowned. "It's been a rough couple months. Accumulative stress can do a lot of damage."

I wanted to protest. I'd had two weeks' rest since my last mental battle, and for Unbounded that was enough time, with the help of a little curequick, to regenerate completely. So maybe it was something more. All the Renegades knew about the shiny miniature snake—a type of mental binding—Delia had planted in my mind during our last battle and had voted to keep me active but under regular mental checkups with Ava. Knowing Delia as well as I did, I wasn't sure it had been the right decision.

Ritter walked toward us, the grisly wound on the side of his head still bleeding. I knew the request he would make before the words came. "Can you deal with those guys or should we take them with us?"

"I can do it," I said. "But even if I remove memory of us, they're going to know something's up when they wake up hurting."

"At this point, just erasing us will be good enough."

For long moments, I sat there and absorbed, pulling in nutrients from the vegetation around us. One of the best things about the Change was that we were no longer dependent upon eating or drinking but could sustain ourselves completely by absorbing. It was as natural as breathing, and we did it unconsciously, though we could increase our rate as needed. And I needed energy now.

Feeling stronger, I pushed to my feet and steadied myself enough to walk to the first unconscious patrolman. Sinking to his side, I sent in my thoughts. I was getting rather skilled at dropping into the unconscious mind and examining thought bubbles. The ability to insert false memories had supposedly been lost over the centuries, but having glimpsed at what else Delia had hidden from even her own people, that might only be more of her lies. I planned to try my hand at fabricating a memory someday, but the first time shouldn't be on Unbounded agents who would later be examined by the Emporium. Tonight I'd have to content myself in simply removing the memory of me and my companions.

Dropping into the calm blue lake of the man's uncon-sciousness, I dodged a thought bubble, looking for what I needed. There it was, at the point they'd left the gate. They'd heard the shots, and he was reporting it to the guard inside the security room as they ran, so obviously they'd left them-selves some way to communicate, even though the shield would have kicked back on. The patrolman was filled with anticipation since this assignment at Desoto's was normally boring enough to make him wish he were assigned elsewhere.

That was when they'd spotted us—particularly me doing acrobatics over the car and Ritter whirling into his opponents faster than the eye could follow. A tremor of fear mingled with anticipation rippled throughout the patrolman's body, making him feel alive and tingly.

I reached for the thought bubble, extracting the memory at the moment we came into it, making sure I took it all. Pulling it toward me, it vanished. I had no idea where the memories went after I extracted them, but it really didn't matter. I looked around briefly, hoping to discover secrets, but he was a low-level Emporium soldier, prevented by his fierce sense of loyalty from becoming too curious.

"We'll need to put them beyond those trees," I said before reaching into the other man's mind. "Just where the van comes into view. If we're lucky, they'll think the Hunters jumped them at that point and won't guess that I took away their last memories."

"We'll leave something behind from the Hunters," Stella said. "Not something too obvious. I'm tempted to leave a couple of the Hunters themselves, but we don't want to be responsible for their deaths. I don't know what the Emporium will think of why the Hunters didn't take the guards, though. If the Hunters had knocked them out, they would have taken them prisoner."

Ritter shook his head. "As long as the Emporium doesn't suspect anyone was ever inside the house, it really doesn't matter now. We can't change things."

By the time I'd finished with the second man, most of the Hunters had been thrown into their van, and Ritter was carrying the first Emporium patrolman to the location I'd indicated. "Tell him to go about ten feet to the left," I said to Mari when Ritter stopped. She nodded and shifted next to him.

Stella grabbed the arms of the second man as Mari reappeared to help her. Ritter passed them at the halfway point, unfazed by their rejection of his offer to help. "Go get yourself some curequick," Stella told him. "Or at least a little morphine."

Since we weren't in any impending danger and we didn't have any other jobs to accomplish right away, I knew Ritter would let his body heal at its naturally speeded-up rate without using the addictive curequick.

Ritter grunted, but instead of going to the car, he came to where I had staggered to my feet. "We'd better get going. We may still run into more trouble." He hesitated a second before asking, "Are you okay?"

"Me?" I forced a laughed. "Last I checked, you're the one

bleeding. Who was it that said not to get shot? You're lucky he didn't blow your brains out."

"Next time I'll move faster." As he put an arm around me and led me in the direction of the car, practically supporting my weight, his presence hit me like a punch to the gut. In a normal life I wouldn't have been able to break into someone's mind, the bullet would have hit Ritter straight on, and he would have died. Really died. Because in a normal life he wouldn't have the Unbounded gene. I wanted to weep with the tragedy of mortality.

Almost at once, the emotion passed. In my old life, I wouldn't *live* the way I did now. Or fight. Or love—with the knowledge that we had two thousand years ahead of us.

"You're not going to let me forget this, are you?" he asked, his voice the gentle mixture of amusement and determination that he reserved only for me.

"Not on your life." He might still look gory, but that only made him more attractive. What's more, I didn't care what my attraction said about me.

Stella was to drive the Hunters' van with Ritter riding shotgun, while Mari and I followed in the rental car. As Mari started the engine, a glimpse of white drew my attention to the trees near the unconscious Unbounded. I concentrated on it. Definitely a life force. A face moved into view, peering at us from behind a tree. If my impression wasn't mistaken, it was Walker, the blond guard from the security room. He hadn't been outside earlier because I'd been checking, and I didn't think he'd seen us get into the vehicles, so he wouldn't be able to identify us. Hopefully, whoever he reported to would lump us in with the Hunters.

If he had unwittingly led the Hunters here and didn't know of the Emporium or the Unbounded, he was in for a rude awakening when the man Mari had temporarily killed with the knife came back to life inside the hour. Nothing we could do about that now.

We left the van with the Hunters' unconscious bodies in front of the Austin library and headed toward the airport, taking all their weapons with us. My older brother, Chris, our mortal pilot, met us at the plane. His dark blond hair stood on end as if he'd been running his hands through it while he waited for us, and now concern filled his gray eyes as he caught sight of Ritter's bloodied head. But all he said was, "I thought this gig was supposed to be boring. Jace is *so* not going to be happy that he missed all the fun."

I gave him a crooked grin before collapsing into one of the plane's nine front-facing passenger seats. "Maybe we shouldn't tell him."

"What about the information?" Chris asked. "Is it what we thought?"

Though he'd been addressing me, it was Stella who answered, obviously having read the information as I transmitted it. "Yes, Desoto really is going to supply Iran with plutonium."

Chris met her gaze, and without trying I could feel his attraction for her. I'd noticed it before, but with his wife dead less than four months and Stella's husband gone just over five weeks, he hadn't seemed inclined to act upon the feeling. Yet I knew he had been lonely since Lorrie's murder and that Stella was great with his two kids, and I'd recently started worrying about him making a move. Stella had already lost one mortal husband, and I didn't think it was an experience she'd ever want to repeat. I didn't want to see Chris hurt.

"But they won't use the plutonium, right?" Chris said. "It's the threat of war the Emporium wants. That'll make them billions through those defense contracts."

Stella sank down into the seat next to me, placing her computer bag near her feet. "Unfortunately, their plans go much further than mere threats."

CHAPTER 3

EVERYONE WAS SUBDUED AS WE LEFT THE SAN DIEGO AIRPORT AND started toward the new headquarters that we had lovingly dubbed the Fortress. We'd made the flight from Austin in well under five hours, but because it was three in the morning, we didn't head directly to the Fortress but to another building nearby.

This second building was just as old and almost as protected as the Fortress itself, but it was closer to more businesses, so our unusual comings and goings were less obvious. On the outside it was little more than an oversized garage—and the inside was no better. In fact, except for the hidden security alarms and the underground connection to the Fortress, the place was worthless. But it kept our neighbors near the Fortress from becoming suspicious. Well, as much as was possible seeing that it was one of the largest mansions left over from the founding days of San Diego. Our recent renovations had made it the place of security I had dreamed of for Chris's kids ever since the Emporium had killed their mother.

Stella hit the garage code on her phone, and Ritter guided his Land Cruiser inside. His wound had long since stopped bleeding, but the dried blood was impressive. We grabbed our gear and headed for the wall where Stella placed her palm against the surface under what appeared to be a normal light switch. The wall panel clicked open like a door to reveal a staircase, which in turn led to a corridor deep in the ground that intersected with the sewers. It wasn't exactly a pleasant-smelling jaunt, but it was worth any discomfort to have a back door in case the Fortress was ever breached.

We owed our good fortune to one of the early public works managers in San Diego whose business expertise was only equaled by his paranoia. When the city was still in its infancy, he'd built the tunnels below, reinforced them with concrete against high water levels, and connected them to both the sewers and his newly built mansion. Then he conveniently left the intersections out of the official plans. If anyone in the city's employ had ever known about such a blatant use of city property, they were long dead now. The only copy of the real house plans, including its tunnels, had been given to Ava with the deed of the house more than a hundred years ago when she'd purchased it.

We passed several new steel doors with combination locks and a final one with another handprint reader. We weren't taking chances this time. We entered into the lowest level of the house, a basement lined in more concrete. One section of this sublevel held our workout room, furnished with every weapon available. In another part we'd built a playroom for the children, with a climbing wall, jungle gym, a slide, and a connecting theater. We'd gone too far in making them comfortable, but the poor things deserved it after the horrors they'd endured.

We took the stairs instead of the elevator to the main floor where the hallway lights were on. Benito Hernández, our maintenance man, stood on a ladder in the hallway, a cordless drill in his hands. A painting he was apparently hanging leaned against the wall. He jumped down as we came from the stairwell.

"Shouldn't you be in bed?" I asked. Benito was a hard worker, but I'd learned that he normally guarded his sleeping time as sacrosanct. He'd never once shown interest in joining us for the two-hour training sessions we held each morning at four in the workout room.

"Gotta hang the picture," he said in a thick Mexican accent. "Besides, a bit hard to sleep with all the commotion going on."

"Commotion?" At first I'd suspected he wanted a first-hand account of our doings this night, seeing as he was responsible for the intel we'd obtained from the Emporium thumb drive that had sent us to Austin in the first place, but the excitement radiating from him went beyond his usual gloating satisfaction.

"Yeah, that woman upstairs is waking up. Last night Dimitri said she was ready and he was going to let the sedatives wear off. Everyone's watching her now. Well, not the kids. They're the smart ones. Still sleepin'. Ava said to bring you guys up when you got here."

"Thanks, Benito," I said.

Ritter and Stella headed for the back staircase, and the soft suction I felt told me Mari had shifted away from us—presumably to the medical suite on the second floor. We were lucky that she'd stayed with us on the drive from the airport. She didn't travel well, not since learning to control her ability. She would have tried to shift home all the way from Austin if our scientist Cort hadn't advised her to hold off until we understood her limits better.

"I'm going to check on the kids first," Chris told me, heading to the elevator.

"You okay?" Benito looked hard at me as we followed Ritter and Stella up the stairs. "You seem a little different."

Ever since I'd helped get him off the streets, he looked for ways to make himself useful to me. In Mexico some five weeks back, he'd tried to save my life, almost costing his own. In the end, I'd saved him from being used to kill hundreds of innocent people, and he'd only become more dedicated. That kind of thing left a connection that wasn't easily ignored or severed. I was as loyal to him as he was to me. "I'm fine. Thanks. But we're not bringing back good news, unfortunately."

He frowned. "Well, it's better to know what you're up against. It's a good thing you do here. All of you."

He'd come a long way from calling us vampires, which was a step in the right direction since it looked like he was here to stay. He'd never be a warrior, but he could fix just about anything in the Fortress and could even pitch in for the cook on her day off, so the arrangement worked well for everyone.

Benito turned back at the door to the medical suite, crossing himself and muttering under his breath. Okay, so maybe he hadn't put the vampire idea to rest completely— the woman's regeneration was something he still didn't entirely comprehend—but I could live with that.

In a glass room in a corner of the medical wing, the

woman lay in a raised stainless steel basin that resembled a large rectangular sink. Much better than the coffin I'd awakened in after my accident. She'd been naked during the first week, but Mari had covered her with a small blanket that was now coated in the curequick gel that filled the basin. The yellow gel rose almost to the top, with only the woman's face sticking out. An IV of more curequick ran down from a pole and into her chest.

Ava and our healer, Dimitri Sidorov, who had over a thousand years of experience, were in the glass room with her. Two additional members of our Renegade family—Cort Bagley, the scientist who could see and understand patterns on the atomic level, and Jace Radkey, my younger brother, gifted in combat—stood near the glass on the outside next to Mari. Hardly everyone as Benito had indicated. Missing were Oliver, our illusionist, who was on loan to the New York group; Keene, Cort's half brother, who had newly Changed; and Chris, who was still upstairs with his children. Our three mortal, former black op employees were also nowhere in sight. Probably on patrol or watching the security monitors.

Jace did a double take at Ritter as we walked into the room, his blue eyes narrowing. "Wait a minute. Is that dried blood on your head? I thought this was a snatch-and-grab, no-combat mission. If I'd known there was going to be action, I'd have come with you." He made a face. "Man, I should have known. Erin always has all the luck."

We ignored Jace. His enthusiasm had its uses, especially now that he was gaining a bit of experience to even him out, but indulging him only made it worse.

"So what's up with Norma Jeane?" I asked.

Cort cleared his throat before responding. "She's waking." With his brown hair and lean body, he was the most average-looking of our group, an impression the scientist enhanced through his hairstyle and choice of clothing, but which was blatantly contradicted by striking blue eyes that saw everything. "Glad you made it back in time. We tried to wait because . . . well, we really don't know what to expect."

Meaning Norma Jeane wasn't in our database of known Unbounded and we didn't know where her loyalty lay. We also didn't know what her ability was. Several odd things had happened during her recovery, the most unusual being that while we could detect the woman's life force, neither Ava nor I had success delving into her unconscious memories. Instead of a warm lake and memory bubbles, the lake was frozen over and we couldn't penetrate. It was strange.

I walked up to the glass, behind which the woman lay motionless in the basin except for the occasional slight movement of her head. She'd changed drastically from the smelly, gruesome mass we'd brought back with us from New York after rescuing her from an Emporium prison. A rotting mass, but one that still contained a connection between two of the three focus points—her reproductive system and her heart. Though her head had been missing and her outer flesh had dried to a leathery substance, her Unbounded body had protected the most important parts of herself, allowing for a complete regeneration once she was out of her sealed prison and could absorb.

After only three days of soaking in curequick, we'd had our first surprise when she regenerated enough for us to verify that she was female and not the male the Emporium had indicated before her rescue. The second surprise came four days later when we realized that during at least part of her life, she'd been a famous actress who was rumored to have had an affair with an American president. Kennedy had also been Unbounded, his assassination faked when it became impossible to continue hiding that he wasn't aging. It made sense that they would have sought each other out, both being Unbounded, but their supposed tragic "deaths" only a year apart made me wonder at what lurked behind the public story. Did she know that he had since been really and truly killed in the battle with the Emporium?

Physically, Dimitri estimated the woman to be in her mid-thirties, and given that most Changes occur between the thirty-first and thirty-third birthdays and Unbounded age at two years for every hundred they live, she was probably over two hundred and fifty, give or take a couple decades. So perhaps Ritter's contemporary. She had dark hair and a delicate face—beautiful by even Unbounded standards. No wonder mortals had been so taken with her during her short career.

Cort had a tablet in his hands and was making notes with an electronic pen. "We've activated the one-way glass, so she won't be able to see us. Oh, there she goes."

Her eyes opened. I knew they were blue because Dimitri had checked, though apparently in her professional life, she'd experimented with changing her eye color long before most people had ever heard of contacts. Her Unbounded connections, no doubt.

It worried me that we could find no information on her. We'd contacted Kennedy's Unbounded son in Europe where he worked with our Renegades, but he had no information for us. Though Junior had seen his father after his faked assassination and before his own pretend demise, they had never talked about the woman. He'd expressed doubt about her identity, and he might be right. After all, there were people all over the world who looked nearly identical.

She'd soon be able to answer our question herself.

Dimitri was talking to her softly, his voice coming to us through the speakers above our heads, telling her how we'd found her locked in a bomb shelter below an Emporium building used for imprisonment and experimentation. "You've been here two weeks," he added. He'd shown the same kindness with me after my Change, and I still felt grateful for his quiet support that day.

To the woman's credit, she didn't start crying or asking question we didn't have the answers to. She accepted Dimitri's help to sit up, letting the curequick-soaked blanket slide down, showing indifference to her nudity as many Unbounded did, even the most conservative ones. I felt sympathy for her. Only a short time ago, I'd been the one waking up in curequick and being stared at by the people who would become my new family.

Her eyes went to Ava's and back to Dimitri before she asked the year. At Dimitri's response, she sucked in a quick breath. "Twenty years she had me there. Twenty years." Anger tangled in each word.

"She?" Ava asked.

"Delia Vesey."

"Are you a member of the Emporium?" Neither Ava's voice nor her gravestone eyes showed emotion, but I knew her well enough not to be fooled by the casual tone.

The woman looked between Ava and Dimitri again and slowly shook her head back and forth. "After what they did to me? Not a chance."

"But you were." Dimitri this time.

"If you're asking me if I ever believed in their goals, then, yes, I did. But as long as Delia Vesey controls the Triad, their stated goal of utopia for all Unbounded is nothing more than everyone bowing down to her." Her laugh was low and evocative. "Please tell me you don't work for her."

"We already said we freed you," Dimitri answered.

He continued talking to her, but my attention was distracted by Ava's mental nudge. I let her in. *Are you getting anything?* she asked.

No, and I've been trying since she opened her eyes. I can get inside her mind, and I see the sand stream, but I can't understand any of the thoughts. It's really odd.

Her life force glows brightly. She's not even trying to block. Why don't you come in here and see if that makes a difference? Bring that robe on the counter.

Proximity did make a difference in our sensing ability, as did actually touching someone, but my ability had grown so much that neither was usually necessary. *All right, but it may be related to her ability.*

We'd taken bets as to what that ability might be. Jace's guess was pheromone manipulation, where the person emitted pheromones that made them incredibly attractive to others. An obvious guess considering her reputation—if she was the former actress we'd identified her to be—but I hadn't felt any of that from her so far. And I knew exactly what it felt like to be controlled and manipulated through pheromones. It was a weak ability because most people could resist once they understood what was happening, but often great damage was done before that point.

"Ava wants me," I said to the others. As I passed Ritter, his hand lifted slightly, brushing against my hip. Warmth spread through my body to my extremities. I smiled, feeling rather full of pheromones myself.

Dimitri's voice broke off as I entered. The woman's gaze went between me and Ava, obviously noting a family resemblance in our faces as well as our matching gray eyes and blond hair. I was thirty-one, and at three hundred, Ava was physically six years older, but she could easily pass for near my age.

"My granddaughter," Ava said.

Fourth great-granddaughter, to be exact, but I didn't care to make the distinction. "Hello, Norma Jeane," I said. Up close, she looked even more like the Internet pictures of the actress, complete with the facial mole on her left cheek. Not a scar that her Unbounded genes would have eliminated, but something programed into her genetic signature.

The woman laughed. "Oh, wow, yeah. That's not really my name, you know. I mean, it was for a time."

"What is your name then?" I asked, shaking out the soft white robe in my hands.

"You can call me Jeane. Jeane Baker. I always liked that name."

"Well, there's a shower back there." I motioned to the door behind her. "We have some clothes ready for you. I'm sure you'll be glad to get out of that gunk."

She laughed again. "I actually kind of like it." She slid a hand through the curequick, rubbing it up over her arm and down her breasts. "You have to admit, it gives you quite a buzz."

I reached for her. "Yes, but that means you're already at risk of being addicted."

She sighed and placed one hand in mine and the other on Dimitri's broad shoulder. I pushed mentally at her mind as we touched, but still I saw nothing except the sand stream full of thoughts I couldn't read.

Nothing, I told Ava as I helped Jeane put on the robe. *It's as if my ability simply won't work on her.*

Ava gasped so softly I thought I was imagining it. Dimitri's dark eyes shot toward her, but neither of them spoke as Jeane disappeared inside the bathroom. Then Ava led the way out of the glass room, shutting the soundproof door behind her.

"She's a null," Ava announced, as everyone gathered around us. "Or at least I'm pretty sure of it."

Dimitri blinked. "That would explain a lot. Or at least why you two couldn't see her unconscious thoughts—"

"Or her conscious ones," Ava put in.

"—and why I couldn't use my ability to help her heal faster." He sighed. "That's going to make it tough to learn where she's really from."

"Uh, what's a null?" Jace asked, echoing my own thoughts.

Ava turned toward him. "It's an Unbounded ability that renders other abilities useless."

"So she's using her ability against us?" I asked.

Ava shook her head. "Abilities won't work on a null at any time, even if they aren't intentionally using their ability. If Jeane were exerting effort, anyone within her range wouldn't be able to use their ability."

"You mean you and I couldn't have been communicating?" I found that hard to believe.

"That's exactly what I mean." Ava sat on the edge of a desk that abutted the wall.

"Can they target it?" I could just imagine a battle where the Emporium had a null with them that could weaken our strongest fighters. A massacre wouldn't begin to describe the ending of that scenario.

"Some can." Ritter pulled a chair from the desk and straddled it backwards, laying his arms on the backrest.

"How far is their range?" I hated the idea that Jeane—or anyone—could limit my sensing just by being near me.

The others shook their heads, as if no one wanted to risk a guess, and then Cort said, "It's one of those less common abilities. Range should vary with the strength of the individual."

"There's a null with the Renegades in Italy." Stella folded her arms over her stomach in a gesture that had become familiar since her miscarriage. "I'll put out a call. But Jeane showing up here now worries me, especially in light of our discovery in Austin."

"Why don't we discuss that now?" Ava said. "We can fill in the rest of our group later."

More chairs scraped the tile as people retrieved them from the corners of the room and brought them over. When we were settled, Ava looked at Stella. "Want to give them a rundown? I haven't read all the documents yet, not like you have."

"The short version, please," I said with a half smile in Stella's direction. I'd photographed the documents, and I knew it would take days for me to read and understand them. Even channeling her ability, I couldn't digest electronic documents the way she could.

"And use short words," added Jace. Mari giggled at that while Ritter gave him a hard stare.

Stella winked at Jace. "I'll try. Mr. Desoto has several US defense contracts. He also has been secretly supplying Iran with plutonium. Everyone's heard the rumors about Iran, and apparently the fact that they have weapons-grade plutonium is true. Desoto has partnered with the Emporium, and they now have controlling shares in all Desoto's companies, as well as several other companies who hold defense contracts."

"Once it gets out," Dimitri said, "about Iran having plutonium, those companies will make billions."

"Only one thing could make them more money than the threat of war," Ritter said, his voice nearly a growl. "And that's war itself."

"Exactly." Stella nodded, her dark eyes angry but her voice still calm. "And that's why what we discovered tonight isn't as surprising as it might seem on the outside. Desoto plans not only to supply more plutonium to Iran but has also agreed to help them use it on a target."

"That's crazy!" This from Jace, but the same thought radiated from everyone present.

"It is crazy," Stella said. "Because they know that America and the other nations can't sit back and do nothing. That's why the plan is for Iran not to use the weapons themselves, but to set up a rebel faction of terrorists to take the blame."

"They're going to wipe out Israel," Cort guessed.

Stella nodded. "Israel and several US targets in Iraq."

No one said anything for long moments, staring at each other with a mixture of dismay and disbelief. We knew the Emporium cared little for mortal lives except for the comfort they could lend to their supposed godhood, but this seemed to go beyond anything they'd ever planned.

Ava stood up from the desk. "We can see that despite their failure in New York with our new president, the Emporium is gearing up to enact their ultimate plan to reveal their nature to the mortal world. If they succeed in Israel and Iraq, many people will die, including Americans living in the regions and the soldiers we're bound to send later. There will no doubt be a lot of political changes here that we can only begin to imagine. I'm sure they've had this in the works for decades. This war must be their ultimate goal, but it's possible that our upheaval of their plan to place one of their own in the presidency has pushed up their schedule. That means they haven't had time to prepare for everything, and that's where we come in. We have to make sure they don't succeed."

We all nodded our agreement, a feeling of determination taking over the incredulity in the room.

"Stella," Ava continued, "I want you to set up a conference with our allies via satellite. We'll need their take on what to do, as well as intel on any operatives they have in the area. I know you've been up all night, but I'll need you to transmit the documentation as well so they'll be prepared for our powwow."

"I slept enough on the plane." Stella opened her computer bag and pulled out her neural headset, switching on the Wi-Fi that would connect her with her ultra state-of-the-art computer system in the conference room.

"I'll also put in a call to President Mann. If the Emporium has people they plan to move into place with this action, maybe with his help we can block them." She gave a long sigh. "Cort and Jace, I need you to keep an eye on Jeane for a while until I send up Marco and George. You can take her to the room we've prepared, but don't let her have free reign of the Fortress just yet."

Her eyes fell on me and Ritter. "Why don't you two get cleaned up? Grab a catnap if you need one and meet up in the conference room in two hours. By then I will have talked to our allies, and we should have more of an idea of what we need to do."

Ritter and I left the room together, heading for the

stairs, the threat of nuclear war feeling like a burden on my shoulders. "I can't believe the Emporium is starting a war," I murmured. "I mean, this isn't just us they're fighting, and it won't be only a few random victims. They'll be killing thousands and thousands of people."

Ritter stopped and turned toward me, his face grave. "Millions actually. But war is big money, and the Emporium never has cared about mortal lives. They've had a hand in every war I've ever seen. It's exactly what I'd do in their place."

A chill rippled through me. If the Emporium cared so little for human life, what atrocities would America suffer if the Emporium Triad managed a takeover?

"They couldn't do it if the Iranians weren't on board," I said.

Ritter nodded, the muscles in his jaw clenching and unclenching. I knew he felt the same helplessness I did at the situation—and neither of us did helpless well. "Iran's hatred of Israel runs so deep that it's amazing they haven't done anything before now. And whatever Iran manages to do against the US in Iraq will make Iraq that much weaker for a takeover later. Even if it doesn't work out, I can see why the Emporium is willing to take the risk. Either way, they'll get big money. We're talking trillions."

I had to admit that it sounded logical. Hateful, immoral, and evil but still logical. Give certain Iranians plutonium and encouragement and they would be the perfect pawns. Even with their influence, the Emporium didn't have enough power yet to stand a chance of inciting countries like France, England, Germany, or Russia to acts of war. But Iran, with its holy wars, unstable regime, and splintered terrorist groups? Yes, it was perfect.

"We can't let them win," I said. "I only wonder how far we'll have to go to stop them."

He gave me a smile that showed regret. "As far as we have to."

He was right.

Ritter's eyes ran over me. "Uh, they don't need us for two hours. Are you really going to take a nap?"

I knew what he wanted—I could feel the energy flowing from him. My own exhaustion vanished at his thoughts. "I'll race you," I said.

Minutes later we were down in the training room, stripped down to tank tops and shorts, our escrima sticks flying and sweat dripping from our bodies. Ritter was deadly beauty in motion, and channeling his ability, I was almost a match for him. I didn't always borrow his ability during our training sessions, though, because he wouldn't be there at every operation I participated in. I was determined to hold my own.

Even with his ability, I seemed to tire more easily than usual, just as I had after the fight in Austin. What was wrong with me?

At last, Ritter succeeded in tripping me, and I grabbed him so we fell together onto the mat. He covered me with his weight, and the desire that was always burning inside both of us when we were together leapt to full flame. I drank in his emotion and sent my own back to him as I wrapped my arms around his torso and brought my lips to his.

"Mmm," he said, kissing me back until every inch of my body cried out for him. "That's even better."

"Well, in Austin, you said I owed you. Consider this"—I kissed him hard and long—"your payment."

"I thought you didn't hear."

I laughed. "I always hear." I kissed him again for good measure.

"So everything's set. Two weeks, right?"

"Last I heard." I knew he was counting down the minutes until our relationship was official. Ritter hadn't wanted to wait to get married, but my Change had already ripped everything familiar from my mother's life, and I couldn't deprive her of planning and attending her only daughter's wedding. Cort, who was licensed in at least twenty-five countries to perform marriages, would be conducting ours at the little church my mother had arranged in Portland.

Rolling us over until we lay side by side, Ritter propped his head up on his elbow, frowning. "You don't sound too excited."

I sighed internally, wishing he hadn't gone and ruined the moment. Deciding that I loved Ritter had only been part of the battle. He was an old-fashioned man, which wasn't surprising given his age, and he was more than eager for a physical relationship. So was I. The catch was that every Unbounded union—unless with a sterile mortal—resulted in offspring. While Ritter would be thrilled if I got pregnant, there were two issues regarding children that made me unready for the risk. Thankfully, Stella and I had come up with a possible solution.

"Well?" Ritter kissed me again.

I inched closer to him on the mat, reaching over to smooth a strand of his damp black hair. He'd dunked his head in the corner sink before our bout, and there was no sign of his wound or the blood that had previously drenched him. "I love you."

And I did. But I wondered what I would do if I couldn't

get the hang of channeling Stella and using nanites to prevent ovulation.

Renegades were particularly careful of their children and extended posterity, watching over all of them for six generations to see if they underwent the Change. In my mind it was a huge responsibility, but that was only the beginning of a much darker issue. Even with gene manipulation and altered sperm, we still had a fifty percent chance that any child we had together might be mortal. I was already struggling with how I would have to watch Chris and his children grow old and die before I'd aged another two years, and the idea of that happening with my own child seemed beyond horrifying. I loved my niece and nephew, and I'd always thought I'd have a child or two one day, but my Change and my new lifestyle had made that seem impossible.

"Good." Ritter seemed satisfied with my response and kissed me again. For a very long time, I was perfectly happy not thinking about anything else.

CHAPTER 4

AFTER A LONG, HOT SHOWER IN MY SUITE ON THE THIRD FLOOR, I was feeling rested again, but I wasn't surprised to find Ava waiting for me in my sitting room when I emerged from the bathroom in my robe. I went toward her. "Thanks for coming."

"You seemed to think it was urgent." Ava remained by the door. "We have ten minutes until the others will be down-stairs to hear the result of our meeting, and I'm expecting a call from the president before then."

"You're planning to send us to Iran, aren't you?"

"If we have to. Stella says the plutonium will go in by way of Lebanon and Syria, so stopping it en route might be possible, but so far Iran itself does seem to be your most likely destination. However, it's definitely not my first choice. One of our European Renegades was born there, and he visits regularly to check on his interests. He has people he trusts, so he's looking into the chatter now to see if there is any new information. Perhaps even a way to stop the plutonium before it enters the Middle East."

"I'm not sure I should be involved."

Her brow arched. "Exactly what happened in Texas?"

Sinking onto the couch and pulling a leg under me, I began telling her about the battle and the mental force I used on the Emporium soldier and how drained I'd felt afterwards. "And before you chalk it up to stress, I know something's different now." I hesitated for a heartbeat before adding. "I want to look inside the box." I meant, of course, the box in my mind where I'd secured the snake Delia Vesey had inserted into my unconscious mind during our last encounter with the Emporium in New York City.

Ava moved away from the door at last and sat beside me. "Do you think that's wise? We haven't been able to remove it, and if it has changed inside the containment box, it might be impossible to seal it back inside."

I unwrapped the towel from my hair, letting it slide to my lap. "I have to know. I'm worried I'll be a danger to the others, especially on an operation this important."

Delia had created that thing, that piece of whatever, and I had no idea what it might be except that it was similar to bindings she'd put into other people's heads. Those bindings, also manifesting as thin snakelike threads of shiny black, hid certain thoughts from other sensing Unbounded— particularly Ava and me so we couldn't ruin their plans if we captured the operative—but they also seemed to allow her mental access to that person from a greater distance. Maybe even control them. As far as our research went, we'd uncovered no way for the binding to be removed except by the person who created it.

"If there is any possibility that she could take control of me," I added, "we have to know. Maybe that box I made isn't as strong as I thought. I want you there to watch me open it. I have to know if there's been a change."

"We've checked the box every couple days." Ava's words came with anger. Not directed toward me, but at Delia, who seemed determined to use me to her own ends.

"Not inside it. It's different now. I feel . . . pressure. Especially after last night."

She didn't question me further, for which I was grateful. "We'll look at it after the meeting." I also knew that even if I changed my mind, she would insist on following up on my first gut instinct. That was what made her a good leader. She listened to us.

Ava took up the towel and began rubbing it over my scalp and down to the ends of my shoulder-length hair in a motherly gesture that was as unexpected as it was appreciated. I relaxed into her hands. Being with her like this reminded me of my grandmother back in Kansas. So far, the Emporium had left her alone, but it worried me that she'd chosen to stay behind.

A beeping sounded from Ava's cell phone, and her hand left my head. "Hello? Yes. I'm ready." Covering the receiver, she said, "Stella says the president is ready for me. I'm going to take the call in the conference room."

"I'll pull on some jeans and meet you downstairs."

"All right." She handed the wet towel back to me and arose, starting for the door, where she paused. "Have you told Ritter about the change you're feeling?"

I shook my head, feeling a bit ashamed. I didn't want him to consider me weak, and I certainly didn't want him to pull some macho stunt and insist that I stay where he could protect me. As much as I admired him, he couldn't beat Delia. Not alone.

Ava's lips pursed. "We can wait on that until we find out if there really is a difference."

I nodded. She left then, leaving me clutching the towel. I closed my eyes, focusing inward to my own consciousness. There was an area that was much the same as anyone else's, except I was inside my own thought stream and it seemed much larger, more like a band of asteroids than a stream of sand. There was so much space between pieces of sand, or my awareness so small, that I often didn't notice any thoughts at all but the ones I was concentrating on. In one corner—if I could call it that—there were two black boxes I'd created that were similar to the black snake, constructed from my thoughts and manifesting as a smooth, shiny substance. Inside one of these boxes, I'd stored away my acrophobia, taking it out nearly each night on the roof of our building to stare it into submission. I'd conquered it—or at least the paralyzation caused by it—but the fear never disappeared entirely. The other box was the one I'd made for Delia's evil little present to keep it isolated from the rest of my mind. On the outside, the box appeared unchanged from every other time I'd examined it.

Wait. There was something different. Two thin shoots of blue light seeped from the box, wavering and weak, traveling a short distance before disappearing altogether. Did that come from my box or from the snake inside? The other box containing my acrophobia didn't have anything radiating from it, and it had been there longer. Whatever the light was, I didn't like the look of it, but I would still wait for Ava before I opened the box. Where Delia was concerned, it paid to be careful.

I dressed slowly in jeans and a long-sleeved aqua T-shirt. I pulled on the gold chain Ritter had given me in New York along with its three gold rings. I tucked it between my breasts where I always wore it except during training. The weapons he gave me might be his way of courting, but, for me, this is what had made us real. The two simple gold bands had belonged to his mother and little sister, both murdered by the Emporium. I was now the keeper of his most beloved memories. Sometimes I worried that I couldn't be enough.

But I was going to try.

The third ring, the one with the diamond, was for our official engagement, proof that he was trying to learn my language just as I was trying to learn his.

As I emerged from my suite, Mari caught up with me. Today her long, dark brown hair was free around her shoulders, framing her heart-shaped face. Her eyes resembled deep shadows. "I can't believe all of this, can you?" She shivered. "I don't know anyone in Israel, but I looked up how many people live there and my mind keeps adding up all the deaths. Over eight million. That's the population of New York, give or take a couple hundred thousand. Or almost the populations of LA, San Diego, San Jose, San Francisco, Fresno, Sacramento, and Long Beach combined! Add that to the number of people all over the world who might be affected—so many numbers that my mind wants to count and categorize. I just—" she broke off with a groan. "Oh, let's talk about something else. Let's see . . . uh, I got a call from Oliver this morning."

Oliver Parkin, her Unbounded cousin we'd sent on loan to the New York Renegades. I really didn't want to talk about the arrogant new addition to our group, but I would if it calmed Mari down. "How is he?"

Mari wrinkled her nose. "Same as ever. A snotty, know-it-all jerk. Only talked about himself."

"He came through in the end when it mattered," I reminded her as we started down the stairs, which was usually faster than waiting for the elevator.

"Well, believe it or not, I actually miss him. I just hope he doesn't get himself killed."

I grinned, knowing that was a big admission on her part. "If there's one thing Oliver's good at, it's self-preservation. Besides, their leader knows what she's doing, and she promised he won't be in danger. If he can help them rebuild, sending him is the least we could do."

"He's probably driving them nuts." There was more than a little satisfaction in her tone.

"I'm sure he is."

We made it to the main floor conference room just as Keene McIntyre did. Apparently he'd finally decided to drag himself from bed or wherever he'd been and put in an appearance. He was dressed in jeans and wore his brown hair long and shaggy—probably to hide the disappearance of the vertical scar that had once gouged deeply into the edge of his face from his jaw to his hairline. The whole careless appearance did nothing to hide his lean good looks or the corded muscles running along his bare arms. Mari nodded at him and went inside, but Keene came to a stop and faced me.

"So what do you think of our mystery lady?" he asked. Keene was our scientist Cort's half brother and formerly an Emporium agent. His Unbounded ability was yet unknown to me—and probably to himself—and as far as I knew, he hadn't revealed to the others that he'd recently Changed. Ava knew, of course, since she shared my sensing ability, but he didn't seem in a hurry to make any official announcement.

The secret irritated me because we all lived in the Fortress together, and it was obvious to just about everyone that he was avoiding us. I wasn't sure Cort even knew about Keene's Change. There had been a lot of rivalry between them when Keene was still trying to please their father, who was one of the Emporium Triad leaders, but the brothers had always come through for each other and had ended up on the same side. It bothered me that Keene might not share something with Cort that would mean so much to him. Cort had lost too many siblings in his half millennium of life.

I shrugged. "Didn't get much of a chance to talk to her, and it doesn't look like any of us will with what's going on."

"I don't like that she's not in our database, and I never ran into her in all my work with the Emporium. She obviously wasn't a Renegade, but she was prominent enough in the mortal world that we should have noticed her existence. That means someone must have done a lot of cover up. I know you have reservations about this sort of thing, but I think you need to break through her shield and see what she's hiding."

His green eyes seemed sharp enough to penetrate clear through to my inner thoughts, and I found myself instinctively strengthening my shield. "Then you haven't heard. She's a null." I took a step toward the open door. No one else had appeared in the hall, which meant we were the last to arrive.

"A null," he mused. His eyes now seemed far away, as if searching for a memory he couldn't quite place. "Interesting."

I nodded and continued into the conference room. The space was long and narrow, dominated by a large mahogany table that was wider than average and large enough to fit twenty people if we put two at each end, though we normally didn't. Retractable monitors were set at each place, and some of these had been raised in preparation for our meeting. Benito had been at his picture hanging in here, so we had several peaceful seascapes that made me long for a vacation. All the others in our group were already present, except Chris and our mortal guards. And Benito, of course, who hopefully was back in his bed dreaming by now.

I sat in the high-backed chair next to Mari, the soft, black padding cradling my tense body. Keene settled next to me on my right at the end. Across the table from us, between Stella and Cort, Ritter drew my attention. His hair was wet from his shower and parted on the left side, the strands curving around to graze a mole on his right cheek. He'd shaved since I'd last seen him in the training room. He wore all black, and even his broad shoulders and muscled torso didn't hide the bulges of dangerous weapons hidden in special pockets of his clothing. His eyes looked black in the artificial light of the room, locking onto mine, and a sense of rightness asserted itself in my mind. I lifted my brows slightly, acknowledging the connection that ran between us.

"I just got off the phone with the president," Ava announced from her seat at the head of the table, drawing my attention from Ritter. "He's not happy that I won't give him the particulars of the plutonium transportation, but the leaders of the other Renegade cells agreed that we cannot risk him calling for any action that may alert the Emporium. The papers state that the plutonium is reactor grade and not just weapons grade. That's a significant added risk. In an accident with the plutonium, the radiation would kill any mortals within miles and endanger the operation. However, I have given the president the names we found in the documents, and he will be discreetly investigating those. If we are successful with the plutonium recovery, he believes he'll be able to permanently remove those people from office and perhaps have them jailed. We have identified twenty-two people so far, but he is still going through them." She paused for effect. "Needless to say, getting rid of these political leaders will help our cause immensely, but without the proof offered by the plutonium, it's highly doubtful we'll succeed. Everything is riding on getting our hands on the plutonium."

"So we're going to Iran?" I asked. "Or Lebanon?"

Ava shook her head. "We thought so at first. The documents you photographed identified the plutonium as being produced in Venezuela, but we had no idea of the location, and given what happened the last time at Desoto's, we can't risk going back in to check his other files. However, we've had a break." She looked at Stella, who sat kitty-corner to Ava, gesturing for her to continue.

Stella brought up a photograph of a dark-skinned man on our monitors, this time using the keyboard that was built into her place at the table instead of her neural headset. "This is Shadrach Azima, who was born in Iran four hundred years ago but has been working in Italy with our Renegades there for the past century. He's a healer, and he's made a lot of friends in Iran using his ability, so he was, of course, briefed about what's happening."

She paused as his picture slid to the side of the screen and a map of Venezuela appeared. "In comparing the names of the Iranian officials involved, he believes the plutonium is being made here." The map enlarged, and a dot appeared in the northeast of the country. "It's about thirty miles west of Guayana City in an old steel plant near the Orinoco River.

By the way, that's Guayana City in Venezuela, not to be confused with the nearby Republic of Guyana. We believe the factory is operating with full approval of government officials, which isn't a real surprise since we know Iran has been courting South America to get around UN sanctions. We also know that Venezuelan authorities have been anxious to increase their nuclear infrastructure, which is probably what they've negotiated from the deal."

Ritter frowned. "The Russians could be involved as well, at least as far as a nuclear power station. They've been open about their aid to Venezuela in that respect."

"Maybe." Cort leaned back in his chair and tented his hands over his stomach. "Though I doubt they're aware of the end destination of any plutonium produced in Venezuela." He gestured to the map on the screen. "With all the fuel reserves in Venezuela, it's doubtful that those in charge are concerned about nuclear power. It's clearly weapons they want."

"That's understandable," Jace said. He was also leaning back in his chair on Mari's other side, with one foot up on the table. "I mean, that's the only way to be considered one of the big boys, right?"

"At any rate," Ava said, "there are complications in having the factory located so close to a highly populated city."

"How many people are we talking about?" I asked.

"About a million." Stella sighed and shook her head. "But the location is a definite advantage because getting into Venezuela without raising alarms will be far easier than in Syria, though I'm working on a route there as a backup. We have allies in Israel, who have more than eight million reasons to help us."

Ritter leaned forward, touching his screen to zoom in on

Guayana City. As the area magnified on all our monitors, he said, "I'm assuming there's an airport nearby?"

"Yes. The flight plans are already filed," Stella answered. "By the time we get there, we should have clearance to land." There was no annoyance in her tone, but sometimes I wondered how she put up with those of us who processed information so much more slowly than she did.

Ritter's eyes went to Ava. "When do we leave?"

"You'll need to be at the airport by nine. That will get you to Guayana City by this evening. You'll have Erin, Mari, Jace, Stella, and of course Shadrach will meet you there. He's familiar with the area and the factory." She paused before adding, "I know you could use also Cort and Dimitri, but I think I'll need both of them to paint a picture for the president and his people about what's involved in plutonium production and the possible effect on mortals. With plutonium involved, I wouldn't feel comfortable sending you without Dimitri, but Shadrach is also a healer." She looked at Dimitri, who stood against the wall behind Stella, his arms folded across his broad chest. I knew he shared in making the important decisions for our group, though most of their discussions were private and Ava always took the lead in our meetings.

"I did work briefly with Shadrach in Africa fifty years ago," Dimitri said, "and he is one of the best. I'm sure he'll be able to take care of anything that may arise." Since we all considered Dimitri the best Unbounded healer, his confidence was reassuring.

I could see from Ava's unshielded thoughts that she would like to take Mari with her as well, but Mari was too inexperienced at combat to send in on any operation alone, and Ava couldn't channel her ability like I could, so Mari would be of more use to us. "We'll stay in regular contact, of course," Ava added, "and Stella should be able to learn anything you need to know by way of satellite. Once the plutonium is secure, we'll make sure the president is given the location of the plant. This can't be allowed to happen again."

"Can't we blow it up?" Jace asked, pulling his foot from the table. "Make sure they won't use it again?"

Cort cleared his throat. "Too dangerous. Plutonium originates in nuclear reactors, produced by the capture of extra neutrons by uranium, and then undergoes a series of decays to get what they need for a nuclear weapon. We have no idea what sort of byproducts they're storing, or what else they're producing. I doubt they have extraordinary safety measures in place, so it's possible they've already contaminated the area for miles around. They'll probably need to send in experts to clean it all up. "

"Our focus is on the plutonium they're sending to Iran," Ava said. "This is the immediate concern. The government will have to deal with the long-term repercussions of Venezuela's participation in this whole thing."

"I'm assuming Chris will be flying us to Guayana City?" Ritter had something in his hand and rubbed a thumb over it. His gaze flicked to me, and I wondered what he held.

"Wait a minute," I said as his question about Chris penetrated my thoughts. "Are we going to have to transport the plutonium?" Because I didn't want my mortal brother anywhere near it. He wouldn't be able to heal as we could.

Ava shook her head. "We're hoping to secure it in the country and have it picked up, but if we do have to fly it out, the containers should be safe enough."

I felt sick. So much could go wrong, especially where the Emporium was concerned. "Cort could fly us instead."

Chris wouldn't be happy if he learned I was trying to cut him out of the op, but I'd risk his wrath if it meant protecting him.

"Much as I'd like to come along," Cort said, "Chris is the better pilot."

I stifled irritation. You'd think someone who'd lived half a millennium could have concentrated a bit more on his flying lessons if he was going to take the time in the first place to learn.

"We'll be fine," Jace said, his face confident. "We'll make sure we won't have to transport anything." He winked and gratitude flooded me. *I'll always have him,* I thought. And it would be a long time before we lost Chris and the kids to the disease of mortality.

Ava slapped a hand on the table, interrupting my introspection. "Okay, everyone, meeting's over. Pack your gear. Shut the door on your way out. Erin, Dimitri, and I have some business to attend to before the flight."

She meant the snake. I stifled a shudder. It was time to see what was happening inside that box.

CHAPTER 5

"I'M GOING TO CHECK ON JEANE," CORT SAID, A LITTLE TOO EAGERLY. No doubt excited to learn firsthand about nulls. I was glad he was unaware of my own little science project.

Jace snorted. "Better make sure she hasn't thrown herself at Marco. If she weren't so drop-dead gorgeous, she'd be a big pain in the ass."

Cort laughed. "Oh, come on. She was only teasing you about running away to the Bahamas."

"Her hands were a little too familiar to be all tease," Jace countered. "I know a come on when I see it. Not that I'm fooling myself it's me she wants. I think she's just a bit stir-crazy after being locked up for so long." He turned to Mari and Stella. "Let's get some grub while we talk about what gear to bring to Guayana City. I need to build up my strength with a double helping of Nina's omelets."

Keene followed the others to the door, his eyes running between me and Ava, as if calculating what might be wrong.

I didn't know how I felt about working with him on this trip. Though I'd made my choice between him and Ritter, I still experienced a lot of discomfort in Keene's presence. I shouldn't because he'd never asked for anything I wasn't willing to give. Unlike Ritter who wanted it all.

Ava held Keene's gaze and something seemed to pass between them that puzzled me. His gaze jerked away as he hurried from the room.

Ritter had stood but made no move toward the door. "I'd like to stay," he said quietly.

Ava tilted her head, studying him for a long moment. "All right."

Standing, Ava came around the left side of the table to where I sat in the second seat. "Come closer, Ritter," she said. "Something's going on with Erin, and before she goes to Venezuela, we have to be sure it won't jeopardize the mission."

Ritter showed no surprise. "I agree."

My gaze snapped to his, realizing that he'd felt my unusual drain in Austin. But was it his own ability that told him I was a weaker opponent, or was there some other connection growing between us? Because these days it seemed I could feel him more than ever.

"We're going to open the containment box in Erin's mind," Ava continued. "We want to see if there's a notable difference in the construct Delia left inside her. There is a slight possibility that Delia can control Erin through it, so it's probably a good thing you're here. Your job is to make sure Erin doesn't act on any commands Delia might have implanted. Dimitri will observe her on a healer's level, while I observe from inside."

Nodding, Ritter stood behind my chair, his face immobile

but his surface emotions glowing with concern. I didn't believe he'd hurt me, but I hoped if something happened, he'd do what was necessary to keep everyone safe.

I reached out to him, slipping past his barriers. *It's okay,* I put into his mind. He nodded as I added, *But close your shield tightly just in case.*

Dimitri sat beside me and took one of my hands that were pressed against the top of the table. His touch immediately soothed and relaxed me. I stared into the healer's face. He had dark hair, a narrow nose, a trim mustache, and brown eyes—calming eyes with a wide oval shape that I'd inherited from him, my biological father. I'd long ago come to terms with how he and Ava had used my parent's infertility to create me, and in fact I was deeply grateful. Without Dimitri's genetic material, I would have been seven generations removed from Ava, which meant no chance of carrying the active Unbounded gene. No chance of ever Changing. But they had interfered, giving me not only life, but a chance at near immortality. My existence was uncertain now, that was true, but it was also exhilarating.

His calm pervaded my body. I took a slow, deep breath and let it out again. Though Ritter was behind me and I couldn't see him, his life force was a glowing beacon to me despite his strong mental shield. I would know it anywhere.

"Ready?" Ava asked, slipping into the chair next to me and taking my other hand.

I nodded and opened my mind to her.

"Dimitri," Ava said softly, "please monitor her vitals and let me know of any change. You know what to look for."

I was glad someone did because I had no idea what I was doing. I felt a tremor of terror. Delia hadn't put this thing in my head to help me. She wanted me dead. She wanted to use me first, but ultimately, she wanted me dead.

That's because you're a danger to her, Ava told me. *Show me the box.*

In my mind I led the way, kneeling next to the shiny black container I had created. *See the two blue threads of light?* I asked, hoping they were in my imagination.

I see them. Her tone was different now. Fearful? It was hard to tell. *You are stronger than she is,* Ava added, and I knew my own fear was showing too plainly.

Clamping down on my emotions, I reached out to the box, running my thoughts over it. Warmth filled me, coming from whatever was inside. I lifted the lid, opening it as if it had hinges on the back, though there were no seams.

Instead of the short, thin, snakelike thread that I'd imprisoned inside two weeks earlier, Delia's construct had doubled in width and now coiled in on itself, around and around, filling up all the space in the box and squishing into the corners. Ava gasped, or I did. It was hard to tell where her thoughts ended and mine began.

The black snake started writhing as we watched. An end slipped over the edge of the container.

Panicking, I pushed my thoughts along one of the blue lights that seemed to be more solid now. Was Delia connected at the end somewhere, or was it just a gateway she could enter later? I'd find whatever it was and sever it right now.

No! Ava told me, even as Dimitri's hand squeezed mine.

"Whatever you're doing, you really should stop," Dimitri said. "You're losing strength. Very fast."

He was right. As I pushed out my thoughts, using my ability, my energy burned like gasoline on fire.

Look at it. Ava's voice forced me back to awareness of the snake, which now spilled over the top of the box on three sides, multiplying at a tremendous rate. Aloud, Ava said, "It's growing as Erin uses her ability. The box stemmed it before but now it's spilling out, and—"

We'll never get it back inside, I finished her thought.

Not as the box is now, she agreed, *but you can make the box a little bigger and a lot stronger. It's made of your thoughts so you can change it. I'll help. Show me what you did.*

I touched the smooth sides of the container, stretching it taller. Ava followed my actions, pulling it wider and reinforcing it with her own thoughts. Now to replace the spilled parts of the snake.

"Whatever you do, don't touch it," Ritter said.

A chill spread through me. He'd closed his barrier, but somehow I'd sent him a glimpse of what was going on. Had I sent it to Dimitri as well?

"Use the sai to put it back in," Ritter ordered.

I followed Ritter's instinct, and a mental version of the sai he'd given me in New York appeared even as he finished speaking, one in each hand. The pair roughly resembled a trident without the long handles. The foot-long middle blades were smooth and blunt while the two four-inch side blades were much shorter and curved outward, serving as a hand guard. Sai were usually meant for striking and blocking but were the right weapon for this job. Carefully, I hooked the shiny coils and dumped them back into the box. As if becoming aware of its danger, an end of the snake launched toward me, but I blocked it with a sai, twisting and pushing it down into the writhing mass.

Ava slammed down the lid. Coils pressed against the cracks until I smoothed more shiny construct over them, sealing the box so there were no gaps. Ava went behind me, reinforcing my work, leaving a silver sheen of her own thoughts over my silky black ones. At last we stood back to observe our efforts.

The blue lights were dimmer now but still active. *That's it feeding on you,* Ava said. *The box stops it almost completely.*

Not completely enough. Or it wouldn't have grown so much. I opened my eyes at the same time she did.

For a moment no one spoke, and then Ritter put a hand on my shoulder. "Well?"

I swiveled my chair to face him, and as I let go of Dimitri's hand, a weakness crashed down on me with a weight that I fought to hide. As Ritter stared at me anxiously, I began pulling in nutrients, absorbing through all my pores. I caught a hint of omelet on my tongue. After a few seconds, I began to feel new strength, but the blue lights didn't go out.

Ava stood and paced a few steps, a worried frown on her face. Her chin-length blond hair had a bit of natural upward curl at the ends, and the light seemed to make the strands move like the snake in my head. I blinked away the image. "We made the containment box bigger," she explained to the others, "but that thing has definitely grown since New York."

"It feels like a parasite," Dimitri commented. His healing ability didn't allow him to connect mind-to-mind, but he was aware of everything that affected the body, and he could even stave off death for days in mortals who were fatally wounded. "I pushed back, but it didn't seem to have any effect." He frowned, shaking his head slowly. "It's not something I can cure or remove." There was an unspoken apology in his voice.

"It's not your fault," I said.

"It's draining you." Ava walked a few more steps, her clenching fists betraying her level of concern. "Even as we were building the box, it fed on your effort."

Ritter sank into Ava's abandoned chair. "She can't go to Venezuela then, not if it endangers her."

"The box is holding for now," I protested. "I admit I was worried about going on this op, but a few days shouldn't make a difference. The box will last that long. I might not have the endurance I used to, but I'm still—" I broke off, feeling abruptly self-conscious.

A grin broke through Ava's concern. "Still better than I am." Her gaze transferred to Ritter. "She *is* better. Without her, we wouldn't be able to send Mari in because she's not the fighter or the strategist Erin is. Even if I went with you myself, we might not be able to uncover the exact location of the plutonium without Erin's ability to break through shields."

"We'll make do," Ritter growled. "We can't risk her."

"I'm going," I said, standing and moving away from my chair for a show of strength.

Easy, Ava warned in my head.

I didn't look her way but remained staring down at Ritter, whose scowls didn't hide the fear and anger inside him—not from me, not with his shield down. No wonder that blue light didn't vanish. Even when I didn't try, I used my ability.

"We're talking eight million people," I whispered. "I can do this, Ritter. I have to. I just won't use my ability unless we really need it."

Ritter's jaw worked. "What if during the op, that box ruptures? Ava won't be around to help you put it back together." *I can't lose you.* This last thought from his mind sent fear rolling through me. It was a possibility. I'd seen the coils, and while they had more space now to grow inside the larger box, one day it wouldn't be enough. Briefly, I caught an image from his mind—a sword coming down on a dark-haired woman in a blue dress. Blood spilling across the wood floor. I knew she had been Ritter's fiancée hundreds of years ago, but thoughts of her and guilt over her death hadn't tortured him for months until this fear for me.

"After this op, we'll get it out," I said. "We don't have another choice." *If* we could even get it out. That possibility I kept to myself. Ultimately, I worried that it would be just me and Delia in a fight to the death—and that meant I had to learn to control that thing inside me. Either that or go so far from the Fortress that my friends and family would never be in danger.

Ritter was about to speak when the door behind us burst open. Jeane stood in the doorway, looking sexy and in control, her red blouse unbuttoned far enough to show that she wasn't wearing a bra, and her gray pants at least two sizes too small to be comfortable. Oddly enough, they looked great on her curvy figure.

Ritter was already at the door, a pistol in hand pointed directly at her head. "Don't move," he snarled.

Cort appeared behind the woman, an apologetic smile on his face. "Sorry about the interruption. Jeane insists on seeing you, Ava." To Ritter, he added, "She's not armed. You can put that down."

Ritter took a step back but didn't put away his weapon. I also stood ready, though I couldn't help noticing that Dimitri was still sitting calmly in his chair.

"I just want to know how long you're going to hold me

here like a prisoner," Jeane said in a high, breathy voice as she moved into the room with a swaying walk. Her eyes didn't meet Ava's but caught on Ritter's and held. "I'm really no danger to you."

Ritter ignored her. "We'll need to find another option for Erin," he said to Ava. "Cort might have some ideas he can share with you while I return Jeane to her room."

"You mean the one with the lock on the outside?" Jeane asked, her tone sharpening only slightly. "No, I don't think so. I'm finished being locked up. It's obvious you don't want to kill me or you would have already." She pushed back a mass of dark hair that already reached her shoulders as a result of the curequick and her Unbounded metabolism. The rest of her body slowly and seductively shifted with the movement. "You guys just put a blindfold on me and drop me somewhere if you aren't going to believe that I want to work with you."

Ritter crossed the space between them, his hand clamping down on her arm. "At this point there are many more reasons to keep you than to let you go. Are you coming nicely, or do I have to carry you?"

That almost made me laugh. He *had* carried me the first day I tried to run away.

Jeane attempted to pull her arm from his grasp, and when that didn't work, she glared at Ava. "What do I have to do to prove that I hate Delia Vesey as much as anyone here? After what she's done to me, I swear to you that I fully intend to see her dead."

"I'd like to believe you," Ava said, "but for now we'll need to detain you a while longer. However, you're right that we don't intend you harm."

"Unless you determine I'm an enemy." The breathiness

hadn't quite disappeared, and her voice was still high, but I had the feeling we were closer to seeing the real woman now.

Ava inclined her head. "Yes. You are correct." If we made that determination, it would mean sending Jeane to our prison compound in Mexico for rehabilitation or eventual execution.

"Look, we'll talk about this later," Cort said. "I'll walk you back, Jeane. There's too much going on to discuss this right now." He offered her his arm. "If you'll come with me?"

She hesitated only briefly before taking his arm with a delicate hand and then turned to stare at Ritter until he released her. "Thank you," she said, her voice full of mockery.

They'd almost reached the door when Ava barked, "Wait."

Cort stopped immediately, nearly tripping Jeane. "Yes?" he asked.

Ava's touch was in my mind. *Look,* she told me. *The blue lights. They're gone.* Sure enough, nothing glowed from my box, which meant, as I understood it, that my snake was no longer feeding.

"Ava?" Dimitri asked.

Ritter had raised his gun again, waiting for Ava's command. She gestured for him to lower it.

"Please sit down, Jeane. I would like to ask you what you know of bindings. And especially how to get rid of them."

Jeane's eyes met Ava's, one side of her mouth twitching upward with an expression that was half smile, half smirk. "Bindings don't work on me, if that's what you're thinking."

"Sit." This time it wasn't a request. Ava motioned to Cort. "That chair by Dimitri—help her find the way."

Cort walked Jeane to her chair before going around the table to sit across from us. Ava sat at the head of the table, and I settled into the first seat on her left next to Jeane. Ritter remained in front of the door, the weapon back inside the folds of his clothing but his feet apart in readiness. Everyone was tense and alert—everyone except Jeane, who I couldn't read at all.

"Why do you hate Delia so much?" Ava asked in a deceptively calm voice. Underneath I sensed the same excitement that I felt. If being near Jeane stopped the snake from feeding, perhaps she was the key to eliminating it completely.

Jeane gave Ava an open-mouthed smile and tossed her head as though she were in front of the cameras. "She imprisoned me and let me rot almost to death. Do I need another reason?"

"Why did she do it?" Ava asked. "What did you do to merit such attention? She made it clear to Erin before your rescue that she occasionally let you regenerate partially to prevent a complete death. Obviously, she had some idea of future plans involving you. Which, unfortunately, makes you suspicious to us."

Jeane sighed and leaned back in her chair. "I'm a null. She used me when she wanted to make sure someone else couldn't use their ability against her. She also tried to breed me." Her nostrils flared and her jaw clenched. "But it turns out that nulls are infertile."

We all stared at her in surprise. Copious fertility was a huge problem for people who could live two thousand years, but not having any progeny at all meant no growth, which was death for us as a race. No one to bestow your amassed wealth on, no family businesses to pass on to children through many centuries. No descendants to look after and protect. Or mourn. I'd never heard of such a thing.

"It's true," Jeane said. "Not something we advertise. Of course that didn't stop Delia from trying."

I felt the pity emanating from Ava, even if Jeane wasn't aware of it. "What do you know about bindings?" I asked.

Jeane shrugged. "Delia uses them all the time. She creates them by using a piece of her own thoughts. Or maybe it's more than just her thoughts because it gives her greater control over the person than she had before. Anyway, the bindings prevent people from revealing certain secrets. All her closest associates have them. She tried to do one on me, but it didn't take, of course."

"Do you know how to remove them?"

Jeane's blue eyes glittered with an emotion I couldn't name. "I'm assuming you have a binding you need to get rid of, but all I can say is that I don't know how. Most of Delia's assistants either died or remained faithful. Those seemed to be the only choices available." Again the mocking tone. "Except for me, apparently."

Ava was silent for a long while, studying Jeane. Finally, she came to a decision, which I silently agreed to. "Delia placed a binding in my granddaughter's head."

Jeane leaned suddenly forward. "Let me guess—the representation is a snake."

"That's right."

"She always uses snakes." Jeane rolled her eyes. "Little imagination, that one."

Ava nodded and continued. "This is definitely not a typical binding because it isn't there to prevent Erin from spilling any secrets, but it *is* growing, and neither of us has been successful in removing it. However, we have been able to contain it somewhat by using a similar binding made from Erin's thoughts."

"If Delia isn't hiding information, then she's using the binding as a portal, and once it's large enough, she'll be able to connect with it and control you." Jeane's eyes met mine as she shook her head. "I'm sorry. There's really nothing I can do."

"Well, it stopped feeding when you came into the room," Ava said.

Jeane relaxed again in her seat. "Ah. Well, yes. By now the binding has some power of its own, but it will be interrupted when I'm around. It can't feed without its link to Delia, however thin the connection between them might be. The effect is more apparent if I'm trying."

All at once Ava's presence disappeared from my mind. I could no longer sense Ritter, and even my friends' life forces were suddenly snuffed out. A deep sense of loss came over me, as if I'd lost the ability to speak or to walk, to touch or to see. Blinded as if I'd been cast into a dark pit.

"Stop it!" I said. Mentally, I cried out at the gaping blackness that now existed where before I'd experienced an entire range of feelings and perceptions. Everything in me that was Unbounded begged to permanently erase this new risk.

Jeane only smirked.

I launched myself at her, my hands going around her throat. Her chair went hurtling backward with my momentum—with her still in it. I went forward with her, exerting more pressure on her neck. Her chair slammed against the wall and we stopped with a jolt.

I pushed harder, but my mind was still dark.

Jeane tried to fight back, but she was weak and slow. She barely had a hand up before my ballistic knife was out of my boot and aimed at her heart. It wouldn't permanently kill her, but it would give her a lot of pain and me more than a little satisfaction. It would put an end to her effort to null us.

I heard Ritter come toward me but still couldn't feel him with my mind. I felt frantic, unmade.

"Okay!" Jeane choked past my grip.

All at once, it came flooding back. The life forces, my connection with Ritter. Ava in my mind.

"Don't," I gritted, "do that again. Ever." With tremendous effort, I made myself release her.

The others were staring at me with different levels of surprise—Ritter with a slight smile playing on his lips. Only Ava really understood my reaction because she knew what our gift entailed.

"Okay," Cort said slowly and soothingly, as if I were a wild animal, "I'm assuming that Jeane just gave you an example of a targeted nullification."

"Right." I sat hard in my chair, still gripping the ballistic knife. The safety it represented soothed me.

"I'm sorry," Jeane said, pulling her chair back up to the table. I noticed she was closer to Dimitri now and as far from me as she could get without moving to another seat completely. "I didn't mean anything by it. You didn't have to go all Amazon on me. There are some people who enjoy having a break from their abilities." Her gaze went to Dimitri, suddenly shuttered by lowered lids. "Imagine spending the night with a woman whose body doesn't cry out for comfort or healing but only for your touch." Her eyes went to Cort. "Or imagine not having to see connections and patterns for just one night while you lose yourself in the arms of a beautiful woman."

Next, she rotated in her chair to focus on Ritter, which made me want to tear her eyes out. "Imagine not having your senses divided while you make love to the woman of your dreams, concentrating only on the pleasure instead of the dangers that might be lurking around the corner. You can't turn off your combat senses, but I can. That allows you to feel other things more . . . profoundly." She rolled her neck, laughing lightly, the sound full of promise, but she faced the table again when Dimitri and Cort responded only with expressions of discomfort and Ritter with a slight sneer. "Anyway, I meant nothing by my demonstration."

Despite her annoying behavior, I knew what had to happen. "She'll come with us," I said to Ava.

Behind me, Ritter bristled, but it was Ava I had to convince. He wouldn't be in charge until Venezuela.

She doesn't seem to have much fighting ability, I added silently to Ava, *and she'll only be a pain to Marco or whoever stays behind.* Aloud, for the others, I added, "There are bound to be Emporium agents guarding the plutonium factory. We might be able to use her."

"Assuming she can be trusted." Ritter of course, and I would be a liar if I wasn't glad that he didn't want her along.

Jeane's lips tightened. "Look, if this hurts Delia, I'm in. After that, I make no promises. I don't much like your hospitality." Her hand stroked the red welt I'd imprinted on her neck, though it was already starting to heal.

Ava looked at Dimitri, obviously seeking his opinion. There was more between them, an unspoken attraction, but I hadn't yet determined if they were aware of it themselves. He arose and came to stand between me and Jeane, placing a hand on my face. "I don't feel the parasite feeding now, so I can verify that much. But it's still there. Like a heavy, cancerous mass. Keep in mind that having Jeane along is only a temporary fix—like your box."

"I think it's a good idea," Cort said. "The patterns around Jeane seem to be the opposite of the binding. She may even be the key to getting rid of it altogether."

"How?" Jeane and I spoke at the same time.

Cort shook his head. "That I can't say. We'll need to experiment."

Ava stood abruptly, her decision made. "Okay then. Jeane goes to Venezuela."

CHAPTER 6

FOR A MOMENT THERE WAS SILENCE AS EVERYONE ADJUSTED TO THIS new plan. "But you go too, Cort," Ava added before any of us could weigh in. "Ritter won't be able to keep an eye on her, so that will fall to you."

"What about our trip to Washington?" Cort asked.

"I'm sure the president can rustle up some authorities on plutonium and nuclear weapons, even if they don't have the experience you do. If not, well, keep your phone handy." Ava's gaze went once more to Dimitri. "Guess we're flying commercial to DC."

"Won't be the last time." His grin was warmer than the exchange called for, and I wondered if there was some private story behind it.

"Help Jeane get ready," Ava said to Cort. "Stella should be able to set her up with some clothing. You have less than three hours to get to the airport." To Jeane, she added almost as an afterthought, "Ritter will have full authority on this op. He won't ask you to do something twice."

Jeane gave Ava her open-mouthed, innocent smile. "He won't have to. Once is all he'll need." Sexual overtones oozed from the words.

Without replying, Ava motioned for Cort to take Jeane away.

"I'll go order our tickets," Dimitri said, following them out the door.

Ritter stepped close to where I still sat, bending over to whisper in my ear. "Next time push an inch lower on her neck. It'll hurt more—right before she passes out."

I snorted a laugh, wishing we were alone so I could show him just how much I appreciated his statement. But already Ava was standing by the door, her arms folded as she apparently waited for Ritter to leave.

Ritter's hand passed casually over my lap, depositing something small and warm and hard. My fingers closed over it. "I told you I'd get you another knife." His breath was hot on my ear and sent fire running down my neck. "It's special. Don't touch the tip."

The courtship of a combat Unbounded required the gifting of weapons that were valuable or important. Accepting them was paramount to accepting a proposal. This had first caused me turmoil, but I was long past that. I gripped the small casing. "I'll be careful."

He left the room so fast my eyes had trouble following the movement, but my mind followed just fine. Wherever he might go in the Fortress, I could maintain at least some thread of mental connection with only minimal effort.

Was that what Delia was able to do with me through her binding?

Ava left the door and leaned on the table next to me. "I don't trust her," she said. "Not completely, though I believe her hatred of Delia is real. It'd be different if we could see her thoughts and know what her intentions are."

"Are you thinking she's a plant?" I furrowed my brow. "I don't see how Delia could have planned that. She didn't know I'd get away from her in New York, much less bring Jeane with me."

"I agree, but that doesn't mean Jeane's plans line up with our own. I'm only letting her go because it's safer for you. At the rate that thing is growing, there isn't a lot of time left."

"That's really why you're sending Cort, isn't it?"

She nodded and put her hand over mine on the table. "Erin, you are the most powerful sensing Unbounded I've ever met besides Delia, but I would be lying if I didn't say I was worried."

"When Jeane nulled my ability," I said, "I felt like someone had put my eyes out. I can't seem to stop using it even when my shield is up."

"That's no surprise. It's just another one of our senses. You don't think when you smell or taste something, do you?"

"How do Ritter, Cort, and the others stand not being able to sense?" And to think I'd once complained of the intrusion of others into my head.

Ava laughed as she patted my hand and pushed off from the table. "I know what you mean, but I imagine our friends feel every bit the same way about their own abilities as you do about yours. You've channeled most of them. Next time pay attention to how you feel about losing their abilities when you're finished." She held up a hand. "But go easy on the channeling until Venezuela, especially if Jeane isn't nearby. We can't have that snake bursting out of your box."

I came slowly to my feet, clutching Ritter's knife like a

lifeline. "I'm going to build another box around the first one, just to make sure."

"Well, I've lined it with my own binding, but that's probably a good idea. Mine doesn't have any life of its own the way Delia's seems to."

I left the conference room feeling a little at odds. I was glad to be going to Venezuela, but the idea of depending on Jeane made me nervous. If she could stop the blue lights, she could also choose not to block them. We still had no confirmation of her loyalties.

Though I should probably join the others in the downstairs kitchen, especially to say goodbye to my niece and nephew, the roof called to me. Not because I wanted to be anywhere near the height or to experience the terrible fear, but because I wanted to prove to myself that I could control something. I took the carpeted stairs, running as fast as I could from one floor to the next until I reached the third floor. But as I moved toward the utility closet that we'd remodeled to give roof access, emotion flared from the small upstairs sitting room that intersected the hallway. I halted as I passed the room.

Chris and Stella stood near the couch in each other's arms. Stella had her eyes closed and her mouth was open as Chris kissed her. They pushed closer, the intensity of their kiss exploding until I clamped my shield shut. Even then I could feel something, and the bright glow of their life forces told me neither of them were bothering with shields.

Obviously, Stella was getting over her husband's death.

Chris's hands roamed over her back, pulling her tightly to him. Stella's hand crept under his shirt.

I cleared my throat and they sprang apart. Immediately both their shields came down tightly over their minds.

"Uh, a little late for the shields," I told them.

Chris grinned at me. "Hey, Erin." He looked at Stella again as if I hadn't interrupted anything private. "I'd better go tell the kids goodbye and then get to the airport to check on the fueling and flight plans." He squeezed Stella's hand in farewell before sauntering into the hallway, winking at me as he passed. His bright whistle filtered back as he headed toward the elevator.

I waited until the glow of his life force moved to the next floor before confronting Stella. "What was all that about?" She was my best friend, but Chris was my brother, and my first loyalty had to be with him. "I know you're not in love with him."

Stella sighed, her beautiful face grimacing in distress. "Look, it's not what you think."

"What do I think?"

She rubbed her hands over her face. "It's rather hard to explain."

I waited. That was the best thing to do with Stella. She liked people to understand as much as they were able, even if they could never process information like she did.

"You know that Bronson and I . . . we weren't physical before his death. Not really for years, at least not on a regular basis. He was just too sick most of the time. Even the baby, well, that was a good day because Bronson had received treatment from Dimitri. I—"

"This is about sex? You're using my brother for sex?"

She colored. "No! Of course not. It's nothing like that."

Though her shield was tight, I could feel the sincerity in her surface thoughts. Moreover, most Renegades were born in a time when commitment was ingrained, and one of the main differences between us and the Emporium was that Renegades valued relationships and family above all else. They didn't mess around unless they planned to stick around. I'd seen Stella's devastation at her mortal husband's death; she'd loved him deeply and wholeheartedly. Enough to stay with an aging, sick man who looked more like her grandfather than her husband. A man who apparently hadn't been able to satisfy her physical needs. "Then what?"

"I, uh—it's complicated." Pain crossed her face, and from inside the depths of her shield an emotion leaked out: agony, the black color of despair. I knew she'd let me see it on purpose. "I miss him so much," she said softly.

"Chris is my brother," I reminded her. "He's also in mourning."

"Then what's so wrong about us comforting each other?"

"Do I really need to tell you?" Because someday she'd recover and go on with her very long life, but Chris was in search of a mother for his two children—and looking to replace the love he'd had with Lorrie.

"I said it's not what you think," she repeated, pushing past me. "You need to believe that. I'll meet you downstairs when you're ready to go. I still have to look through the clothing shipment we got this week to see if what else I ordered for Jeane arrived. Apparently Ava's sending her with us."

I watched her go, wanting to yell after her, but Chris was a big boy and I couldn't live his life for him. I couldn't blame him for wanting Stella; every man who saw her did.

Deciding there wasn't time for the roof and any more inner reflection, I went to my own quarters next to the suite Chris shared with his kids and grabbed the bag that I'd packed earlier. My black bodysuit that I sometimes referred to as my catwoman outfit and the similar but heavier metamaterial suit were already inside, along with an extra change of jeans, two more shirts, and an assortment of weapons.

Maybe it was the emotions brought on by Chris and Stella's makeout session, or Ritter's gift of the small knife, but now I tucked in a red dress that was both elegant and impervious to wrinkling. A girl had to hope for some downtime. I tried not to remember that red normally didn't bring me luck; I liked the color and planned to change that. Pulling on my long leather jacket, I slipped my sai into their special pockets in the lining and strapped my machete around my waist. My nine mil was already in my holster and the backup pistol was in my boot near my ballistic knife.

I felt fully dressed now and ready to face anything. Well, anything except my brother's love life and Delia's snake.

On the main floor, I found Mari, Jace, Ava, Dimitri, and the kids in the dining area that was separated from the kitchen by a huge granite countertop where our cook Nina laid out breakfast each morning at six. We usually ate together every morning after training, but it was only a social thing and a link with our mortal employees rather than a necessity. Thankfully, the old woman used warmers—probably having learned that people who didn't need food to survive wouldn't eat if the meal wasn't perfect. It was an arrogance I couldn't see any way around, but Nina had taken it all in stride.

I poured myself a cup of her rich, gourmet hot chocolate with plenty of fresh whipped cream.

"Erin!" my twelve-year-old niece, Kathy, waved wildly from one side of the long table. "Come over here. We're talking to Great-grandma." To the computer in front of her, she added, "Aunt Erin is here. She's coming to say hi."

Kathy's brother, Spencer, jumped up from the space next to her. "You can have my seat. I'm finished eating." More like finished talking, I knew. He grabbed his plate and passed me on his way to put it into the dirty dish bin, grinning with satisfaction. He looked younger than ten, his freckled face still plump with baby fat, though the rest of him was mostly skin and bones. Both children were blond and had their mother's blue eyes. For a long time, I'd seen Lorrie's face every time I'd looked at Kathy, but that was happening less and less now that months separated us from her death.

I sat down by Kathy, only to have my hand licked by Max, the family dog, who really belonged to Jace, but who, for some incomprehensible reason, loved me the most. I wiped my hand on a napkin. I wasn't a dog person, but Max had once saved my life so I owed him.

"Hey, Grandma," I said to her face on the computer. Meredith Martin was almost eighty. Her cropped hair was white and her skin sported a myriad of wrinkles, but she was spry and her eyes bright.

"Good morning, Erin." The old woman smiled, and I felt a pang of nostalgia for the days when I had gone to her house just for the fun of talking to her. Before we had to worry about Emporium assassins.

We exchanged a few pleasantries before I said, as I always did, "So, when are you coming here or going to live with Mom and Dad?" My parents were living under false identities in Oregon after the attempt on their lives, but short of throwing Grandma into a trunk and forcing her to leave Kansas City, there wasn't anything we could do further to protect her. She liked meeting with her friends and walking down the streets where everyone knew her.

She didn't want to start over. Ava had said to give her time, that family would eventually take precedence. I was trying to be patient.

"Well," Grandma said, and I felt a sliver of hope, "I do miss all of you. I think that when I go for your wedding, I might move in with your parents."

"That'd be great. They miss you a lot." I tried to keep the relief from my voice, but my grandmother's smile told me she'd seen it for what it was. She knew me too well.

"Erin, I'm fine. These two young men are seeing to that." She gestured to the two security officers Ava had installed in the house next door, who were on constant lookout for her. Grandma Martin always went to their place to communicate with the kids on secure equipment, so the calls couldn't be easily traced or overheard, but there was still a risk.

"We should go," Mari said from the counter, where she had returned for seconds of bacon. With a last nudge of my leg, Max hurried toward her. He'd become our group mascot of sorts since he'd moved in and knew how to work the system in a way that resulted in the most bacon possible.

"Gotta go, Grandma," I said.

"See you in two weeks."

My stomach flopped at the mention of my upcoming nuptials. "Yeah."

"Bye, Great-grandma." Kathy clicked to disconnect the call.

I arose and nearly spilled the cup in my hand when Kathy hugged me. "You'll take care of Dad, right?" she asked.

"Yeah. Of course. Jace and I will."

"Good," Kathy said, "because he sometimes forgets he's not like you." The children had accepted the near immortality thing a lot easier than most mortals. Almost every day they asked Cort if he'd made any progress on a way to activate the Unbounded gene in their own bodies. He'd told them it was impossible, given the generations that separated them from an Unbounded ancestor, but their hope never dimmed.

Most Unbounded eventually realized that leaving their mortal families behind was the only way the people they loved could have a normal life. One day when Kathy and Spencer married, my goal was to see them set up far away from the Emporium's view—and far away from the danger we Renegades faced daily. Maybe Chris could even be convinced to leave and take on a new identity. I wouldn't be able to be a part of their lives, which devastated me, but it was a sacrifice I'd make willingly so they wouldn't have to live with the constant danger. I didn't think distancing myself would help when I eventually had to attend their funerals.

Leave it, I told myself. I didn't need to think about funerals now. To Kathy, I added, "See that your brother obeys Becka, okay?" Becka was Nina's granddaughter and the children's nanny who Chris had stay with the kids when we all went out of town.

"You kidding?" Kathy laughed. "Spencer has a crush on Becka. He does everything she asks."

Like father like son, I thought. Chris would do anything for Stella. I hoped Chris at least had an idea of what he was doing.

Ritter strode into the room. "Let's move."

A few minutes later, we retraced our steps through the basement and underground tunnels to the warehouse where Ritter's Land Cruiser waited.

"Do you know that I can get practically anywhere in

town using these tunnels?" Jace said. He'd memorized all the maps Chris had created of the connecting tunnels and sewage lines while we'd been in New York and had made a few more of his own. "That guy who built the Fortress might have been paranoid, but he was also a genius. We'll never get trapped in there."

After loading most of our gear into the top carrier, we piled inside the SUV, with me riding in front next to Ritter. The three other women took the middle seats while Cort, Jace, and Keene settled in the rear. Stella was strangely quiet and for once her headset was off and her laptop zipped tightly in her bag. She didn't look at me.

"What's wrong with her?" Mari mouthed over the seat at me. I shrugged because it wasn't my place to tell her. Stella was still my best friend.

Mari lasted all of five minutes in the SUV before she said goodbye and shifted ahead to the plane. I wished I could go with her. Jeane wasted no time in spreading out her belongings on Mari's vacated seat.

We were early arriving at the airport, but the plane was already fueled and ready to go. This aircraft was the corporate jet, not the smaller plane we'd taken to Austin, and inside on the right were two small tables with four seats around each, and on the left side of the aisle, two seats bordered yet another table—for a total of ten seats and three tables. A small kitchen, a bathroom, and a storage area were also located on the left side. A cargo area that looked like sailors' berths stacked impossibly close together was situated at the back of the plane on the right side just past the restroom. We typically used the bunks to transfer unconscious Emporium Unbounded to our compound in Mexico, and I was glad it was empty for this trip.

Of course, with the way I felt about Jeane, maybe they wouldn't stay empty long.

Ritter cast me a sympathetic glance. "I'll be up front with Chris if you need me to shoot anyone."

"The sooner you learn how to fly this thing, the better."

He laughed, knowing too well how I felt about letting my mortal brother head into danger. "Don't let Chris hear you say that. He'll stop teaching me."

I slid into the single seat across from Stella, not wanting to watch Jace flirt with Jeane or to hear Mari's chatter. Cort would have to make sure they behaved all on his own. Keene was already dozing in the back set of seats, his eyes shut and a baseball cap pulled down over his eyes.

Stella reached into her bag and pulled out an extra neural headset that matched her own. She extended it to me. "You want to practice?"

I almost took it but remembered in time. "The snake. It grows when I use my ability. I'd better not."

The nanites we'd injected into my body yesterday to emulate birth control were still there, though probably not doing what they were supposed to since I hadn't connected with them today. Even with the advances Stella and Cort had made with the new nanites, they still couldn't avoid an Unbounded immune system on their own and would be ejected before long. They were better and far more complicated than the programmable tracking devices we all used just inside the skin of our upper arms, but they could be directed only by a technopath—or someone channeling that ability.

"I thought Jeane's presence should keep it from feeding."

"It seems to—at least when I'm not consciously using my ability—but I'm not sure about anything else." I'd been building a second box around the first one holding the snake, and it was almost completed, but I didn't want to make matters worse before I had to.

"You've only got two weeks before you have to get the hang of the nanites. Unless you're going to be a celibate bride for the next couple decades until you decide to have children." Stella smiled. "Or you and Ritter could have a baby. There's always that option." The smile didn't reach her eyes, and for a moment I recalled quite vividly the suffering bleeding from her as she wept over her lost baby, the last gift from her dying husband.

I took the headset and opened my mind. Jeane was close enough that the two blue lights hadn't started up again as they had when I'd gone upstairs at the Fortress. I reached out to Stella. Still no blue light.

Okay. I placed the thought into her mind. I was tempted to look into her thoughts to see if she was thinking of Chris, but I stopped myself in time. She was my friend, even if she had my brother on a string. I hoped I wouldn't have to choose between them if their relationship went sour.

"Do what I showed you," she said. "See if you can get them to behave. Make sure you send those pulses so your body thinks they belong."

Channeling Stella's ability, I connected mentally to my body and all the nanites. It was as if thousands of little cameras came to life. Then I sent complicated pulses to the nanites and to all the nerves in my body, signals the nanites would echo for approximately the next twenty-four hours. These pulses would fool my body so that it wouldn't systematically expel the nanites as it did all foreign objects, especially ones that used the body's own electrical system to obtain power as these nanites did. But the signals needed to

be altered slightly every day because our bodies still eventually figured out they were foreign.

Satisfied it was working, I began directing the nanites
to my ovaries. That was when I noticed the thin blue lights
emerging from the box of snakes. Cursing under my breath,
I dropped the connection with Stella. "It's feeding. When I
exert more effort, they must increase their power enough to
slip past Jeane. I can't risk it."

Stella nodded. "Especially not if Delia's at the other end."

Maybe if I were seated next to Jeane, but then I still
doubted it. She'd have to exert her ability in an equal amount,
which would make it impossible for me to connect with
Stella. Any way I looked at it, the thing had to come out.

I glanced up to find Jeane staring at me. Even as I met
her gaze, her life force winked out of existence as if she
consciously exerted just the tiniest bit of her ability around
her own body. *The quintessential invisible woman,* I thought.
At least to sensing Unbounded.

Something definitely wasn't right about Jeane. I couldn't
see her thoughts or feel her emotions, but I did know that I
would be a fool to trust her.

CHAPTER 7

I DOZED UNTIL WE LANDED IN HOUSTON TO REFUEL, WHICH WAS thankfully quick, but over the Gulf of Mexico and the Caribbean Sea, my exhaustion had vanished. I didn't want to admit that Jeane's presence could have that much influence, but the change was so notable that I had to admit her presence was helping.

But I wasn't about to give her any satisfaction by telling her so.

Our flight had been less than ten hours, including refueling, but getting through customs at the airport in Guayana City took another hour, even with Renegade connections and a few well-placed bribes with Venezuelan officials. It wasn't something we could hurry since our cargo wasn't exactly on the approved list of items allowed into the country, but Ava's contacts ultimately came through. Soon we were camped in a cheap hotel located on the western edge of Guayana City.

"Here? Really?" Jeane said when she saw the narrow room

with its stained carpet and dingy gray bedspreads. "This is their deluxe suite?"

"It's not as if we'll be sleeping here," Mari told her. "It's just a base camp while we wait for our Iranian operative. And the Emporium won't exactly be hanging out in a dive like this. Think of it as going incognito."

"Slumming, you mean." Jeane leaned over and blew dust off a picture frame on the wall to prove her point.

Ritter turned his back on her in apparent frustration. "Azima's flight won't arrive for a few hours yet." He picked up a large duffel holding his favorite SA58 FAL assault rifle, laid it on the foot of one of the queen beds, and unzipped the bag. "That gives us time to scope out the factory. See what kind of security they have on the outside."

"According to the building renovation plans that were filed," Stella said, "they have several layers of entry before reaching the actual place where they produce the plutonium. It won't be easy to get in." She began setting up her computer on a small square table that was barely large enough to hold two laptops. The molded plastic chairs looked like something you could pick up at a hardware store for less than ten bucks each—and every bit as uncomfortable.

Satisfied that his rifle had made the trip intact, Ritter straightened. "Our best bet is to take the plutonium *after* it leaves the factory but *before* it leaves Venezuela."

"Shadrach said he had contacts here." Cort carried Jeane's suitcase in one hand and his duffel in the other. "Maybe they'll be able to help." After looking around, he dropped the bags against the wall, pushing them over slightly with his foot as Jace and Keene added more duffels to the pile.

"Even so, they won't allow any special visitors, not with

the plutonium about to go out, so we'd better hope he has something to bring to the table. Something more than just an address." Ritter's words showed his reluctance to depend on an unknown entity.

"Shadrach Azima is a capable man." Stella said. "I've known him a long time. He's joining us precisely because he has something to share."

Ritter relaxed marginally at her words. "Hopefully, but I want to make sure we have a backup plan—and a way out if things screw up."

"I still think the employees are our best bet," Jace said. "Or at least an angle we can work."

We'd already hashed all this out on the flight over and really could finalize nothing until Azima arrived. Every plan we'd come up with so far depended either on getting Stella into their computer system so we could disarm everything long enough to get the plutonium or taking the cargo once it left the factory. The one thing we all agreed on was that we needed to seize the plutonium before it reached Lebanon or Syria. Pinpointing the exact location of the plutonium would be up to me, hopefully with help from Azima. That meant using my ability.

"We'll know more once I get a feel for the setup." Ritter's eyes scanned the group. "Jace and Cort, you come with me. Keene and Mari, you track down the leads Stella has on the people who work at the factory. We'll report back in two hours."

I stared at him. "I can't pinpoint a location inside the factory if I stay here."

"We won't be getting close enough for any of that. We'll all go back together once Azima's here."

I knew what he was doing, and I hated it. But he was the

leader, and I couldn't challenge his decision in front of the others. "Can I talk to you for a minute alone?" I didn't keep the ice from my voice. Everyone else was suddenly very busy, their eyes elsewhere—except for Jeane, who stared at us with a seductive smile on her face, as if watching us somehow gave her a thrill.

"Sure." His tone was as solid as my ice.

We went into the hall, and I started to put space between us and the room, but Ritter stopped me. "Better not to get too far from Jeane."

I whirled on him, keeping my voice low but forceful. "That's what this is about, isn't it? Her and that snake in my head."

His brow furrowed, and he shook his head slowly. "This is about protecting the most vital part of our plan. Without you, Erin, finding that plutonium is going to be a hell of a lot harder. Yes, if that thing weren't eating away inside you, I'd want you with us, but it is there and we need to work around it. I certainly can't be dragging Jeane around the factory, can I? And you going without her right now is a risk."

My shoulders slumped as all the indignation left me. He was right. I hated it, but he was right. If I endangered myself before we knew where to focus my ability, I might not have enough energy to complete the mission.

His expression didn't show pity, for which I was grateful. "Cort will fill in for you, and you babysit Jeane for him. Choke her again if you need to. That should cheer you up."

I grinned despite myself. "I wonder if her ability would still work as a barrier to Delia if she was unconscious."

"It might be worth looking into." He stepped closer to me, ignoring a couple that had emerged from one of the nearby rooms. "I'll be back soon." It was a promise that slid over my skin like his bare hand, reminding me of our future together.

"Be careful," I said.

He answered seriously. "I always am—now." Because there had been a time in the recent past when he'd cared for little but revenge. Now he had me, and that made the difference between a life of recklessness and what might actually be considered a future.

He went back inside the room for his rifle, and I contented myself by kicking the wall for several long seconds. A man at the other end of the hall stared at me, his thoughts screaming that I must be on drugs.

Pulling my mental shield more tightly over my mind to block out all the unshielded mortals in the hotel, I reached for the door just as the others began filing out. As he passed, Keene's eyes dug into mine, but I didn't hold his gaze.

"Mari," I said, "don't let Keene talk you into anything crazy."

"I'll take care of her," Keene answered.

I wasn't really worried. Scoping out a few factory employees shouldn't be dangerous. Mari could always shift back here, and Keene could take care of himself. He'd already come back from the dead several times—and that was before his Change had made him one of us.

I felt Ritter moving away with Jace and Cort, our connection strong despite my shield. By contrast, Keene was completely dark to me. As he and Mari moved away, I stopped him. "What do you know about Delia and her bindings?"

Keene's eyes narrowed as he studied me. "I never heard of them. Sorry."

I wanted to ask him if he knew what his ability was, but I couldn't break his confidence because Mari wasn't aware of his Change. Keene's brother, Cort, shared their father's ability in science and seeing the patterns in atoms, thus being able to invent new drugs, treatments, and even machinery, but Keene had a different mother, a mortal one, though her parents had been Unbounded. Keene believed his father had loved her, but Cort hinted that their father had been responsible for her death after she'd become terminally ill. The difference in opinion was still a source of disagreement for the brothers. I believed Cort, but I envied Keene's faith in a man who had treated him like a second-class citizen—a mortal—for years.

"I still have a few contacts inside the Emporium," he said. "I'll put out a few feelers about bindings when we get back."

"Thanks." I didn't have to ask him to keep it off the record. Keene worked with us and he felt like family, but there was a large part of him he kept locked away. It reminded me of Ritter when I'd first met him. Keene never expected anything, and in return he didn't share all his comings and goings, even when they sometimes concerned the group.

Stella glanced up from the table as I moved into the room, her headset blinking. "I'm into the hotel's computer, but there's nothing we can use. I'm checking the other locations they have connections with. The firewalls are a joke."

They probably were for Stella. "Great. Let me know if you find anything."

My forced inactivity wasn't really Jeane's fault, and I tried not to glare at her as I approached the bed where she sat. Her eyes followed me, more wary now that most of the others were gone. I felt a twinge of guilt at that, but her next comment killed any sympathy.

"I don't blame you for being mad about not going," she said, tossing her head. "I'd sure like to get him alone." Him, meaning Ritter, of course.

I bit back a retort because alienating her further wouldn't help my cause. "Tell me everything you know about Delia." I might have to stay with Jeane, but I intended to put the time to good use.

"Delia," Jeane said, as if deep in thought. She started to stretch out on the pillows but at the last moment wrinkled her nose and settled for bringing up her stockinged feet onto the worn coverlet. "She is definitely the strongest of the Triad members. Stefan Carrington is the face, the one apparently in charge, and Tihalt McIntyre is the brains. He's actually much like Cort, though he doesn't have the conscience his son does—or either of his sons apparently."

"Delia," I reminded her.

Jeane laughed. "She controls both Stefan and Tihalt. Oh, Stefan is strong, but Delia controls more of the little things, and those are what make up the whole. Everyone is afraid of her. Together Delia and Stefan are the Emporium." She smiled, revealing all her teeth. If I tilted my head I could see her throat. It was an unprotected expression, one that seemed trusting, but it unnerved me. "You Renegades should concentrate more on removing them than taking down the entire organization."

I had no love for Stefan, who because of Delia's manipulations thought I was his biological daughter, when in fact Jace had been the beneficiary of his stolen sperm—not something I had shared with him yet and hoped not to for a long time. But I had already determined that Delia was the most dangerous of the two. I'd thought I was approaching a point that I could best her, but what happened today with that snake in my head had changed everything.

"And how can we get rid of Delia?" I asked, noting that Stella was now watching us and not her computer.

All gaiety fled from Jeane's face. "Kill her. That's the only way she'll be stamped out for good. Otherwise, at full life expectancy, she'll terrorize the earth for another three hundred years."

Jeane arose from the bed. "But it's not a simple sword that will kill her. To get that far, you'll have to make it through her people and then through her shields. I've seen her hold a dozen combat soldiers in place with the strength of her mind."

"She can't hold me." Not unless I allowed her to. Or at least she couldn't before the snake had grown.

Jeane stepped closer to me, staring into my face. We were about the same height, but she had a fragile look about her that had nothing to do with being imprisoned for two decades. I didn't fool myself that the fragility extended to her mind.

"You could defeat her," she said. "And I'll help you."

We stared at each other for a few minutes. I still felt nothing from her except the glowing of her life force, and that was something that emanated from every living thing in differing degrees, insects to humans. Yes, she could hide that telltale sign much like a sensing Unbounded could, but she could also nullify the Unbounded around Delia, and maybe Delia herself, so that I'd have a better chance at beating the old crone.

Provided Jeane didn't have some alternate plan that involved handing me over to Delia.

"Can Delia block you?" I asked. Because though Jeane could nullify others' abilities, my experience had shown me that the stronger an ability became, the more it over-rode others with a similar ability. Delia had once bested me, but I'd more than held my own at our last encounter. And that meant I'd grown. If Delia were stronger than Jeane, she should be able to override the woman's effect on her ability. Maybe.

"No ability can work around me when I don't want it to," Jeane said, but she had hesitated an instant too long, and that told me all I needed to know. Jeane wasn't sure.

"After this is over," I told Jeane in a voice I hoped Stella couldn't hear, "we'll go after Delia." It was my only choice, really, but before I put myself in Jeane's hands, I wanted to be sure I was strong enough to block her ability or at least its effect on me. Of course if I practiced blocking Jeane right now I would also be allowing the snake to feed, which was a bit of a problem.

"Uh, Erin," Stella called, "you're not going to believe this."

Jeane and I turned together. We were standing so close that our arms brushed, and I stepped away. "What is it?"

"Remember that guard from Austin? Walker-something? Well, guess who's here? The stuff you gave him in the coffee is definitely registering on my system."

I blinked. "He would have had to leave Texas right after his shift."

"Must have already bought a ticket," Stella agreed. "Unless he's secretly wealthy and has his own jet. I didn't even scan for him on purpose. It's an automatic thing I have set up."

"He could be Emporium," Jeane said.

I felt a grudging admiration for the woman that she even

had an inkling as to what we were talking about. Apparently, she'd managed to get at least a basic briefing from someone—probably Cort.

"It does seem unlikely that he'd show up here unless he was involved with the Emporium or this whole mess," I agreed. "Where is he?"

Stella stood with her phone in hand. "A couple of miles. The range isn't very far." With a glance at Jeane, she added, "I'd better go see what he's up to."

"I'll do it." I started for the door, excited for something to do. "Guess you're with me, Jeane."

"You sure?" Stella looked at me doubtfully.

She meant if I could babysit Jeane and find Walker at the same time. "We'll be fine," I said. Jeane wasn't a match for me in combat, even without my ability, and the tracking chip in her arm would help me recapture her if she ran. Besides, I might die of boredom if I stayed in the room a minute longer.

"I'll send the link so you can track him on your phone." Again Stella glanced at Jeane, and I knew the link to her would be there as well.

"We'll call you when we find him." I checked to see that I had my phone, the local currency Stella had given me at the airport, and as many weapons as I could carry in my jeans and blouse. The weather was about ten degrees hotter here than in San Diego, and that made wearing my long jacket and my boots a bit conspicuous, even at eight thirty at night. Fortunately, I didn't need them for weapon concealment.

All the cell phones in our group were satellite phones, which meant that if there was no cell tower nearby, they would automatically connect to any available satellite, so we had service virtually anywhere in the world. The phones opened only with a code and a fingerprint, and any variation or tampering would fry the memory instantly. Even so, we were careful. You could never be too cautious where the Emporium was concerned.

The dark streets were busy with cars in this section of town, and several handfuls of pedestrians also walked to their destinations under the streetlights. With a few notable exceptions, the style of clothing didn't appear too different from that of San Diego; most people sported jeans and T-shirts, though a few seemed dressed up for a Saturday evening out. The people themselves didn't look all that different either, although there were more dark heads and olive complexions, but much of the architecture of the surrounding buildings was notably foreign to me. There were signs in English as well as Spanish, which only seemed right because most of San Diego did the same these days. There wasn't much vegetation besides the occasional flurry of palm trees, though I'd seen jungles from the plane. In all, the place was rather disappointing on my foreign radar.

Jeane stretched. "What a beautiful night." She had traded her red blouse and gray pants for a fancy, glittering white top and a pair of breezy patterned culottes that showed the bottom third of her legs. Strappy matching sandals assured me that everyone would be looking at her and not at me, which was the way I liked it on an op. "Is he close?"

"Not really. And I don't see any taxis. Are your sandals going to hold up?"

She shrugged. "I don't know. Stella gave them to me."

"Then they'll be fine." I really didn't care if they were. I quickened my pace. "So you were a movie star."

"It was a lot of fun, but sometimes very tedious. All those people expecting something. Mostly a piece of me." She gave a low laugh. "I think the next time I choose to be famous, I'll try politics."

I snorted. "What makes you think that would be any different? They wouldn't just want a piece. They'd want it all."

"There is that." She shrugged, apparently not overly concerned.

I let a few seconds go by before asking. "So, what happened to the real woman? Or are all the records forged?"

"Oh, she was real enough. I stumbled across her while searching for someone who looked like me. I needed a new identity, and she just happened to match my criteria. We really did look a lot alike. As a teen, she could pass for older, and I was young for my age—I Changed right before I turned thirty." She flashed me a glance. "Before you ask, that was three centuries ago."

Three centuries put her closer to Ava's age than Ritter's, though since he was only thirty years younger, I guess it didn't make much difference. Still, for some reason I didn't understand, it made me feel more cautious about her.

"It helped, of course," Jeane continued, "that she was one of those throwaway kids. No one really too interested in her. We lived together for three months while I sort of learned her life." A dry chuckle. "I think I rubbed off on her just as much. That was when I started with the acting."

"What happened to her?"

Our footsteps on the pavement were the only sounds for a few moments besides the muffled conversation from a group in front of us. Finally Jeane spoke. "The plan was to pay her off. Give her a nice chunk of money so she could go away somewhere and have fun. Money was nothing to me. It was the human experience I craved. Someone with a real emotional connection to the mortal world, even someone with connections as weak as hers. It wasn't like I was going to be able to step into just anyone's life."

"Where is she?" I asked again because that hadn't really been an answer.

"She was coming to see me on a set, and she was killed in a car accident." Jeane shook her head, her face full of tragedy that I knew was contrived. "It's sad, really."

You had her killed, I thought. I couldn't really prove it, of course, but if she really had murdered the girl, she wouldn't fit in with the Renegades in the least.

We walked in silence for several more blocks, the people thickening as we passed restaurants and bars. Many were obviously tourists enjoying the decidedly great weather. "He's close," I said, glancing at my phone. "Maybe in that restaurant."

"Oh, good, I could use a drink or two . . . or six." Jeane laughed.

With our metabolism, it'd take at least that many to get the mildest buzz. Which would be gone in minutes. I wasn't sure it was worth all those trips to the restroom. "Do you know Spanish?"

"Of course." A flip of her head. "But you won't need it. Not here. They'll speak English. I hear they have great beauty parlors here in Venezuela. I wouldn't mind getting my hair bleached. It's a pain having to do it several times a week. Too bad I can't use nanites like your friend Stella."

She seemed to know an awfully lot about us for having only awakened this morning. I wondered who'd been running off at the mouth. Cort liked to teach to an audience, but he was careful. *Probably Jace,* I thought.

"You can't die your hair blond," I told her. "Not yet. You haven't been dead long enough."

"Oh," she said dismissively. "Like these mortals would figure anything out except that I resemble a deceased actress who would be ancient now had she lived. No, it won't be a problem."

It would be if she planned to stay with us. Ava had very strict rules about keeping a low profile, and any way I looked at it, Jeane didn't approach that ideal. She'd have to go to Europe. It was the only answer. But maybe she'd been close to death for so long that her brain hadn't regenerated completely enough to understand the stakes.

I held the restaurant door for her and motioned her inside. The place had a bar along the right wall, and on the left side, tables crowded together in a narrow, dimly-lit space. I wasn't claustrophobic, but it was stuffy enough that eating here wouldn't be my first choice. No wonder so many of the women had shed outer shirts and wore only tanks with thin straps, their skin glistening with moisture.

While I looked around for Walker, Jeane somehow cleared a couple of stools at the bar with nothing more than a smile. "There," I said, slipping onto the high stool. "Near the back by that hallway. He's the blond in the brown shirt talking to the older guy with the messy facial hair." Both were obviously American, not so much because of their pale skin but because of their uncomfortable demeanor.

Jeane twisted to look. "Hunters," she hissed. "The older one at least."

"How can you tell?" I took a sip of whatever drink Jeane had requested for us, casually glancing again at the pair.

"Dumb look in his eyes, that atrocious striped shirt, bad hair. You name it."

Now that she said it, he did look like a lot of the Hunters I'd had the misfortune to meet. Their leaders weren't all that way, but as with the witch hunting or lynch mobs of the past, Hunter numbers swelled by targeting the poor and uneducated, breeding them on hate and fear. However, Hunters also decried gun control and increasing government regulation, and on these subjects the Renegades were in complete agreement with them.

I spied what might be the symbol of a hunter with a rifle on a baseball cap lying on the table, but it was too far away to be certain. If I were Emporium, it would be enough to kill him, but while I didn't like Hunters, the Emporium agents he might capture in the future were enough to prevent me from acting against him. Fortunately for Walker and his companion, there were no Unbounded in the restaurant at the moment besides Jeane and me. Of course that didn't mean there weren't other Emporium agents.

Angling toward Jeane so I could watch the men, I took another gulp of the amber liquid, wincing as it seared a pathway down my throat. They were arguing about something, but we weren't close enough to hear their low, urgent voices. Every now and then both glanced nervously at the tables around them. I reached out tentatively with my thoughts—more a simple letting down of my own shield as opposed to exerting my ability. At once all the thoughts around me rushed in and the life forces tripled in brightness, leaving me momentarily stunned. I shut down again, leaving only a conduit opened to the blond. He was still shielding. I could get through if I tried, but that would mean the snake would begin to feed again. For now, I'd just take those surface emotions—which told me he was upset and angry with his companion. The way his eyes kept sliding to the door definitely told me he was expecting someone else.

The young man's eyes met mine briefly as he stood and threw a tip on the table, but I shifted slightly, putting Jeane between us. "Looks like they're leaving," I told her. "Get ready to follow."

I rotated further as they walked past the bar, keeping my back to them but watching for any sudden moves. When they passed us without incident, I let out a breath I hadn't known I was holding. The older, hairy-faced man was shorter than the blond guard and walked with a bit of a bowlegged swagger. They looked awkward together, as if they didn't belong. Walker was white collar and university-bred, while Hairy Face appeared as if he should be working as a day laborer in a construction job, spitting tobacco through his front teeth.

I threw some of my Venezuelan bolivares onto the bar and stood to leave. As Jeane followed, a drunkard's hand grabbed at the sleeve of her blouse. He said something to her in Spanish, his desire wafting from him like bad cologne.

Revulsion filled Jeane's face, and she leaned close to him, her hand disappearing under his baggy T-shirt that piled on his lap as he sat on the stool like a castoff belonging to a gorilla. "Bug off!"

His eyes widened, and he grunted with pain as she twisted whatever she had hold of. He jerked away, tumbling off his stool, squealing like a baby pig. Next to him, his companion jumped to his feet, reaching for something—probably a knife. This was getting ugly, fast. And each second Desoto's security guard and his Hunter companion were getting farther away.

CHAPTER 8

I THREW MY KNEE INTO THE DRUNK'S SWARTHY FACE AS HE recovered enough to launch himself at Jeane. His eyes rolled back as he collapsed, his eyes staring at me with dazed confusion.

I whirled toward his companion, whose dark face was punctuated with an ugly sneer. "Don't," I warned.

He came for me anyway, the knife not quite out of his pocket, and I jabbed my fingers at his throat, hooking one of my feet behind his and yanking it forward at the same time my fingers met flesh so that he tripped backward, falling over his stool and gagging. Then I grabbed Jeane's arm and pulled her from the bar before the man could recover and remember his knife.

"Didn't anyone ever teach you about keeping a low profile?" I said through gritted teeth. "I should have left you with Stella." Preferably tied up or unconscious.

"He touched me." Jeane tossed her head, the thick dark

strands falling around her face. She had a lot of curl that I once would have envied; now it and she were just liabilities. Well, except for the snake thing.

"Besides, I knew you'd take care of them," she added in spite of my silence.

As if I had a choice. I stifled my anger and checked my phone. "They went that way. On foot, I think."

Jeane kept quiet as we moved up the dark street, which was a good thing for both of us because a half block in front of us, two shadows detached themselves from the wall. They moved smoothly and fast—almost unseen like Ritter and Jace. I didn't need to probe them to see their natures.

"We have company," I said. "Unbounded."

Jeane sucked in a tiny breath as I released the tight hold I had on my shield, allowing the glow of their life forces to reach me. Dim instead of bright like the mortals in the restaurant—blocking and doing a good job of it. They'd probably been there when we'd entered, but with my shield drawn tight and my reticence to use my ability, I hadn't noticed them before. I silently cursed at the snake in my mind and hoped my error wouldn't be a fatal one.

Before I could decide if we should attack or flee, Jeane said, "They're following the Hunters."

They were in fact heading in that direction. All at once things clicked. Walker and his companion had been waiting for someone at the restaurant, and either these men were who they'd been waiting for or they were the reason the contact hadn't arrived. I was betting on the latter because though Walker had been involved with the Emporium at Desoto's mansion, he hadn't shown Stella's device to the Emporium agent there. I didn't know what Walker's angle was or how he was involved, but I was going to find out.

"We can't let them get Walker," I said.

"What do you mean? They're probably friends. Maybe he's a recruit." Jeane stepped delicately over a beer bottle on the sidewalk, looking for all the world as if a camera were following her every moment.

"No. I don't think so." I stepped up the pace. My bet was that Walker had learned about Unbounded from the Hunters he'd led to Desoto's mansion, but that he hadn't fallen to all their rhetoric. He might not even know for sure that some of the patrols at Desoto's were Unbounded—at least I hadn't detected that in his mind.

I was also betting that both of the agents in front of us were gifted in combat. No way could I take them on alone without using my ability to either channel one of them or to incapacitate them with a mind blast. I was glad I had reinforced my snake container.

I put on my phone's wireless headset and placed in a call to let Stella know where we were and about the Unbounded. "I think they're an Emporium hit team."

"Good to know," she said. "I'm tracking all of you. The Emporium agents are a complication, but we knew they'd be around. You want me to call Mari and send her to you?"

My gut relaxed a little at that. With her ability, Mari could "find" me anywhere I was, a link so far she'd only been able to develop with me and Dimitri. "Maybe. Tell her to get ready just in case." Mari was reliable, though inexperienced, and a far better companion than Jeane. Plus, she knew her way around a knife. With Mari, I could also shift out, though that would mean leaving Jeane, and as irritating as it was to be with her, I needed her for now. Letting her fall into Emporium hands again was not an option.

"Walker is with a Hunter," I told Stella. "Or at least we think the man is a Hunter."

"Well, we've known Walker might be involved with them since our run-in with the Hunter's back at Desoto's. You think Walker's one, or just working with them?"

"Not sure, but obviously there's some connection. I may bring him in for questioning. Assuming he isn't killed in the next five minutes."

"Try to see that doesn't happen. Keep the line open. I'm calling Mari now."

We'd fallen into step behind a group of people, but they turned a corner while the Unbounded continued ahead. A man and a woman, I saw now, both wearing dark clothing and jackets I knew hid swords in back sheaths that would have called far too much attention had it been daylight. They slowed as we moved into a section of town that was darker and plainly deserted except for Walker and the Hunter, who my phone indicated were just ahead, down a street on the left.

Sure enough, the hit team turned in that direction. As we reached the narrow intersection, I motioned for Jeane to duck behind the parked cars along the right side of the street so we could get closer without being seen. She looked incongruous squatting there, her lips pursed sourly. Ignoring her, I slid past the first couple of cars and then darted to stand against the wall of the building behind us where the light didn't quite reach. Jeane was behind me, moving slowly but steadily.

This street was deserted and a little less than half a block long, though it still had two lanes with space for parking on both sides and sidewalks as well. Five-story apartment buildings loomed overhead. I went faster now, spying Walker as he reached for the door of a new sedan that he'd probably rented at the airport.

The two Emporium agents emerged from the darkness, moving with the stealth of shadows themselves. The man was white, probably American or European, and his female companion, a full head shorter, had olive skin like many of the Venezuelan natives, and her black hair was woven into a braid similar to my own. Both whipped out their swords, looking as if they anticipated, and even hoped for, resistance.

Walker's companion yelped as the hit team appeared next to him out of the darkness, and he fell back into the car with astonishment, his hands up in a warding-off gesture. "You can have our money. Just leave us alone! Please!"

Walker turned, backing to the car as well, but his head twitched back and forth as if searching for help or a way out. He said something, but I couldn't hear what, so I drew even closer, using the parked cars again to hide my approach.

"Why are you here?" The male Unbounded said, almost casually, as if he were amused. "Why were you meeting with Habid Salemi?"

"I don't know what you're talking about," Walker said. "Look, take all our money." He reached into his pocket.

"They ain't after money." Terror filled the Hunter's voice now. "Can't you see the swords? They're devils, just like I was telling you. Sooner gut you and eat your heart than give you a chance to explain."

The Unbounded shared an amused glance with his partner. "Oh, and I thought that's what I was doing—giving them a chance to explain. You feel like eating heart?"

"Hmm, maybe a little," she said.

Walker held up his hands. "Look, I don't know what you guys want, but we aren't a danger to you."

The woman stepped toward him, lifting her sword until it was parallel to his neck, the point inches away from his skin. "How do you know Habid Salemi? What has he told you?"

Walker's chest heaved with sudden terror. "Nothing! I swear. We were going to meet, that's all. He said he had some information he thought I'd want. I'm a journalist."

"An American journalist?" The woman gave a low chuckle. "And what did Salemi say to make you come all this way?"

This wasn't looking good for Walker and the Hunter.

Signaling Jeane to stay put behind the parked car, I worked my way far enough down the street so I wouldn't be heard. "Stella," I whispered, easing out my nine mil, "tell Mari to come on my signal." As I checked my silencer, I flirted with the idea of giving Jeane my backup pistol but decided she might decide to empty its magazine into my back.

"Sorry," Stella answered in my ear. "She hasn't picked up yet."

"Well, send her when you can." I was already retracing my steps back to the parked car where Jeane still crouched. I wanted to learn more about this Habid Salemi guy, and the fact that Walker claimed to be a journalist was very interesting.

"Where is Salemi?" Walker was asking the Emporium team. "He can tell you we don't know anything."

The woman twirled her blade. "Don't worry. We know how to deal with traitors, even those who need a little more care to kill."

The old Hunter moaned. "Dear God, they're going to eat my heart!" Was he really that afraid? Many Hunters I'd met became sniveling weaklings without a group to support them, but I had a hunch he might be one of the rare brave ones, leading the Emporium agents on while waiting for a chance to pounce.

"And what would you have done to us, old man?" The Emporium man flicked out his sword, slicing into the Hunter's shoulder. It was a controlled hit, meant to bring pain but not mortally wounding him. Yet.

The Hunter screamed, grabbing at his shoulder as blood spurted over his hands.

To hell with the snake, I thought, pushing out my thoughts, ramming them against the male Unbounded's mental shield. I couldn't let them kill Walker or the Hunter, no matter how much I despised the old man's ideals.

The enemy's shield held for the moment; obviously this pair had been working on creating stronger barriers. Using the mental reincarnation of my machete would probably do the trick, but that took effort and would feed the snake even more. Better to use a little physical force.

As his sword came down for another slice of the Hunter, I shot the Unbounded in the neck because I was pretty sure he was wearing body armor. My next bullet was supposed to go into the woman, but she anticipated me at the last minute—her combat ability kicking into high gear—and the bullet went wide as she changed position.

The man tumbled away, pulling his own silenced gun and firing. I was already moving, having slipped inside him as his shield wavered with the pain of his gushing neck wound. Channeling his ability, I let off two more shots at the woman without looking, knowing already that she would move out of the way in plenty of time, but at least it would keep her ducking.

Two against one. Me protecting the cowering mortals who would probably flee as soon as they had the chance. Or stab me in the back.

I'd chosen to shoot the man first because of his size, knowing he would be the greatest danger. If I could take him out in a way that still allowed me to channel his ability, I'd be a match for the woman. Even as I had the thought, I felt the man's mind slip from my grasp.

No! I pushed out, but the only thing I received was the last few seconds of agony as his life bled out onto the pavement.

Dead. Temporarily so, but useless to me at the moment. Obviously my training had paid off—or not in this case, since I hadn't wanted him quite that far out of the way.

The woman fired more shots, and Walker dropped to the ground, scurrying under the car for cover. The wounded Hunter wasn't as fast, and she grabbed him for a shield, backing into the shadows across the street, firing steadily. Crouching between cars, I went after the woman, wishing I could shoot her as well. But as long as she had that Hunter, I couldn't use the gun without risking his life.

He would kill me if he had a chance.

I dived between two cars and came up running. Something punctured my thigh, and a flash of white hot pain traveled up my leg to my stomach, making me want to vomit. I dove to the ground next to a car bumper and lay there panting, my cheek pressed into the roughness of the road.

Where is she? I had to find her before she warned whoever had sent her. I pushed out my thoughts. My mind felt groggy all of a sudden, as if a sleeping pill had suddenly gone to work. The blue lights from the snake gleamed brightly, and I had no doubt where my energy was going.

The muffled whizzing sound of the silenced shots had ceased. Either she'd stopped for a refill or she realized she'd hit me and would now stalk me to finish the job. I pushed outward, searching for her life force. *Concentrate.* I tried not to think of the snake growing as it fed on my energy. The pain in my thigh was less now, as my body rushed natural painkillers to the wound at an accelerated rate. I wasn't in danger of passing out or temporarily dying—if I could keep my wits about me.

There. I felt the woman's life force. She was only two car lengths away. I heard steps—the Hunter's clumsy ones. Just two, but it was enough to help pinpoint their progress. I waited, focusing on the dim light of her life force. Touching the shield on her mind, I knew I'd need the machete to get inside her, and more time, which I didn't have. There had to be another way. Feeling around, my hand closed over a couple pebbles. Not the rocks I'd hoped for.

Dropping them, I worked my way to a crouched position. Slipping my ballistic knife from the sheath on my leg, I aimed it upward. Its range was eighteen feet, and she was still far enough away that she probably wouldn't pinpoint the launching point, so if I aimed it just right, she might be fooled into thinking I'd managed to sneak around behind her.

In one, two, three. I pushed the release when she was a car length away. There was a firm click as the knife launched from its housing. It was too dark to follow its trajectory, but if I'd calculated correctly, it should land right about—a solid clunk reverberated in the alley as it landed on the roof of the car she'd just passed.

Go! I vaulted to my feet and jumped toward her, slamming into her and the Hunter. Her gun skittered across the pavement, but she was already whirling, tossing the man to the ground like refuse. Her leg shot out, slamming my hand holding the pistol, forcing it from my grip, but I had a knife in my left hand, the little one Ritter had given me. I swiped it at her, felt the blade bite into her hip. Not deep enough to hit flesh.

She jumped away, laughing at me before she landed a punch to my jaw. I blocked her next punch and landed one of my own, but it was clear I wouldn't be good enough, unless I got inside her head. Ordinarily, I would be able to hold my own for a bit longer, but with the snake sucking my energy, doing so seemed impossible.

And this Unbounded was good.

Where was Mari? I'd already lost my headset in the fight, but Stella would send Mari once she found her if I didn't answer. Whether or not Mari would arrive in time was left to be seen. I pushed harder at the Unbounded's mind without success.

I took two more hits to my torso that didn't hurt all that much through my protective vest, but one to my throat nearly knocked me down.

"Let me guess, you must be a Renegade," she said, before slamming her fist into my face. I didn't block but instead used her distraction to whip the knife at her again. Pain exploded in my mouth, but this time the little knife sank into the flesh of her arm. Again not deep enough to cause a mortal wound, or even a slowing one—except for the poison.

She laughed again. "Really? How pathetic. No wonder you guys are—" As pain abruptly contorted her features, I punched hard with first one fist and then the other. The next instant she was down, giving me time to pull out my backup pistol and shoot her. This gun wasn't silenced and the shot echoed loudly in the stillness of the night.

I'd once again chosen her neck because it was unprotected, and the idea of blowing off her face made me sick. Besides, I'd need her conscious sooner rather than later, and head wounds took more time to heal. Ready with the gun just in case, I leaned over and spat out a mouthful of blood, watching as she gurgled to unconsciousness.

"Fiend!" came a scream from behind me as the old Hunter recovered enough to launch himself at my back, a knife in hand. Just to show me gratitude for saving his life.

The blade sank deep into my right arm and my fingers lost hold of the gun. I turned toward him. Ordinarily, a mortal wouldn't be much of a challenge, but this Hunter surprised me by slamming into me and wrapping his arm around my neck. The knife penetrated my skin as he dug it into my flesh.

I'd been in worse situations, though not with a snake in my head devouring my energy. I reached out to him mentally. It felt like slogging through mud. At last I found his shield—weak, yet strong enough to keep me out in my condition. I summoned the mental image of my machete. I'd have energy for one stab, and then no more. *Get in. Fry his brain,* I thought. I hoped I had enough strength. Desperately I began absorbing, pulling in nutrients from the air. Still, the Hunter's shield held.

He cursed vehemently, telling me exactly what he was going to do to me and the others I'd incapacitated. Slow carving with a chain saw was the entire gist. That was one thing you could always trust about Hunters: they took joy from doing their duty to dispatch Unbounded. I'd been to one of their meetings when they'd planned a killing—

a righteous and necessary killing as they saw it—and first they made the man suffer in order to atone for the sin of being Unbounded. Knives were their preferred method of exacting this penance.

Maybe the Emporium wasn't all that wrong to want them dead.

If I failed, Ritter would never forgive me for leaving him like this.

CHAPTER 9

JEANE CASUALLY EMERGED FROM BETWEEN TWO CARS, PAUSING FIVE feet away. "Drop it." Her voice was icy cold, without its usual breathiness. She was pointing an assault rifle at us, one that looked very similar to the rifle the man I'd shot had been carrying.

"No way," the Hunter said. "I'll be dead the minute I let her go."

Jeane shrugged delicately, her mouth opening in a smile. "Oh, darling, I'll just shoot you both if you don't let her go. She'll recover. What about you?"

His chest heaved against my back and the stench of sour sweat filled my nose. "You wouldn't."

"Actually, I'd love to—shoot you both. I owe her one." She flicked her gaze at me, her expression cruel. "Though I had something else in mind. Look, you let her go, and I'll let you go. But you have only ten seconds. One, two, three, four, five . . ."

With a hoarse sob, the Hunter pushed me at her and ran.

Jeane stepped out of the way as I struggled for balance. She let him reach almost to the end of the alley before shooting him. The sound of the bullet was deafening, but he collapsed without a sound. I couldn't even hear the quiet *thump* of his body as it hit the pavement.

Jeane's satisfied smile as she turned to me would probably haunt me for a very long time. I snatched the gun from her, fire licking across the deep cut in my arm. "You didn't need to do that. You should have just let him go."

"Hunters are vermin. I agree with the Emporium on that."

I couldn't refute her, having had similar thoughts only moments before, and somehow I couldn't find too much pity for the man in my heart. I wouldn't have killed him, though.

"He was inferior," she added, more as an afterthought rather than an explanation.

The comment concerned me. "Because he's mortal?" That would be Emporium rhetoric.

She gave a low laugh. "Because of his morals."

"What about the other one?" Had she also killed him?

"Over by the car." She jerked her head in the direction of the car where the Emporium agents had confronted the men.

Dare I hope Walker was still cowering under the vehicle? Because I wanted to question him. I couldn't see much by the dim light of the single streetlight at the end of the alley, but I looked for his life force and found him more or less where Jeane had indicated, alive and close to the body of the male Unbounded, whose life force was glowing brighter as he healed, but not bright enough to be a concern. Yet.

Using my knife, I ripped my shirt and wrapped it around the wound in my arm, tying it with difficulty. My neck was also slick with blood, but I could feel that it had already stopped bleeding, so the cut hadn't been deep. The bullet in my thigh was the most serious problem, each movement sending a ripple of misery throughout my entire leg, but I would have to deal with that later.

Though the headset had been lost during the scuffle, my phone was still intact, and I called Stella. "Erin," she said, sounding relieved. "What happened? You sound terrible."

"Little complication, but I have two Emporium agents down. You want me to bring them in?" Now that Jeane was close and I wasn't exerting sensing effort, the snake was no longer emitting light. I continued my higher absorption rate, which gave me the impression of breathing or drinking more deeply, and energy trickled into my body. It was easier without a knife to my throat.

"Did they see you?" She was all business again. "Because bringing them in could endanger the plutonium recovery."

I considered it. "One can't identify me. The other I can fix. They'll think they were attacked by buddies of the Hunter." Just the idea of removing another memory made me feel exhausted, but I was confident I could do it if needed.

"Bring the one who saw you," Stella said after a pause. "Leave the other to finger the Hunters for his companion's capture. We don't want to pass up an opportunity to question an Emporium agent, and it's not like it'll make things worse. Besides, you shouldn't use your ability anymore." I was glad she didn't berate me for using it in the first place because it wasn't as if there had been a choice.

I picked up the woman and carried her to Walker's rental car. Hopefully he had the keys because I really didn't want to search the Hunter's dead body for them. I found Walker not only close to the sprawled Emporium agent but cuffed to him. His eyes were crazed with fear.

I scowled at Jeane. "What?" she said with a casual lift of her shoulders. "He was trying to run."

Unceremoniously, I dropped the Emporium woman by the car and approached Walker slowly. "It's okay. We're not going to hurt you."

A sob burst from his throat. "You killed him. You killed them all."

"For starters, these two aren't dead. If you know enough to be here, you know that. And your friend tried to kill me."

"Not my friend." He convulsed with another sob. "I'm on a story. He's a contact, that's all."

"I'll get you free, but I want you to tell me everything."

He nodded, still looking as if he was going to puke from fear. I rummaged over the sprawled body, trying to find the keys to the cuffs. I found them and opened the lock. Walker scooted backward until he hit his rental car, rubbing his hands. His eyes darted frantically up the street, as if calculating his chance for escape.

"Give me the keys," I said. "We've got to get out of here, and we're taking her with us." I thumbed at the apparently lifeless woman. "Someone could have heard those last shots."

He snorted. "If they did, they probably ran away. This is Venezuela. There's more civil unrest here than just about anywhere. People shoot it out on the streets all the time." His voice rose to a painful squeak. "Should have known better than to come here."

I had no idea about civil unrest, but then I hadn't actually listened to the news lately. Little busy trying to stay alive. I held out my hand for the keys, and he practically threw them at me. I passed them to Jeane, who seemed to be examining her fingernails. "Get her in the car." When she stared at me, I felt compelled to add, "Please."

When I was sure she would comply, I turned back to Walker. "Who is Habid Salemi?"

Walker shook his head. "Some Iranian guy is all I know."

"Why did you come to meet him?"

"Just to see if he knew"—he cast a look at Jeane who'd opened the trunk and now grabbed the unconscious Emporium female's arm and began dragging her unceremoniously to the back—"what the Unbounded here were planning."

"And what was that?"

"Something big is all I know. He wouldn't tell me over the phone."

"How'd you get a line on him?"

He heaved a breath. "Look, I was doing research for a story on the president's son. Well, that was several months ago when he was still the vice president. You see, my sister went to school with his girlfriend, and she claimed that something odd happened to him. That he suddenly couldn't remember things they had done together. They broke up because of it, and she was devastated. Asked me to look into him. She was sure someone was drugging him or something."

I knew what he was talking about. The president's son had been abducted and an Emporium agent put in his place, but we'd managed to rescue him at the same time we'd freed Jeane, putting a stop to their plan to gain more political control. Both the White House and the Renegades had taken stringent efforts to see that not a hint of the event was mentioned in the press.

I nodded for Walker to continue. "What happened then?"

"About Mann? Nothing, but while I was researching him, I stumbled over some mention of people who don't die, and that led me to Strout—the guy I was with tonight. He gave me enough information to track down one of the

Unbounded, and I got a job as a security guard for a rich guy in Texas to keep an eye on him to see if it was all true."

The rich guy had to be Desoto, but I wasn't letting on that I knew. "And?"

"And it didn't take me long poking around in their computer system to realize something unusual was going on down here in Venezuela. Not with the Unbounded, but with the rich guy. So I put out a few feelers and found the Iranian, Salemi, who told me he had some information, but that I needed to come here for it." Walker's voice became more confident, slightly tinged with pride. "I talked to Strout and we decided to come here. He has more of an expense budget than I do."

"So you abandoned your job with the rich guy and came down here."

He shrugged. "Strout and his friends ruined it for me anyway. When I told them there was definitely something going on, they came to the house, tried to grab the Unbounded I was tracking. Didn't end up well then." He paused before adding, "Or now."

At least that explained why he'd kept Stella's device instead of reporting it to the other guard at Desoto's. He'd probably thought he could get information from it.

"And Salemi?" I asked.

"He didn't show up tonight. But I talked to him several times during the last week, and even sent him some material he asked for. There's no way he would cut out on me." The fear was back in Walker's eyes, and he curled in on himself. "Those two who attacked us knew we were coming. They might have killed him."

What his story meant was that those stupid Hunters had probably ruined everything for us. If the Emporium knew someone had information about the plutonium, it would be that much harder to steal.

"Get in the car," I said. "Front seat."

Walker's breathing came faster. "Please, just let me go. I won't tell anyone about you. I promise."

"Look," I said, tilting my head at the unconscious Unbounded, "this guy here is about to wake up, and if you're anywhere nearby, you'll be dead. He's going to think you did something to his partner, and I believe you know what that something is. I'm sure your Hunter friend over there told you exactly how his ilk rid the world of Unbounded." I motioned again at the male agent. "He won't be as nice to you as I am, but I'll leave you here if you want." Judging by the strength of the agent's life force that was increasing as his body healed, we had maybe ten minutes before he awoke.

My statement was enough to get Walker into the car. I heaved myself painfully in after him, sliding behind the steering wheel, wondering what I was going to do with him. The woman in the trunk would be sent to our prison compound in Mexico after we questioned her, but Walker was essentially an innocent, his only offense being an unhealthy curiosity and a desire to break a story that would make his career. Being driven wasn't all that bad, and maybe he'd learned his lesson.

"Where do you want to go?" I asked him.

He thought a moment. "My hotel?"

"Might be watched."

"Airport."

"Much better. I'll get you to a taxi."

"We're really going to take him somewhere and let him go?" Jeane said from the backseat. "He can identify us."

She had a point, which meant I would have to do

something about that, regardless of what that snake did in my head. It was either that or lug him around until we got the plutonium, and I already had one millstone around my neck in the form of Jeane.

"It's easier to kill him." Jeane spoke carelessly into the darkness, her face only partially lit by street lamps and the headlights of passing cars. "If we did that sort of thing, I mean."

Walker gazed at her in horror. "You're really going to kill me, aren't you?"

I pulled the car over to the curb. "You have something to write on?"

"Yeah." Terror filled the word.

"Get it."

From his pocket, he drew out a small cell phone.

"Write this. Strout is dead. You barely got away. They gave you something to erase your memory. Go back to the States. Forget the story."

His hands were shaking, but the glance he gave me held relief. Or was it something else? A stab of conscience made me ask, "These guys don't know your name, do they? Or how to track you? Because they *will* want you dead."

"No. I was careful. The meeting place was the only way they had of finding me." Walker frowned. "Are you saying they killed Habid? Man, he was trying to do what was right."

"You just worry about yourself. Now let me see what you wrote." I took the phone and read the note. "That's good, now add your name." After he did, I said, "Nighty night," and hit him hard in the head. Not hard enough to cause permanent damage, hopefully, but enough that he'd have a headache when he awoke. A little pain might go a long way toward convincing him that he should obey his note.

I checked the box with the snake. No blue glow and no sign of it breaking out of its double container. Okay. I reached out gently, slipping into the lake of Walker's unconsciousness. I found the memory bubbles of our conversations and grabbed them. Then I searched for the scene in the alley. Better to leave as much of that as possible, but it would depend if he could identify me. There I was springing into the scene, my features unidentifiable in the dim light. He was too busy saving himself to worry about me. Until I came back to talk with him. I reached inside that bubble, extricating half of it and leaving the rest. It floated merrily away.

There would be big enough gaps in his memory that he'd know something happened, but that would only back up the note he'd written, and he wouldn't be able to report me to any remaining Hunter contacts. He wouldn't even remember Jeane because I'd taken that memory as well. He'd witness Strout's death but would have no idea who killed the man. Maybe he'd give up both his curiosity and his ambition.

Once again there were two blue lights coming from the snake box in my head, but they were much fainter with Jeane nearby. They vanished even as I dropped my connection with the reporter.

We found a taxi driver and overpaid him to drop Walker at the airport. He should wake by then. I hoped. I let Jeane do the talking, and she made up a story in Spanish about her drunken American boyfriend who got in a fight protecting her. I didn't know the language, but images came to me from the taxi driver's surface thoughts. The man couldn't take his eyes off Jeane, and I suspected he'd do her the favor even if we hadn't paid him far too much money.

He gave her a card. "You need anything while you're here, I'm your man."

Jeane smiled, gazing at him beneath half-lidded eyes. "Oh, thank you."

Afterward, we parked outside our hotel, where we checked on our prisoner. She was coming to, so I made sure she was tied tightly, with strips of her own clothing. If I'd been more prepared for our little dance, I'd have brought rope. I gagged her before locking her back in the trunk. I'd leave her for someone else to deal with.

We headed toward the back entrance of the hotel, Jeane appearing as if she'd just returned from a lovely stroll and me staggering and blood-streaked, as though I'd barely survived a mugging with an entire city of gangbangers.

"Look," I said to her, "back there in the alley. Thanks." I didn't add that I'd expected her to run more than I'd expected any kind of help.

She blinked slowly. "Well, it wasn't really for you, though we can pretend it was if you want. I know you're needed to find the plutonium, and the sooner we get that, the sooner we can get out of this hole."

I was confused for a moment until I realized she was still hung up on our lowly accommodations at the hotel, however temporary. I tried not to roll my eyes. Whatever her reasons, she had saved my life, and it was hard to dislike her as much as before.

Stella met us at the back door, taking in my disheveled appearance with a calm eye. Exhaustion washed over me, and I allowed her to help me inside. It was that or pass out. I'd probably held up until then because there hadn't been any other choice.

Inside the room I collapsed on the bed.

Minutes later, as Stella began doctoring my wounds, Mari flashed into appearance, bringing with her a rush of smoke fumes. "Sorry. I came as soon as I got your message."

"What happened?" I asked, knowing it had to be something serious for her and Keene to ignore Stella's phone calls.

Her eyes were bright with exhilaration. "We were searching this condo a few miles west of here that was supposed to house the factory's non-local employees. The whole place was a wreck, and it looks like it's been at least two or three days since anyone was there, judging by the food they left on the table and on the stove. We went through the papers spread on the floor and what's still in drawers—all junk. There were no computers. We were just leaving when Emporium agents showed up to torch the place. We had to hide inside until they left, and then we barely escaped the fire. It took us a bit to recover from the smoke, but we're both fine. Keene's on his way back now." She paused, watching Stella begin sewing up my arm. "Looks like you weren't so lucky. Sorry."

"We managed." I tried not to wince as the needle pushed through my skin. Stella had deadened it with anesthetic laced with curequick, but it still hurt because I hadn't let her wait until it was completely numb. I wanted her to hurry and finish before Ritter returned. Besides, she'd probably have to give me another dose of anesthetic to make it completely numb because our bodies got rid of the drug even faster than they healed.

"Help me get the bullet out of my leg, would you?" I added to Mari. "While Stella finishes my arm. It's numb enough, and you're good with knives."

Mari made a face. "This is different. I can't poke a knife in *you*. If Stella can't do it when she's finished with your arm, we'd better wait for Keene."

"Give me your knife." No way was I waiting for Keene, or for Stella. I'd rather do it myself. Of course, left-handed it might be a challenge, but maybe Mari would get over her squeamishness.

"Oh, I'll do it." Jeane came from where she sat gingerly on the edge of the other bed. She flicked a glance at Mari. "You really are new, aren't you?"

Mari didn't reply but made a mocking face at Jeane as she focused on my leg. Stifling a grin, I watched Jeane dig the bullet from my thigh with unhesitating precision. By the time she'd found the piece of metal, Stella had finished with my arm and began preparing to stitch my thigh. I would have preferred no stitches or needles, but they would help my body heal that much faster, and I didn't have a day to laze around while I recovered normally.

Jeane stripped down to her bra and pants after getting some of my blood on her shirt, which she tossed into the garbage. "I'm going to take a shower, if anyone needs me." The bathroom door clicked shut behind her.

It was only then I thought to ask Mari. "Did you find anything related to someone named Habid Salemi?"

Mari perched on the bed Jeane had vacated earlier, tucking her legs up under her. "His name wasn't on the list Stella gave us, but only a few names were, and those seemed to be local people—food vendors, janitors, building maintenance."

"Did you say Habid Salemi?" Stella's hands had stilled over my leg with at least one more stitch to go. The neural headset she wore blinked madly, and the computer on the table suddenly flared to life, information streaming across it too fast for the eye to read.

I met her gaze. "You've heard of him?"

Slowly, as if it pained her, she nodded. "Habid Salemi is an alias used by Habib Azima, Shadrach's son."

Shadrach Azima, the contact we were waiting for. I stared at her. "Could this Salemi be the same person?"

"It's a common enough name, but I think it must be. It would explain how Shadrach knew about the plutonium being here in the first place."

"I don't suppose Shadrach told you his son was here."

She shook her head. "And I can't believe it's a coincidence."

That couldn't be good. If Shadrach was keeping secrets, I wondered what else he was hiding.

"The hit team I ran into as much as told Walker that they had Habid in custody. They didn't sound too happy about Habid communicating with an American journalist." I looked at Mari. "You didn't find anything useful at the condo? Any sign where they might have gone?"

Mari frowned. "Besides the mess, it looked like they had all left suddenly. Or were taken." Her tone implied that the latter was her conclusion. "That would fit in with what you heard."

"I think—" Whatever Stella was going to say was lost as the hotel room door slammed open. Ritter stood there in the entryway, breathing heavily, his skin glistening with sweat, a wild shimmer in his eyes. His assault rifle was in his hands. He looked ready to single-handedly do battle with a dozen Emporium soldiers.

We all tensed. I waited anxiously for my brother to appear behind him, but Jace was nowhere to be seen.

"What happened?" Stella asked.

"Why don't you tell me?" Ritter's eyes fell to my leg. "I felt—" He broke off, as if momentarily disoriented. "You were hurt. I felt it."

Stella tilted her head at him. "That's impossible. Even if she used her ability to reach for your mind, you were too far out, even for her."

"I *felt* it," he repeated. His black eyes met mine, and the connection between us strengthened through no effort of my own. I believed him because something strange—and wonderful—was going on between us.

Laying aside his rifle, he strode over to the bed, doused his hands with astringent from our medical supplies, and took the needle from Stella's hand. His touch was surprisingly gentle, though his eyes hadn't quite lost their wildness. He pulled through not one but three more stitches, neater and smaller than Stella's, knotting the last one off deftly.

I eased my good leg off the bed, feeling remarkably better now that there were no more needles in my immediate future and the curequick was pumping through my veins.

Or was it because Ritter was here?

We sat side by side on the bed, not quite touching, but it felt as if we were.

Jeane chose that moment to emerge from the bathroom, wrapped only in a towel. She gazed at Ritter from beneath her lowered lashes. "Oh, so that's what all the noise was about." Her voice was calm and breathy, but the quickness of her exit from the shower told me she'd been worried.

"It's good you're back," Stella said to Ritter, ignoring Jeane. "Because Shadrach will be arriving soon, and we've just realized that one of his mortal sons is here—possibly in trouble. Shadrach might have an agenda he neglected to tell us about, and that means getting the plutonium might not be his first priority."

"Well," Ritter drawled, "we'll have to change that now, won't we?"

CHAPTER 10

I'D SWALLOWED A HEFTY DOSE OF ORAL PAINKILLER AND TAKEN MY own quick turn in the shower before Shadrach Azima arrived. He was alone, but Mari had shifted to the roof of the hotel with a set of night vision binoculars so she could warn us if anyone else approached or looked suspicious. Keene, who had finally arrived while I was in the shower, was standing watch down the hall.

Shadrach was a distinguished, elegant man with straight dark hair, deep brown eyes, a sensuous mouth, and glowing dark skin. Although he wore gray slacks and a white button-down shirt with several buttons opened, I could easily imagine him in bright ceremonial robes of some sort, surrounded by a harem of adoring women. At four hundred years old, he was the mortal equivalent of thirty-eight and had aged well. He seemed young and full of vitality.

Stella, stripped down to a white tank top and tight-fitting black pants because of the heat of the room, motioned Shadrach to enter. She exchanged the usual Renegade greeting of bumping fists, stepping away when he made a move to kiss her cheek. Though many men were attracted to Stella, she favored only a choice few with physical affection, and Shadrach's casual attempt told me that Stella had known him rather well during her time with the group in Italy.

Shadrach frowned, obviously not pleased at the rebuff. "Has something happened?" He looked around at our faces, noting our solemn demeanor. His eyes snagged on a deadly-looking Ritter who stood near the door, his assault rifle once again slung over his chest. I was near the window wearing my black bodysuit, with all my weapons and gear intact. We weren't taking any chances with him.

Only Jeane watched him without ire or concern from her seat on one of the beds.

Stella was quite a bit shorter than Shadrach, and younger, but she looked completely in control. Her manner and the neural headset she still wore made her seem regal. "Why didn't you tell us your son was here?"

Shadrach looked around for a chair and sank into it, dropping the case in his hand to the floor, his face aging in a matter of seconds. "It's true, he's here. Against my wishes." His aggrieved tone now held vestiges of an accent that four hundred years hadn't been able to excise completely from his speech. "That's part of how I knew the plutonium was here."

Sounded reasonable—too reasonable to have been withheld from us.

"What's the catch?" Stella regarded him calmly.

Shadrach heaved a long sigh. "Years ago I began investigating some of my competitors in Iran. I could tell they were up to something. There was too much excitement in different circles—the wrong circles—for them to slip under the radar. Big sums of money were flying through the banking establishments like water through a canal after a heavy rain." He gave a mirthless laugh. "I had no idea about the plutonium then, only that something big was in the works. Habid decided to figure out for himself what they were doing and perhaps get us into the action. He is the youngest of my sons and the only one by my current wife, his Iranian mother. She still lives in Iran, and I visit as much as I am able from my base in Italy." Shadrach's voice softened, the love he had for the woman apparent. "She is very protective of him and tried to make certain he doesn't take part in my businesses. However, Habid doesn't respect his mother's wishes. He is mortal—too young to know if he'll Change—and he has a desire to prove himself to his brothers. So two years ago, he took a job with one of my competitors under a false name. Eventually, they brought him here, along with others from Iran. Habid contacted me last week about the plutonium."

"*That's* how you learned about the plutonium?" I asked, coming to my feet. "What if it's not the right plutonium? From the sound of it, your friends in Iran are all chomping at the bit to get ahold of the stuff. For all we know there could be a dozen of these factories."

"Hardly." His gaze skimmed mine before resting again on Stella. "I knew immediately that this was far more serious than just my competition in Iran, and I began investigating more deeply. My son also realized we couldn't allow them to take it to Iran. He said he had a plan to expose them. We talked once more, but I haven't heard from him since."

"So where is the plutonium?" Ritter strode toward the man, one hand gripping his rifle, the other clenched. "When are they moving it? How many guards? By land or by sea?" When Shadrach didn't answer, Ritter's expression hardened. "Do you know *anything* useful? Why are you even here?"

Shadrach's nostrils flared. "Habid will know. If we rescue him, he'll be able to help us. And you know why I'm here. I want to save my son."

"So basically you called us here on a rescue mission." Irritation filled Ritter's words, and I knew it wasn't because he didn't want to help Shadrach's son but because we'd been played. "You told us you had vital information."

Shadrach stood, straightening his shoulders. Even then, he seemed small compared to Ritter. "There is still time to intercept the plutonium at a later date if we fail here. The information you have proves that. But stopping it here would be far safer and easier than back in my country. So, yes, I want you to help me save my son, but I believe our best chance to get the plutonium is here. Or at some point before entering the Middle East. He'll be able to help us do that."

Stella met Ritter's eyes as if to say *Dial it back.* His nostrils flared before he eased away.

"The problem," Ritter said, his voice calmer, "is that we believe your son and all of the employees he lived with have been taken to an unknown location after he agreed to meet with an American journalist."

Shadrach nodded. "That's what I feared."

What went unstated, though all of us knew, was that without Shadrach's son, our chances of finding the plutonium before they shipped it out had gone down drastically—especially now that the Emporium was aware of his spying.

"Getting him back won't be easy." Ritter walked over to the small table and gestured for Shadrach to follow. "Provided he's still alive."

"You think they'd hold them at the factory?" I asked.

Because from what I understood about plutonium factories, the entire sum of which I could probably print on the palm of my hand, was that there was a limit to the exposure workers should have, even while wearing protective suits. "I'd think they'd be a lot more trouble there. The factory won't be set up for that, and the fear of exposure would make them harder to handle. So the employees they took from the condo are either dead or they're keeping them somewhere else."

The others nodded. "But where?" Stella asked.

"The woman agent," Ritter said. "She might know the place." We both glanced toward the bathroom. While waiting for Shadrach, he'd brought in the Emporium agent I'd captured and put her in the bathtub in case we needed her for questioning. She was conscious—barely—and Stella had shot her up with curequick and bound her neck. Stella had also given her a pillow, which was more than I'd felt like doing after she almost killed me. But Stella was nice that way.

Maybe she wouldn't be so bad for Chris.

"She's not just going to tell us what we want to know," I said. "I'll have to break through her shield, and it's still pretty strong, even considering how hurt she is. I can do it, though."

"No need. She'll tell me." Shadrach's smile was back, but it was a frightening one that sent a chill crawling across my shoulders. "If there's one thing I learned in my native country, it's how to make people talk." Something he had in common with the Emporium, apparently, and which further blurred the lines between them and us.

Suddenly my leg and arm ached, and my lip hurt even worse. I wanted nothing more than to curl up in one of the

beds here and sleep for a week, regardless of the room's ques-
tionable cleanliness. Of course, sleep would have to wait.
I just hoped that while I waited the snake didn't take away
too much of what was me. Because that's what it felt like at
the moment.

I looked up to find both Ritter and Shadrach staring at
me, both with equal expressions of concern, though I was
sure I hadn't let out so much as a sigh.

"I'll get the woman," Ritter said after several more seconds
of studying me.

I really hoped Shadrach could convince her to talk
because I honestly didn't know if I was still capable of
breaking through a strong shield. Of course, Ritter could
snap a few bones and that might make her weak enough.
I shuddered at the thought. It was one thing to consider
torturing someone who had hurt you or those you loved,
but it was another thing altogether to actually do it. Ritter,
Shadrach, Stella, and all the older Renegades had seen too
much of that. Maybe it made them a little less human.

And what if it has? My Unbounded genes certainly didn't
care. They exulted in the difference of near immortality and
denied me the comfort of self-pity or collapsing on the bed
in a shivering lump. They would fight the snake and Delia.

I would fight.

Ritter came from the bathroom, his hand gripping the
woman's arm. He'd untied her legs so she could walk but left
her hands secure. He shoved her into the chair Shadrach had
vacated. "Where did they take Habid Salemi?" His voice was
controlled, though I could feel anger rolling off him.

The woman shut her eyes and opened them again,
reminding me somehow of Jeane. Her brown hair was still
tightly bound in a braid, exposing the angular beauty of

her face. Her dark eyes were on the large side, but they held no innocence. "I don't know."

"What about the rest of the employees?"

"I don't know."

Ten more variations of the questions, and still the same answer. The woman didn't show anger, but her eyes burned with the loyalty of the truly converted. She believed in everything the Emporium stood for. Ritter nodded, as if predicting the outcome of more questions. He nodded at Shadrach, who already had a needle prepared with liquid from the case he'd brought.

"You really will tell us." He flicked the syringe for emphasis and then injected the substance into her exposed neck above the bandage Stella had tied there.

"Your truth drugs won't work on me," she said, as if we hadn't already known. Shadrach's face wore the same frightening smile as before. "Oh, I know your metabolism works too fast for the drugs to have much effect. However, this isn't a truth drug. You should know that Habid is my son and I will do anything to get him back. As a healer, I understand how to both soothe and cause incredible pain."

She glared at him, clamping her jaw shut as if daring him to do his worst. Almost, I felt a grudging admiration for her. In the space of a heartbeat, her eyes grew impossibly wide and her mouth opened in a scream. Shadrach grabbed a pillow from the bed and clamped down over her mouth to blot out the sounds. Her body jerked back and forth with terrible agony, contorting as if she were changing into something inhuman.

Sickened, I jumped to my feet. "What are you doing? Stop! I'll get inside her mind. You don't need to—"

Ritter crossed to me. "Shadrach's injection isn't doing

this—something else is going on. He only gave her a euphoric. We usually have better luck getting information that way."

Jeane arose from the bed in a fluid, catlike movement, her eyes intent. "I've seen this before at Emporium headquarters. She's taken something."

The woman's screaming had ceased, though her jerking continued for several more seconds. Shadrach lifted the pillow and laid his hand on her cheek. Her eyes stared at me, unseeing, her face still locked in agony. The healer took his hand from her cheek. "Her insides have turned to mush. I haven't seen anything like this except in biological warfare."

By the time she stopped moving and slumped in her chair, her life force was almost completely extinguished. But not gone. No poison we'd ever encountered could kill Unbounded. "We'll give her curequick," Ritter said. "You should be able to help her regain consciousness fairly quickly. We need the information sooner rather than later. We can't wait."

Shadrach shook his head. "Even with my help, her recovery will take days."

"Of course," Jeane said. "That's why the Emporium equipped her with it. Probably glued it to the side of a tooth. Delia was testing the drug at the time I was made a prisoner. I didn't think it would be successful because word got out about how horribly painful it was, but apparently this woman—and maybe everyone connected with this project—is loyal enough not to care."

"It's like the cyanide capsules given to pilots in the 1960s," Stella mused. "What a horrible way to die."

"But effective," Ritter said. "By the time she's awake, that plutonium will be long gone, and everything she knows will be old news."

The whole thing frustrated and repulsed me. "Why haven't we heard of this before?"

Ritter met my eyes. "Probably because it's only reserved for their most important operations. If we'd had any clue, we would have checked her for it while she was unconscious."

We all stared down at the pitiful figure. Gray liquid was now leaking from her eyes and mouth in a gruesome manner I hoped wouldn't be echoed in my future nightmares. Ritter tossed a blanket over her, and together he and Shadrach carried her back to the tub.

"What now?" I asked when they emerged. I wished I'd used my ability to investigate the woman's mind, snake or no snake, before she'd regained full consciousness, though I knew there was no guarantee that I would have stumbled on the right information, even if she possessed it.

Even as we spoke, her colleagues might be moving the plutonium. Worse, the whole route would be changed if the Emporium so much as suspected it was us and not the Hunters who'd taken the female agent. I had a wild vision of us going into the factory, guns blazing, but it wasn't realistic, not if it meant risking the Emporium blowing up the place or escaping. Without a viable plan, we were blind.

Ritter scowled. "We can have Erin read the people coming out of the factory, but if we can't find the plutonium, we may have to catch up with it in Syria."

"What about Habid?" Shadrach's voice sounded old.

Ritter was about to speak when Stella said, "Uh, Ritter, Cort's calling. He's been trying to contact you. I'm putting him on speaker. Go ahead, Cort."

"Thanks, I was getting worried." Cort's voice came not

from Stella's headset or her phone, but from the speakers on her laptop across the room.

"We've been a little occupied," Ritter responded.

"I figured."

"What's up?"

"Movement in front of the factory. A dozen soldiers arrived, heavily armed. Emporium by the look of it. Not replacements, apparently. Just reinforcements. Then a guy from the factory came out and examined someone still inside the van. We glimpsed a wounded soldier. Lots of talking, but they're obviously blocking signals because our spybots picked up nothing. Then the van drove away—with half of the extra soldiers. But not out to the main road. It went past the factory on a dirt trail."

"You follow it?"

"I sent Jace. He's on foot, but they can't go very fast. He should be able to keep up."

My brother was fast, but I hated the idea of him being out there alone.

"You told him observation only, right?" Ritter said, echoing my own concern.

"No, I told him to light himself in flames and do acrobatics. He knows what's at stake."

"He'd better."

Cort cleared his throat. "You coming?"

"We're on our way. Let us know if anything else happens."

"Will do." The line went dead.

I paced a few steps. "The wounded guy in the van must be the guard I shot."

Ritter was already heading for the door. "I'm thinking those other soldiers might be going to where they've taken the employees."

"Not taking the plutonium somewhere?" Jeane asked.

"No" Ritter said. "They're reinforcing the factory, and that means something important is still there. But they might be moving it soon. Either way, we have to get over there."

"Only six extra soldiers dropped at the factory with the others going elsewhere?" Stella shut her laptop, tucking it into her bag. "They don't know we're here, then. They must think they're only up against Hunters."

Ritter's smile was almost as disturbing as Shadrach's had been earlier. "Sounds right to me. Let's go. Everyone out."

"What about our guest in the bathroom?" Stella asked.

Ritter grimaced. "She doesn't need a babysitter. Contact Mari and Keene. Tell them we're all leaving."

CHAPTER 11

RITTER'S ARM BRUSHED MINE AS WE HEADED TO OUR RENTAL SUV, the others trailing behind. It was the first semi-private moment we'd had since getting on the plane in San Diego. Electricity sparked at the point of contact, settling deep in my bloodstream.

"You all right?" he asked.

I knew he wasn't referring to the wounds but to Delia's snake.

"No blue lights." I hadn't checked inside the outer box, but I was confident the inner box was still holding strong. I hadn't exerted too much sensing effort during my fight with the two Emporium agents. Not compared to past events. "I'm ready for whatever, if that's what you're asking."

"I know you are."

Of course he did. The link that had formed between us was beautiful and more than a bit terrifying because it meant so much. I wanted to take his hand to pull him closer. I wanted to wrap my arms around him and feel his body next to mine. We'd been waiting to be together for what seemed like forever.

His eyes slid over my face as if to say, *We're almost there. Piece of cake,* my eyes said back.

We only needed to stop a nuclear war first. Oh, and face the most powerful woman in the world to purge the snake from my mind. What was I worrying about?

Keene and Mari were already waiting for us at our SUV. Keene's green eyes ran over my face, as if noting the damage there. I hadn't seen him yet since his return from the employee condo, but he appeared no worse for his brush with the fire, except for the lingering smell of smoke. Again I wondered what his ability was, or if he even knew. He wouldn't be the first to discover it in the heat of battle. If he'd learned anything during his confrontation with the Emporium tonight, he hadn't shared it with us yet.

I turned to open the door and found Mari watching me with Keene, the slightest frown on her face. She smoothed it over immediately, but it made me wonder if something had happened between them. Mari hadn't seemed interested in men since her Hunter husband's betrayal and brutal death, but I sort of hoped she and Jace would eventually get together. Not that I blamed her for any fascination she might have with Keene. Though I'd chosen Ritter, I understood Keene's attraction only too well.

The SUV was rather a tight squeeze, and somehow I ended up between Shadrach and Jeane in the middle seat. Ritter drove, and Stella rode in front with her computer and other equipment. Keene and Mari were in the back. We wouldn't have enough room for everyone once we caught up with Jace and Cort, unless Mari shifted back to the hotel instead of riding.

Shadrach surprised me by putting his hand over mine as it rested on my knee. "May I?" he said. "You are in pain, and I can help."

So could a bottle full of painkillers, but I let him continue. The only experience I'd had with a healer was Dimitri, and I was curious.

Shadrach closed his eyes, and I knew he was feeling his way mentally through my body, finding the wounds and directing the healing. He couldn't see internal thoughts or influence people as I could, only feel his way, tracing veins and pathways, finding what needed repair.

"It's healing well already," he murmured, his voice warm and assuring.

I wished I dared push my thoughts into Shadrach's brain and follow his process as I had Dimitri's, but I didn't dare risk feeding my unwanted mental passenger.

After five minutes, my headache eased and my arm stopped burning. Another five and the throbbing in my leg faded. He continued for another five minutes until my phone buzzed. I grabbed it, recognizing the different vibration pattern as belonging to Jace.

"Hey, Jace," I said. "You all in one piece?"

"Last I checked. Are you with His Deathliness?"

"Oh, yeah. We've been waiting to hear from you."

"Well, tell him I followed them to a place they seem to be guarding very heavily."

"Let me put you on speaker." I clicked the button.

"Okay, so, this place is little more than an old stone house with a second-floor addition. Looks like a warehouse of sorts now. No one here is dressed in protective gear, and they haven't taken in or out anything that could be the plutonium, but they're guarding something inside. Wait. Hold it a minute." A long pause. "Okay, they're putting one, two, three—let's see . . . about a dozen men in the van I followed. They're not tied up or anything. They're heading back toward the factory." He waited several seconds before adding, "The soldiers who came in the van are staying here, though."

"I'm putting in a call to Cort," Stella said.

Ritter nodded sharply. "Have him be on the lookout for the van. Might be heading there." After glancing at Stella's monitor where we were tracking Jace's locator chip, he added to Jace, "We should be near your location in seven more minutes."

We were already going faster than was probably safe on this narrow road in the dark, but I felt the SUV's speed increase. "What else do you see?" I asked Jace.

"Nothing. I'm out in the middle of the woods and that's about it. They've got at least one guard on the roof and a couple around the perimeter, but most are inside. I see lights on the second floor through a lot of narrow windows. There are at least a dozen windows on each side, and the building's not that big."

"Sounds like where they've taken the employees from Habid's condo," I said.

"What employees?" Jace asked.

By the time I'd finished explaining about Habid and the missing factory employees, Stella had found a route that didn't pass the factory but would bring us close to Jace's position. "But are you sure we should go there?" she asked. "What about the factory?"

Ritter hesitated only a second before saying, "Cort can handle the factory for now. He'll alert us if he sees them moving anything out. Let's go see what they're guarding at that house."

I knew it was a gut feeling, not something he was sure about, but Ritter was a master strategist and his gut was usually better than most intel.

Stella peered into the darkness. "Turn left on the next little road. It's small, so don't miss it. I'll let you know when we need to douse the lights."

Cort reported in, letting us know the van had returned to the factory with a group of men he guessed were the night shift workers. "Different workers are coming out now," Cort said. "Most are getting in the van. They're being escorted by an armed guard. But a few must be local employees because they're leaving in their own cars. No guards for them."

"They're letting some people leave?" Mari asked. "Why?"

Ritter glanced in his rearview mirror, though he couldn't possibly see Mari inside the dark cab. "I don't know. Maybe they're only concerned with workers who've had recent contact with Habid. They can't know how much he's told them about his dealings with the American reporter."

"Habid shouldn't have contacted that man," Shadrach said.

"Well, the reporter's out of the picture now," I said. There was a possibility that Walker would be picked up by the Emporium, but he'd seemed to understand the danger. Surely he'd taken a class at some fancy college that taught him not to leave a trail when he researched semi-immortal killers who planned to start the next world war.

"Turn off the headlights," Stella said. "We can drive on this road a bit more as long as we can see, but Jace's location is high enough that if they have a guy on the roof, he'll notice the lights long before he hears our engine."

She let us go another few miles before signaling Ritter to pull the SUV behind a clump of trees near the side of the road. The vegetation here, so close to the river, was lush and plentiful, except for on the road itself, which had been cleared at some point—thankfully, since we were using the overhead satellite for our phones and Stella's equipment and needed a clear path.

Stella packed her laptop in a small carrying case and slung it across her shoulder while the rest of us climbed from the vehicle. I texted Jace to let him know we were coming. As we approached his location, I released the block I was holding over my mind in order to sense any life forces nearby. Ritter looked at me, and I shook my head. No sign yet.

We fanned out, moving silently in the night. Shadrach's ministrations had eased my pain, and the curequick hummed through my veins, giving me energy. I felt eager and anxious to do battle again, despite the lingering discomfort in my thigh. Tiny, dim life forces filled the bushes and vegetation, revealing a plentiful assortment of animals and insects. I didn't try to block them. The faint star-like lights were beautiful in their own way, and there were no accompanying human thoughts to complicate my emotions.

I signaled the others when I spotted Jace, and we angled toward him. "The van came back about a minute ago," he told us when we reached him. His blond hair was out of place, but he wasn't breathing heavily from his recent sprint. His broad grin told me he was having fun. He jabbed his thumb in the direction of the building. "Bunch of guys got out and went inside."

"It's the workers who just finished their shift at the factory," I said. "Or most of them." Though the building itself was draped in shadow and its features unclear from where we stood, to me it was shining with life forces. With a little effort, I began counting. "Twenty-six inside. Plus the guy on the roof and the two outside under the trees. We get a little closer, I might be able to tell which of those inside is Habid." Six of the life forces inside were dimmer, which meant Emporium soldiers or someone else was blocking thoughts.

"I don't think Habid's here," Jace said. "If they know he's a spy, they'll have no use for him at the factory anymore. Besides, if he's in there, how are we going to get him out?"

"We're going in." Ritter altered his position slightly so the moonlight shone on his face. "At least some of us. Stella, am I right in assuming that place doesn't have any electronic shield or blocking signals?"

"Nope, it's clean." She already had a device out of her bag and was punching buttons on it. "I'm sending in a bot right now, but I'm pretty positive we can use the radios."

He grinned at me, as much in his element as Jace. "You feel like climbing, Erin?"

"Live for it." If I could get inside, I knew I could find Habid. Stella had shown me a photograph back at the hotel before Shadrach's arrival, but he should be easy to identify even without that. He'd be the only guy who was mentally blocking but not carrying an assault rifle.

"Erin, Mari, and I are going to get closer to the house after those guards pass," Ritter continued. "Jace, you make sure the guards stay away. Rustle the leaves if you have to. Take them on a little chase. As long as they don't see you, they'll decide it was an animal. We shouldn't need much time to break into a place like that, and I'll give you the signal when we're clear. Only Erin's going inside. She'll be able to avoid everyone and get close enough to Habib to get through his shield and communicate with him. When she's ready to get out, Mari will be close enough to let Erin channel her ability so she can shift back to us. I'll be ready to initiate a direct assault in case Erin needs a distraction. Last resort, of course."

"What about my son?" Shadrach's voice was hoarse.

Ritter turned to him. "If Habid's in there, I doubt they're letting him walk around free so he can rile up the other employees. Breaking him out will endanger the mission. We have to get the plutonium first and then come back for him."

Shadrach nodded, but the darkness didn't hide the pain in his expression. I knew that pain well. It was a fact of our existence, one that we were doomed to experience. Everyone we loved would die, unless we were lucky enough for one to Change. It was why our group of Renegades were closer than family.

"We'll maintain radio silence except for the absolute necessary."

I felt guilty as Ritter said this. The only reason we needed the radio instead of using me to communicate was to diminish the banquet for Delia's snake. Truthfully, I had begun to wonder if I could best Delia at all, and thinking that way meant I was halfway down the path to defeat, which scared me.

Ritter glanced over the group. "Keene, maybe you'd better move closer with us so you can keep an eye on that guy on the roof in case he gets any ideas." Ritter paused, looking at Jeane. "You stay with Shadrach," he said almost regretfully. "You won't be able to go inside with her anyway."

As he had in Austin, Ritter led the way, with Mari and me following. Keene also came along, though he angled away from us, moving as close as he could to the building while still maintaining a direct view of the roof. The going was easy; in most spots the trees and shrubbery grew clear up to the house. After a while, we left Keene's life force behind, and moments later, I became aware of him climbing a tree.

I wanted to check on Jace, but the brightness of the life forces coming from the building had increased as we approached, and I had to clamp down a bit to maintain my equilibrium. The snake box in my mind was shooting out blue again, now that Jeane and I were separated, but that couldn't be helped. My energy level was high and I barely limped.

Ritter studied the building before pointing to the second window near the left end. "Anyone up there?" When I shook my head, he motioned. "Go, then. You shouldn't need a crowbar this time." He had a gun out, but it was a tranque, and I knew that if he did find anyone, he hoped to deal with them and still somehow maintain anonymity.

"Can't I go with her?" Mari asked. "I could back her up."

Ritter gave a grunt of dissent. "Too many people inside. Easier for her to sneak around on her own and shift out quickly before anyone sees her. Besides, you suck at climbing."

I stifled a laugh. Mari didn't see the point of practicing climbing when she could simply fold space and appear wher-ever she wanted. I was tempted to shift up to the window myself and avoid the battle with my fear of heights, but it simply wasn't an option because I couldn't see well enough what to grab on to. Without a rope and grappling hook, I'd likely end up on my butt. Better to do it the old-fashioned way.

Mari touched my arm as I left the bushes where we crouched, her way of saying good luck. Her mind was open and inviting, but I didn't exert the effort to connect with her. I was marginally aware of Keene somewhere behind us, high in the tree, and I was glad to have him help cover my approach to the building. He'd be equipped with night vision goggles and would be able to follow my progress. I could see the guard's life force on the far side of the roof, glowing dimly, but I might lose track of him depending on what else drew my attention.

The outside of the building was mostly lined with stones of varying shapes and sizes, dirty and worn now, and in many places overgrown with vines. Directly next to the house was a stone pathway, and circles of rocks set off trees and other decorative vegetation that was now mostly weeds. One of the trees had fallen over, crashing into a short flight of stone stairs that led to an elevated patio. I suspected the place had started out as a home belonging to some plantation owner. There had once been windows on the lower floor in the back, but these had long ago been replaced with brown-painted metal. I crept over the stones, steering clear of the moonlit patches that would make me visible to anyone watching from the building.

Reaching the back wall of the house, I pulled out one of my knives from my thigh sheath, and slipped the flat of the blade between my teeth. I might arrive at a point where I couldn't reach the knife, and since my teeth certainly weren't going to help me climb, I might as well put them to good use.

It was easy going, the rough, mismatched stone offering plenty of handholds. Even so, my heartbeat elevated and I couldn't help thinking about the height. *Not really that high,* I tried to tell myself. The building was short for two stories and the eaves were wide and sloping. I could probably jump from the upper window without hurting myself. It wasn't as if I could die if I fell. Well, provided the guard on the roof didn't hear me hit the ground.

My fear was locked away tightly in my mind, but thinking about it reminded me of the snake, ever feeding on my strength. Could the presence of that growing monstrosity somehow release my fear? A sense of danger hummed through me at the thought, and for an instant my vision grew blurry.

Don't look down.

I refocused on the window above and reached it with little effort, encountering nothing more harrowing than my increased heartbeat. I extended my ability, double-checking that no life forces were inside the room we'd chosen. Then I secured myself against the low-hanging eaves, spit the knife from my mouth, and began prying at the tiny window. The muffled sounds were loud in my ears, and I hoped the guy on the roof didn't come to investigate.

Ritter was right that I didn't need the crowbar or to channel his ability. After cleaning off the caked paint, I popped the lock without difficulty and began to ease up the window.

The knife in my hand slipped.

I grabbed for it, knowing the clatter on the stones below would attract the guard's attention. My fingers closed around the handle, but my stomach twisted with the ever-present vertigo as my left foot shifted on the stones. I struggled to maintain balance. Impossible.

As I started to fall, I scrabbled desperately to launch myself toward the window. It wasn't going to be enough. Then I felt a push, and the next second my face slammed none too gently against the glass.

What?

My fingers locked around the edges of the window. Heart racing, I waited for something more. Nothing happened.

I sent out my thoughts, but the guard was on the front side of the roof, so he hadn't heard anything.

Had I imagined the push?

A feeling of dread washed over me. Maybe I was losing it. Maybe that snake—now feeding eagerly judging by the brightness of the twin blue lights coming from the outer box—was doing something else to me. If so, could I trust myself to finish this op?

Instinctively, my thoughts reached for Ritter, finding his mind without a barrier. He was thinking of me, urging me to go inside. He knew I would complete the job, that I was the only one who could.

Shaking myself back to my senses, I pocketed the knife and squeezed through the window into a dark room. The flick of my penlight showed me that double bunk beds lined each of the side walls, leaving a narrow path in the middle. Two metal lockers followed the beds and the door loomed beyond. Smaller than any dorm room I'd ever seen. More like a prison.

I crept to the door, pushing out my thoughts. No one in the immediate hallway, but I could see glowing life forces on both sides of the hall—probably belonging to other workers who were in their own cramped cubicles.

Extending further, I felt for any blocked thoughts, but all of them were downstairs. Peering into the hallway, I eased out. The corridor was dim, lit only by the pale wisps of light coming from under the doors. I started down the hall on high alert, checking to make sure none of the life forces were near the doors. Their thoughts rushed at me like loud voices from dozens of television sets. Many words I didn't recognize, but the abundant images were clear.

They were scared.

No, not just scared but completely and utterly terri-fied. They didn't understand why they'd been brought here. They were especially worried about seeing their families again once the project was over. At least a few were contemplating escape, despite the guards' guns.

But if the plutonium was ready for transport, wasn't the job almost over? Or was the Emporium planning on also supplying another country with nuclear weapons? Maybe bloodthirsty Syria or Pakistan? At this point, I wouldn't put anything past the Emporium.

I eased down the short, narrow staircase. The stairway opened immediately into a spacious living room, where four men lounged on a couple of couches and an easy chair. One of the couches looked new, but the second one and the chair seemed decades old. All the men were Unbounded. Their gazes were fixed on a TV that was blaring in some Arabic language, but they'd kept their assault rifles within easy reach. Beyond the living room, I sensed two more people in what I assumed was the kitchen. They were chatting and laughing in another language I didn't recognize. But I knew it wasn't Arabic or Spanish.

Could one of them be Habid?

Hugging the stair wall closest to the living room, I pushed at the shields of the people in the kitchen. One felt like black granite, but the other was softer. I pushed against it harder. And then with even more effort. I could feel it weakening. I conjured my mental machete, sliced open a tiny hole, and slid inside.

The man I entered was not Habid but an Emporium guard, and he sat at a table across from another guard, playing cards. I watched the sand stream of the man's mind, but nothing useful appeared. His thoughts were on the card play and on the Venezuelan hooker he planned to visit the next day.

If the six blocked minds were all Emporium guards, where was Habid? Either he wasn't here or they'd beaten him to a point where blocking was the least of his concerns. None of these men were likely to be sensing Unbounded anyway, and Habid would be able to determine that. So, back upstairs or down to the left where I sensed yet a few more life forces?

Prisoner. I formed the thought in my imaginary hand and held it near the guard's thought stream. In a blink, the mental nudge was sucked inside. Not two seconds later, he thought about their prisoner. Main floor, down the hall, last room.

I pulled away from his mind, refocusing on the living room. I'd risk being seen when I crossed the space to the hallway where the additional rooms were located, but I could minimize my chances of being spotted by timing my movements with the television plot. Before moving, I waited until the volume rose and the hero was fighting off a dozen gruesome aliens.

I paused after reaching the hallway, my gun drawn. Not much against six assault rifles, even with Mari's ability for backup. Thankfully, the men didn't see me. I moved silently, glad that my soft-soled shoes were as good as bare feet for slinking around. Only two of the rooms here were occupied, one with four life forces and the other with only one. I assumed the other rooms were for the guards themselves.

The door with the one life force was locked, and I pondered for a moment what I should do. The keyhole looked like one of those old kind that I'd seen in the eastern US, where one skeleton key opened every room in a house.

Mari could probably pick it in an instant, but I couldn't waste the time or trust that the prisoner himself wouldn't alert the guards by reacting.

No, I needed Mari. I reached for her. Better that I stay connected with her now anyway. At any moment the guards might decide to come this way.

I'm here, I told Mari. *Almost finished.*

I hoped. A lot depended upon what I found behind the door.

CHAPTER 12

MARI'S THOUGHTS WERE FULL OF QUESTIONS, BUT I COULDN'T answer them now. Just by linking with her, I felt the drain on my energy increase.

Channeling her ability, numbers filled my head, and I instinctively chose the right ones that would help me fold space. Not too far. Just inside the door. Shifting, I reappeared with my gun ready. The dark room stank like blood, sweat, and human waste, making me gag. The only light came from a dimly glowing clown that had probably once been a child's nightlight. The illumination barely extended beyond the upturned plastic bucket it sat upon, but the room appeared to be the same size as the one upstairs, minus the bunk beds.

I heard a gasp from the corner near the faint light and then, "Who's there?" The words came in English, which surprised me.

I flicked my penlight in the man's direction. He lay on a cot with a thin mattress and one blanket. He was blond with an unshaven face and hair that was plastered to his head with dried blood. His face was cut and bruised so deeply that even if I'd known him, I might not have recognized him. But the blond hair and pale skin told me he was definitely not Habid.

"Sh." I put my finger to my lips. Now, I'd have to remove his memory of me. First, I might as well get some information from him. "Where's Habid Salemi?"

"Can you get me out of here?" he asked, holding up his tied hands. "Please. They're going to kill me. They're going to kill all of us. As soon as they don't need us anymore."

"Who are you?" I kept the light on his face but pulled my gun closer to my body so he wouldn't see it. His terror was already evident, and even if he attacked me, he couldn't do much damage with those tied hands.

"My name is Crandall. Dr. Francis Crandall. I was hired to oversee the development of some plutonium which I thought was going to be used for a power plant. But I was wrong."

I frowned. Another innocent. "Look, tell me where they took Habid."

Crandall's head shook back and forth. "He's not here. They took him yesterday. I think they may be going back to Iran."

Iran? Why drag him all the way there, unless they had some other use for him? Or unless they wanted more information from him. "What about the plutonium?"

"It'll be finished in the morning, and then that's it—for all of us. Please, I heard them talking. They're going to kill all of us because of Habid. We didn't even know he was talking to someone."

"Why aren't you with the others?"

He made a face. "Habid approached me. He told me what the plutonium was really meant for. I tried . . . I tried to stop them." His face crumpled. "Please, I have a wife and a two-year-old daughter back in the States. I was just a consultant. I was only supposed to be here two months."

I felt sick for him and for the fact that I would have to leave him behind. "I need to know about the plutonium. Tell me everything, and I'll try to come back for you. But you understand that I can't do anything now, right? If they realize you're gone, they'll know we're here and we'll miss our chance to stop this."

"Who are you working for?"

"I can't tell you that, but we are the good guys."

"How do I know you're telling me the truth?" Despair oozed from him in waves.

"You don't. But I'm not the one who did this to you. You know they're terrorists. Isn't that enough?"

He gave a sharp nod and then winced. "After Habid told me what was going on, I did some checking." He choked, coughing with a wet hoarseness that sounded painful. "I found a schedule. I think they're moving it in the morning. If . . . if I figured the days right." He paused, turning his head toward the wall where several fat dark lines marked the plaster, lines I suspected were made with his blood. "A boat is picking it up near the factory. There's another boat offshore. From there, I think a plane or something." Again the hacking cough and one of his fists clutched his chest as he struggled for breath. "No transport approval—nothing like you need for this stuff. That's how I knew Habid was telling the truth."

"Thank you." As he'd talked, I saw in his mind the documents he'd found, including a map. I wished I could take a picture of it with the little camera I carried, but I satisfied myself by memorizing a few landmarks.

He pulled out a letter from under his thin mattress, holding it out with a shaky hand. "Please, if you can't make it . . . if you can't get back to us in time . . . will you see that my wife gets this?"

I took the letter, trying to block his despair before it consumed me. "I will."

"Habid was going to meet with a reporter, you know." His voice was barely audible now, and I realized that when he'd given me the letter, he'd also given up most of his hope.

"I know." I leaned in and touched his arm, wanting to give him something to hold onto. "I talked to the reporter a few hours ago."

A flash of optimism momentarily drowned out his fear, but it was accompanied by a thought of his little daughter that filled me with deep sorrow.

"I'm sorry." With that I stepped closer and slammed my elbow down on his head, knocking him out. He never saw it coming and the effect was immediate, but that didn't make me feel any better. I wished I could have tranqued him, but the drug, especially prepared for Unbounded, would probably kill him in his weakened condition.

Stepping closer, I put my hand on his forehead and dove into his unconscious. It was easy to locate the thought bubble containing the memory of me. He'd never know I was there. Except for the missing letter. I replaced it under the mattress and started to channel Mari's ability.

On second thought, I crouched down, retrieved the letter, and pulled out my camera to take a picture of both sides. I couldn't give him peace of mind, but if the worst happened, I could give closure to his family.

I saw the approaching life force before I heard the steps in the hallway, and I reached into Mari's head, making sure it was safe. The door was already opening as I shifted out of the building, appearing where I had left Ritter and Mari, still crouched as I'd been by the prisoner's bed. They turned toward me simultaneously, and I could feel their unasked questions.

"Habid's not there." I hesitated before adding, "He might be dead. The guy I talked to thinks they may have taken him back to Iran. Hardly seems likely, but maybe Shadrach might have an idea why. Anyway, they're moving the plutonium in the morning, probably before dawn. They're using the river." I reached out and put my hand on Ritter's arm, using the physical link to boost our mental connection. I pushed a memory of the map at him while it was still fresh in my mind. He'd be better at remembering it and knowing where we should overtake the boat.

I wanted to say more, to tell them about Crandall and the letter to his wife. But there wasn't time for any of that, and I didn't want Mari to carry the load I felt now. I took a deep breath. "We'll have to come back and free these people after we get the plutonium. The Emporium will have no use for them then."

"Don't worry. We'll rip the doors out if we have to." Though his face was in shadow, I knew Ritter understood that something had happened to make me upset about the prisoners. Maybe I would tell him later. For a moment I thought he would ask about the snake, but he didn't and I was grateful. The blue lights had faded somewhat now that I wasn't delving into people's thoughts, but I needed to get back to Jeane soon.

Ritter led the way out. As we moved forward, a heavy

weight seemed to crash down on me, and it was all I could do to keep up. I stumbled and would have fallen, but Keene joined us, the brush barely moving in his wake, and steadied me.

Or at least I thought he did. When I looked, he wasn't touching me. Prickles ran over my skin, the feeling intensifying when he didn't meet my gaze. Was that my imagination or did I feel stronger now that he was near?

"We're done here," Ritter said into his mic after putting some distance between us and the building. "Rendezvous at the SUV."

We continued into the night, walking until I felt numb all over. I began absorbing at a greater rate, and by the time we reached the vehicle, I was feeling better. Or maybe that was because Jeane had joined us and Delia's creation stopped feeding.

Ritter explained what I'd learned, and Stella opened her laptop on the ground and connected to the satellite. Ritter, Stella, Jace, and Keene huddled together over the display, discussing options, while Mari and I sat down on the grass, close enough to see, but not participating in the dialogue. Jeane had settled on the hood of the SUV, her arms around her knees, looking as if she were posing for a commercial featuring vehicles that were meant to be taken to exotic, sexy locations. Shadrach stood aimlessly nearby, his face mournful. I knew he thought his son was dead, and there was little any of us could say that would help him. I felt sorry for his wife and that he would have to tell her that her only son was gone.

"Okay, so that has to be the boat they're taking," Ritter said, extending a forefinger toward a satellite photograph of the river. "It's bigger than I expected, but nothing else nearby really fits the profile. The best place for us to board will be here." He moved his finger to a place downriver. "There'll be at least two ladders, one on each side, but we'll need grappling hooks to get everyone up at once. The only other choice is at the entry point."

"They'll have too many guards while they're loading," Jace said. "But I think we should board farther away than what you're saying. Give them more time to start feeling like they've made it. The river is also much narrower in this area so we won't have as much space to miss them. It's deeper, but we all know how to swim, right?"

I waited for Ritter to point out why that wouldn't be a good idea, but he gave a nod and said, "I think you're right. That is a better location. And it'll give us more time to get into place. But no heroics. We do what's necessary to grab the plutonium and get out."

"Okay." Stella snapped the laptop shut. "We'll have to call Chris and have him meet us at the hotel with the water gear. If he starts out now, we'll be in place in plenty of time. I hope everyone is ready for a cool dip."

"Not everyone." Ritter glanced at Shadrach. "I want you to wait here for Cort. You two will keep an eye on the guards here to make sure they don't hurt the prisoners. If they try, do whatever it takes to stop them. We'll come help you free them once we have the plutonium en route to the rendezvous with whoever Ava and the president are sending for it."

Stella put on her headset. "I'll call Ava to see how that's going. I'll let them know we'll need them soon."

"Keene and Mari," Ritter continued. "I want you two watching the loading. I need a solid count on guards. As soon as they board, you'll come to meet us. We'll probably be out in the river by then, so depending on what signal we send, you'll either pick us up or speed forward to a second location to make another attempt in case we fail." His tone told everyone he didn't think that would be necessary.

"What if you need more help on the boat?" Keene asked.

"We won't." Ritter hesitated before adding, "With Erin channeling, we'll have three using combat, and that should be plenty because Jeane's going with us, and she'll null their agents' abilities. You think you can do that, Jeane?"

She slid down from the SUV, giving him a long stare. "Of course." There was more in her gaze, a question about why he'd decided to trust her, but she didn't voice it.

Ritter must have seen the same expression because he added, "I know you would hate it if they took you back to Delia. They are working for her. Don't ever forget that."

Maybe he wanted her close to help me, or maybe it was so he could put a knife in her if she did anything stupid. I couldn't really say. But for whatever reason Jeane had saved my life, and I believed that, at least for now, she was aligned with us.

"We'd better get into place," Ritter said. "Shadrach, when Cort gets here, he'll use the listening device Stella sent in so you can listen and act against the guards before we get here if you need to." He paused before adding, "If you do go in, be sure you keep one of the guards conscious. They might know where your son is."

Shadrach nodded, his gaze refocusing. I was glad that Ritter seemed to know exactly what the healer needed to hear.

INSTEAD OF CALLING TO REPORT, MARI SHIFTED FROM THE DOCK where the Emporium were loading the plutonium and came to stand with us on the bank downriver where we waited in ambush. "We count nine guards," she said, "and at least two boat personnel. But there could be more. Some were on board before we arrived."

"That's good enough," Ritter said. "Even if there are a few more, it'll be more than a fair fight. Uh, but don't forget to go back for the SUV."

She laughed and vanished with a soft *pop!*

Ten minutes later, I swam into the river with the others. The lush vegetation on the banks was full of insect and animal life, and I was glad that nothing really large registered in the water. I was feeling strong and anxious for a fight, but it was the two-legged enemy I wanted to confront, not the endangered Orinoco crocodile.

"Here she comes," Ritter said. "In exactly sixty seconds, we start. Begin countdown now."

We all carried grappling hooks and waterproof weapons, except for Jeane, whom we'd equipped only with a pistol. I'd worried the wetsuit would inhibit my mobility, but the material was pliant enough. It didn't keep out the cold, of course, but the water wasn't as chilly as I'd expected.

Separating from Ritter and Stella, I let the current drag me slightly downstream, out of the way of the Emporium boat and the huge light mounted on the front. They'd be doing the same on the other side. Jace, who was entering the boat on the same side as me, was already in position several yards upstream.

My watch beeped out sixty seconds. Showtime.

I fired my pistol at an Unbounded guard who stood near the boat railing holding an assault rifle. Without a sound, he toppled forward into the water. Not exactly what I'd intended, but it was good enough. I pulled out my tranque gun, now equipped with a tracking beacon, and shot at the body in the water. Maybe we could find him later and take him to our prison compound.

Swiveling, I launched my grappling hook and pulled myself close to the boat, where I grabbed hold of a ladder and began climbing. Jeane came after me. I saw Jace scaling the boat some distance away. There was no sign of Ritter or Stella, but I knew they were on the other side. I was about to pull myself up when I noticed something grabbing onto the side of the boat several yards away from me. Before shooting, I sent out my thoughts tentatively.

It was Keene, and I saw in his mind that after determining the number of guards, he'd hooked on and ridden the boat down to us in order to be part of the assault team. I had to admit that it was something I might do, but disastrous if he had been caught, and I hoped Ritter didn't come down on him for it.

I reached the top and peeked over the railing, glad to see that the four guards who had been outside on the deck were down. Yet, even as I had the thought, a radio crackled static and a clump of men spewed from the door to the cabin. I vaulted over the side, dragging Jeane with me. I pushed her against the side of the boat. "You stay right here. Remember, focus on them. Not us."

Could she really pinpoint nulling like that? I could with my ability, and Mari had great precision. So did Dimitri with his healing. But some abilities like combat just happened. You used them or you didn't.

No time to worry about that now. My friends had engaged the enemy, even Keene, who had somehow made it the rest of the way up without a ladder or equipment. Bullets zinged, ricocheting off the sides of the boat. I launched myself into the fray, firing at a soldier as he raised his pistol. He dodged behind the cabin, and his bullet went wide. Then he was firing again. I dived away.

In that instant, a weight slammed into me from the side and I fell to the deck, a soldier on top of me. He was bigger than I was and the quickness of his movements were frightening. I reached for Jace, since he was the nearest, and began using his ability. It was odd seeing Jace's fight and experiencing my own at the same time, but we'd practiced enough in training that the double vision was no longer much of a problem. I pulled the trigger of my gun, but the guard hit my arm before I did, throwing off my aim.

The distraction was enough for me to pull out from under him and slam my pistol toward the side of his head. He blocked and my gun skidded across the deck. He went for a shot of his own, but I rammed my fist into his face, momentarily stunning him. Leaping to my feet, I spun, using a kick to free him of his gun. He answered with a punch to my stomach that made my eyes weep.

Why was he still so fast? What was Jeane doing? Twiddling her thumbs?

Feinting first one way and then the other, I somersaulted to the side, bringing up my ballistic knife. He anticipated me and moved like a blur, but I'd fired ahead of him, where I projected he might be. He jolted to a stop and collapsed to the deck with a thump, my knife embedded in his heart.

I wanted to lie there panting, rejoicing over my very lucky shot, but I jumped to my feet. No one was in sight, but I could see Jace in my mind exchanging furious love taps with his opponent. Pushing out my thoughts further, I found

Ritter and Stella together, fighting off two men. Keene was shooting another man—probably the one who had shot at me when I'd first climbed on the boat. With the four who had gone down at first, and my felled man, that accounted for nine guards. If the count was correct, we'd only have the two sailors to deal with.

My gun was lost somewhere in the dark, so I grabbed my knife from the soldier's chest, wiping it hurriedly before replacing it in its housing. Sprinting to the cabin door, I found a short flight of stairs leading up and a longer one going down. I reached out, searching for life forces. There. Up the stairs, two shone brightly. I took the six steps two at a time, reaching a hallway that ran the short length of the cabin. Glass lined one side of the corridor, and I looked through to where two mortals sat before a large window, their hands on a panel that controlled the boat.

They turned as I entered the room, their eyes widening. They weren't blocking, and I saw in their minds that they were both Emporium employees, recently contracted, and they understood at once what my appearance meant for their cargo and their job security.

One went for his gun, but I jumped in his direction so fast that he didn't have time to draw. Adrenaline from the fight zinged through my body, increased by both my Unbounded genes and the ability I was borrowing from Jace.

I slugged the man hard and snatched his gun, stepping into him as I kicked backward at his companion, who was getting the wrong idea about jumping me from behind. The man hurtled backward, slamming into the chairs. I pointed the gun at his face. "Where is it?"

He remained silent, but his thoughts went to the trap-door in the floor, where he customarily hid his contraband.

"Tell me how to open the trapdoor," I said.

"I tell you, I'm as good as dead."

I shrugged. "That says a lot about who you work for."

Where were Ritter and the others? If Jeane had done her job, they should have dispatched their opponents far more quickly than I did. Which meant Jeane hadn't nulled anything. I was going to kill her when I caught up to her.

Taking my tranque from a pocket of my suit, I shot the man. For good measure, I shot his unconscious companion as well. Not being Unbounded, they'd be out at least six hours. I glanced at the trapdoor his mind had indicated. It looked like any other metal section of the floor. I hoped the plutonium really was down there or I'd have to shoot one of the sailors with something else to waken him for questioning.

Closing my eyes, I searched for life forces. Was that a faint burning under the metal floor? And why wasn't it moving? If it was a person, it would be the tenth man I'd counted. So not nine as Keene and Mari had hoped.

My earbud was smashed during my skirmish with the guard on deck, so I had no way of checking up on anyone except mentally. I could see that Ritter was doing double duty, battling his own opponent and helping with Stella's as well. Stella was one of the best fighters I knew, but she couldn't hold up forever against someone both gifted and trained in combat. I didn't dare talk to Ritter, to tell him what I intended, lest I interfere with his concentration.

Jace, though he did seem to be getting the best of his opponent, was inexperienced enough that any communication with him might change that in a heartbeat, so I didn't talk to him either.

Keene was holding his own, even without a combat

ability, and I could only attribute that to his years of training with the Emporium.

I couldn't see Jeane's life force anywhere, and if the greedy glow coming from the box in my head was any indicator, she wasn't nearby. Had she jumped ship and abandoned us to our fate? If so, I'd kill her, and after she recovered, I'd kill her again.

It didn't take me long to find the latch under the control desk that popped open the floor panel. The resulting hole was larger than I'd expected, revealing a steep, narrow stairway instead of a cubby hole or ladder as I'd anticipated. I went down slowly and carefully, holding the sailor's gun ready and trying not to make too much noise on the metal stairs. It descended about twice my own height, landing in a very narrow hallway that was dimly lit by tiny lights set in the floor. If I had the lay of the ship correct, this hidden corridor was behind the passenger cabins below deck. I didn't mind the closed-in space. In fact, I felt more secure—despite the fact that an Emporium agent lurked somewhere close by.

The life force was burning more brightly now, unhindered by layers of metal that had previously separated us. I didn't even have to reach for it. I started down the cramped hallway toward the mental glow. Latches holding panels on the wall bumped my shoulders on both sides as I passed. I was curious about the panels and what might lie behind them, but opening one would alert the guard—if I hadn't already done that. I edged forward, keeping my link with Jace but trying to ignore his fight. I had to focus on what might happen next. Especially with Jeane having gone AWOL.

I set my foot down and a loud creak echoed through the tight space.

The light force moved. Fast.

I brought my gun up as the man came at me, his body a blur. I squeezed the trigger, hoping he wasn't moving too fast for me to hit. A binging of the bullet as it ricocheted off the metal walls confirmed that he was. The figure kept coming. I started to tug on the trigger again.

He stopped two feet away, coming into focus—a young, slightly built man with wispy blond hair, a small face, and crunched features. His blue eyes laughed at me, and my finger on the trigger stilled, and not because of the gun he had aimed at my face. "Oh, it's you," he said. "Hi, sis."

CHAPTER 13

"HELLO, JONNY." I WASN'T HIS SISTER, OR EVEN HIS HALF SISTER, AND if not for Delia's continued deception, he would know by now that I wasn't the daughter of Stefan Carrington. He'd know that the sperm Ava had stolen from the Emporium arrived too late for my mother's insemination, to be saved for a later date. He might guess that Jace was really his half brother, but I'd die to keep that knowledge from the Emporium . . . and maybe even from Jace himself.

Jonny was over a hundred years old, though he looked twenty-eight, and often acted like a gleeful child in a man's body. As a side effect of a forced Change at eighteen, he was aging at five times the rate of a normal Unbounded—so ten years for every hundred he lived. The last time we'd met, his thoughts had told me he was bitter about his life expectancy of only four hundred years as opposed to two thousand. He'd pulled a gun on me then, too, and almost cost Ritter his life.

I was surprised that Jonny was here and apparently in

some form of command position. His gift was speed, a variation of the combat ability, and while he could move faster than anyone I knew, he had only limited fighting skills. I'd thought it likely that I might run into some of the Emporium agents I knew, given our various encounters, but I'd expected an Unbounded with more skill, someone held in higher regard. While Jonny's parentage set him apart, his lack of full ability and his limited life span made Emporium investment in his future less likely. Iran was important in their plan to start a war; it seemed they would have sent someone . . . better.

"Where's the plutonium?" I demanded.

"I don't know what you're talking about." His shield was tight over his mind, so I couldn't tell if he was lying or not. But if I was to get the plutonium, I'd have to get past him, which wouldn't be easy without either borrowing his speed and beating him to the prize or flashing light into his mind and rendering him unconscious. Unfortunately, like so many of the Emporium agents we'd met recently, his shield was stronger than I was at the moment. The snake inside me was feeding faster since I was using my ability, seeming to drain my strength even as I watched. The blue lights emanating from the outer box grew brighter as I summoned the image of my machete and began hammering at his shield.

I upped my absorption rate in an attempt to alleviate some of the energy drain. "I can't let you kill eight million people. Eight million, Jonny. Not to mention all the others who'll die after the war starts. They're women, children, innocents. Civilians. Doesn't that mean anything to you?"

He laughed. "They're mortal, Erin. Their lives are short anyway. It won't make much of a difference, not for long. Sixty million mortals died in World War II, most of them civilians, and look at the world now. Most people don't know or care about what happened back then. Everything continued on well enough without them." He sounded almost as if he'd been there, maybe somehow helped start that war. And maybe he had.

"The people we'll target are replaceable," he added, "and their sacrifice will pave the way to a new world for the Unboundaried. We, who are destined to rule."

That made me angry, especially his use of the full name Unboundaried, as if he had the right to godhood because of his lack of temporal boundaries. "If mortals are inferior because of their shorter lives, what about you? What about what the Emporium did to you, forcing your Change?"

"Shut up." His smile didn't waver, but emotions leaked from him: anger, resentment, regret. His gun hand dipped slightly and then came back up again—too fast for me to react.

"What about your friend who died when they tried to force her Change?" I could see that his shield was weakening as I worked at it with the machete. I had left the real weapon back at the hotel, not wanting to risk it in the water, but the mental image of it remained constant. Jonny's surface emotions dampened. "She was weak. Probably never would have Changed."

"You loved her. What was her name?"

"Shut up."

But my comment had weakened his already battered shield; a tiny hole opened and I slid inside. His thought stream was erratic, bouncing up and down. In his mind, I saw what I'd hoped not to see: a thread of shiny black undulating in his sand stream. Now appearing and just that quickly being buried. The thing was similar to the snake inside my box, and I knew Delia had put it there not only to protect certain thoughts inside Jonny's head but also as a trap for any unsuspecting sensing Unbounded. I'd already made that mistake once.

I also saw the girl he'd loved, her pretty face contorting in unimaginable pain as he'd watched her die. She'd been a volunteer for the program like he had been, despite the lack of knowledge about the possible consequences and side effects. Anything for the good of the whole, for the Utopian dream.

I still didn't know her name because he didn't think of it, his mind overwhelmed with grief that should have lessened after a hundred years.

If I lost Ritter, would I mourn him that long? Would he mourn me? He'd mourned his family longer than that, and I believed what was between us ran far deeper. Why had I waited so long to make him mine?

Regret washed over me.

No, Jonny's regret. I had a future. I wasn't Jonny and his loss wasn't mine. Yet I felt it was, and I understood why he clung to the ideals of the Emporium. Because once he stopped believing, the girl he had loved would have died in vain.

"Don't make another mistake," I said. "Step back. Let me by."

I saw him decide to pull the trigger before he actually did, and I flashed light inside his mind. Crying out, he fell, his thought stream vanishing instantly. I withdrew, feeling suffocated in the lake of his unconsciousness. I tried to take a step, but the next second I collapsed on top of Jonny in the narrow corridor. The feeding snake made flashing a hundred times more draining, and it was fortunate I was still able to see.

As I lay in the darkness, gathering my strength, a radio at Jonny's waist crackled. "ETA, four minutes by chopper. Can you hold them off that long?"

So he'd reported us, and now the plutonium was in danger of being lost. I took Jonny's gun from his loosened grip, tucking it and my other stolen weapon in different pockets. Then I crawled forward toward where I'd first seen Jonny's life force. I wished I could check on the others, maybe tell them where I was, but I had to preserve my strength.

By the time I reached Jonny's hiding place, I was able to stand, steadying myself on the metal lockers lining the walls. The place was an alcove, little more than an indentation just large enough to hold a stiff-looking love seat that had probably been down here since the ship was built at least two decades ago. Nestled next to the couch was a rectangular metal container two feet long, eight inches wide, and about a foot tall. I reached for it, but it was too heavy to pick up, and I had to content myself by lifting a handle on the end and pulling it along the floor on the set of tiny back wheels. The wheels scraped over the metal floor more than they rolled, sounding ridiculously loud to my ears.

Plutonium was a heavy metal at about seven hundred and fifteen pounds per cubic inch. About twenty-two pounds were required to make a bomb. While I had no idea how much plutonium was inside the cask, I was sure the packaging weighed far more than the actual plutonium. The double containers were normally built to withstand a two-thousand-foot drop from an airplane, submersion in water for eight hours, and thirty minutes in fire. A cask would also prevent plutonium leaks during transportation that might cause mortals exposure and endanger their lives. In theory, moving the cask was perfectly safe.

The corridor seemed twice its previous length, and I contemplated opening the box and removing just the plutonium. But I knew it had been packed precisely to avoid forming a critical mass which could then start a chain reaction, so messing with it really wasn't wise. So I tugged the cask along the corridor, realizing I wouldn't be able to get it up the narrow stairs alone. How many minutes had passed?

A soft clink drew my attention to the staircase, and I pulled out a gun, reaching with my thoughts. To my relief, it was Keene, his mind unblocked. He was looking for me.

I felt a rush of gratitude. *Keene,* I pushed into his mind, *I'm here with the plutonium. It's safe.*

He came fast down the stairs toward me, bending briefly to look at Jonny. They had been friends once. "Anyone else?" he asked.

"No. But this is too heavy. Awkward. We'll need one of the others." I wanted to ask how he'd been able to rid himself of his opponent when Stella hadn't been able to, but now was not the time to ask. Maybe the agent he'd faced hadn't been gifted in combat.

"There's not much time," I added.

"I can do it."

He hadn't reached me, but all at once the weight of the container lightened, and my next tug sent it hurtling toward me, and I flattened against the side to let it careen past, wincing as it ran over my toes. Keene leaned over and caught it.

"Keene, you—" I broke off.

"Yeah," he said, irony seeping into his voice. "It seems I share a variation of my father and my brother's ability to see patterns on an atomic level. Not to understand how they interact, but to change them, or at least to increase them. Efforts people make like you did when you pulled that cask. Or I can make physical things change." He glanced at the cask between us. "I start it, and it continues almost on its own."

I remembered beginning to fall at the old house, and how I'd felt something pushing me up as I'd scrabbled for purchase on the window. And imagining the support when I'd nearly collapsed in the woods.

Keene. Had he increased my effort or *added* to the air around me? Or maybe both.

Just now, before he'd spoken, I'd guessed some sort of telekinesis, at least as far as being able to lift something without touching it, but it seemed I was a bit off.

Far off.

I wondered how many generations it had taken and how many experiments the Emporium had conducted to rebirth that ability. And what they'd do to get him back once they heard.

"It's rather difficult to control." In his thoughts, I saw what he wasn't saying, how he'd tried to stop the fire in the employee condo but instead had helped trap himself and Mari.

"Maybe that's just in the beginning," I told him. After my Change, all I'd felt were impressions of emotions, and now I was blasting people's minds with flashes of light or forcing their limbs to move the way I wanted. If I stopped to think about the continual developments, I might go crazy.

Keene inclined his head, apparently not willing to agree but hoping I was right. "Let's get this up."

"They're sending a chopper. We have to warn the others." Oddly enough—or maybe not so oddly—now that he was close, I had enough strength to reach out to Ritter. I found him sprinting toward the cabin, having finished off both his and Stella's opponents.

Emporium chopper coming, I told him. *I've got the plutonium. Joining you now.* His satisfaction mirrored my own.

I turned my attention back to Keene. "It's working on me. Your ability—it makes me stronger."

He shrugged. "You look beat."

"Just don't blow me up."

That got a smile from him. "You'll be fine. I just excited a few atoms."

"Hopefully, they'll go back to the right place when we're finished."

"I'm not promising anything," he said with a laugh.

Together, we hefted the plutonium cask, seeming much lighter now with his effort. I hoped he knew well enough to stay away from trying anything with the plutonium or the cask itself. The last thing we needed was a critical mass.

Now I understood how Keene had beaten the Emporium agent so quickly. He must have experimented with his ability. I was glad for him, glad that he had something more to focus on, an ability that might have some real teeth. And also happy about the very short glimpse I had of him and Mari stuck in a closet at the employee condo. Of course his erratic heartbeat could have had more to do with the fire than her presence, but it might mean something more. A chord of nostalgia rang inside my chest, making me recall the moment I might have chosen to be the woman in his life.

When we made it back to the moonlit deck, Ritter and Jace were readying their rocket launchers. The sound of chopper rotors thumped faintly in the wind.

"Erin!" Stella shouted from the side of the boat where I had boarded. "I need some help here!"

Leaving Keene with the cask, I joined her near a sprawled figure. Jeane. She'd taken a bullet to the chest and was dead—at least temporarily. Her life force barely glowed, so it wasn't a wonder I couldn't see it earlier. Maybe I'd have to forgive her for not helping us out.

Stella had activated Jeane's life jacket and connected a tow rope to the latch. "Once I'm in the water, throw her over. I'll make sure she gets to the shore. I've already called Mari to pick us up. She's tracking us now. Here's the raft for the plutonium."

Stella shoved the raft into my hands. It was nothing more than a thick Styrofoam board that was wider but not quite as long as the cask itself. I laid it on the deck as Stella disappeared over the side. I heaved Jeane over after, making sure she didn't hit the side of the boat on the way down.

"Go," Keene said, appearing behind me. "I'll lower the plutonium." He began unraveling a length of rope.

I nodded, glancing behind him at Jace and Ritter, who were barely visible in the dark. The sound of the chopper was louder now, but they were waiting for a visual to fire. With all the trees near the river, that might not give them much lead time.

I jumped from the boat with the plutonium raft, the shock of the cold water momentarily engulfing me. Triggering my life jacket, I waited as Keene lowered the plutonium. At first I worried that the raft would sink. But as soon as I'd hit the water, little fans in the bottom activated, buoying it— and me—up. After securing the cask as best I could while treading water, I pushed off after Stella. We had to get out of here before the Emporium arrived.

Behind me I heard two loud explosions and saw flashes of light. A chopper careened toward the boat, slamming into it and exploding in a deafening roar and a rush of fire. But there were more chopper sounds that were growing louder by the moment. Kicking hard, I made it to the side of the river where Stella helped me drag the plutonium onto the bank. Keene joined us as another explosion rocked the sky.

Stella carried Jeane, while Keene and I brought the cask. We'd gone only a hundred feet when Ritter and Jace came up from behind. Ritter took my side of the cask. "Speed it up, folks, we're about to have a lot of company."

I risked a glance behind and saw that the boat was burning. Was it wrong of me to hope the Emporium could put it out before Jonny suffered too much? Fire wouldn't kill him, but it made for a painful recovery. Despite all his delusions, I had a soft spot for my would-be brother.

Mari wasn't long in catching up to us, and I breathed a sigh of relief as we loaded the plutonium into the back of the SUV.

"What now?" Mari asked, relinquishing her place behind the wheel to Jace, whose energy level seemed to have increased with the fighting.

"Now we separate." Ritter tossed me a new earbud to replace my damaged one, a line of worry creasing his forehead.

"Cort sent several text messages about activity where the Emporium is holding the factory employees." His eyes caught mine and held. "I don't know what the situation is, but Cort and Shadrach need help, and you and Mari are the only ones who can get there fast enough. Jace and I will join you as soon as we rendezvous with the CIA."

His eyes were asking if I was up to it, so I nodded. "Let's go, Mari." I reached out and touched her arm. I knew my action would signal, at least to Ritter, that I wasn't quite up to my usual strength, since touch enhanced my ability, but preserving what strength I had left was more important than my pride. This was almost over, and then I'd get that monster out of my head once and for all.

CHAPTER 14

WE APPEARED IN THE WOODS BEHIND THE EMPLOYEE PRISON where pandemonium reigned. Guards were everywhere, gesturing with assault rifles at the employees who spilled from the house, half-dressed, to join others who had apparently just arrived from the factory in the predawn morning. Several cars had accompanied the van, and those drivers were begging the guards to let them go home to their families. I assumed those were local employees, who hadn't been held before. Something had changed.

The guards had their mind shields in place, but their countenances were dark and sinister, and I knew they were about to commit atrocities that would haunt me for months to come—if I couldn't stop them.

I searched the trees for the two life forces of our friends and gestured to Mari for us to shift there. We reappeared behind them, far enough away that we wouldn't startle them. "Cort," I called softly to the men, who were little more than shadows crouching under a tree.

He turned, his weapon ready, but no surprise emanated from his surface thoughts, so Ritter must have warned him we were coming. I wanted to tell him about Keene and his ability, but it wasn't my place.

"We listened with Stella's spybot, and the guards have confirmed that the Emporium can't risk any connection to the factory, not if it's linked to Iran or terrorism," Cort said as we approached. The knit cap pulled over his blond hair somehow made him appear deadly, far from his normally bookish demeanor. "Their orders are to get rid of all witnesses and to raze this place. They have a big pit prepared about thirty yards out from the house. We found it an hour ago. They still have an old backhoe there. Looks like they're planning a mass grave."

I couldn't even respond to that idea, but my silence must have testified of my disbelief because Shadrach said, "They've done it before. It's deep enough not to be a problem with small game or the smell, even if they didn't own the land out here."

"All this because your son talked with a reporter?" I was having a hard time believing it.

"It's probably more to hide the origin of the plutonium," Shadrach said. "They're making sure no word gets out."

Mari made a sound in her throat. "Well, they've already figured out that someone knows about the plutonium since we just stole it."

"Which makes this cleanup even more necessary," Cort said, the tightness in his voice betraying his worry. "Gives the Emporium time to concentrate their efforts in other areas before people start connecting the dots. While that might mean they've abandoned the plutonium idea for the moment, it could mean they have something even worse underway."

He stood, keeping behind the tree, though it was so dark where we were that the Emporium agents couldn't possibly see us. "Come on. Let's go."

The employees were in full panic mode, knowing something wasn't right. If they had previously believed they would be released once their job was finished, they understood now that wasn't happening. I could feel their emotional anguish and fear—a loud cacophony, which echoed the crying and pleadings going on in front of the house. I thought of Dr. Francis Crandall, but I couldn't find him in the dozens of milling people. I still had the photograph of his letter back at the hotel with the rest of my gear.

The guards were yelling and pushing the people into a pack, using cruel voices that evoked even more fear. A few bolted, and they met with the butt of a rifle, most needing to be helped up afterward by their fellow prisoners. No shots yet, so obviously these guards wanted all the evidence in the pit so they wouldn't have to clean up stray bodies after the deed.

"We'll hit them at the far edge of the clearing," Cort said, "before they disappear into those trees. Erin, you shift to the right side and Mari to the left. We'll fan out over here. Keep out of sight in the trees for as long as possible. Each of us will take the two guards closest to us. If there is any doubt, talk it out."

Only two? There seemed to be more than eight, but Cort would have made a complete count. I put in the earbud and mic Ritter had given me.

"Afterward, we'll get those people out of here as fast as we can in case more soldiers come."

"There won't be more coming," I said, hoping I was right. "They're too busy trying to catch up with the plutonium."

"Make sure your earbuds are receiving." After we all nodded, Cort said, "Okay, let's get into place."

Reaching out to Mari, I remained crouching and channeled her ability, shifting to the far side of the clearing. The emotions of the frightened prisoners were slightly muffled here, but I was still anxious to relieve their terror.

Yet it was another half hour before the guards were satisfied that they had everyone. Two more cars had arrived, and I counted at least forty-three prisoners. My stomach felt sick as I burned with the desire to protect them. It was agony to wait. Finally, they began moving toward the place where we planned to attack. Slowly and gruesomely. The prisoners had fallen silent for the most part, though occasionally a terrified sob reached my ears.

At last, Cort's command came, and I concentrated, using my anger to hone my aim. My first guard went down instantly, and the second followed before he could turn his weapon to fire. Most of the other guards fell as quickly, but at least one managed to fire two shots, one in my direction and one into the crowd of workers, before crumpling in a bloody, grisly heap, hit by four more bullets from each of our guns.

Terrified screams shattered the air as the employees bolted into the woods. I met up with the others as we ran after them—all but Shadrach, who crouched by one of the fallen guards. We'd made it only a few yards into the woods when Cort lifted his hand to tell us to stop. "They won't trust us now. They'll think we're after them. We'll have to contact their embassies and make sure they know people will be coming in for help." Reluctantly, we started back to the clearing where we'd left Shadrach.

"Wake up!" Shadrach shouted as he shook the lifeless

figure of a guard. "Where's my son?" He began talking and cursing in a language I didn't understand, his grief obviously sharp and painful.

Mari scowled over her shoulder at the dark trees, as if they were responsible for Shadrach's grief. "What if the employees go back to the factory?"

"If they're that stupid they deserve what they get." I didn't really mean it, but my gaze had caught on a figure just inside the clearing who hadn't made it into the woods, and I was steeling myself for who it might be. The man lay face down, blood from a gunshot wound gushing over his back, the flow already slowing noticeably. The guards had apparently claimed at least one victim.

The gunshot wasn't the man's only wound, though. As I knelt and turned him over, sorrow knifed through me. It was Dr. Crandall. I felt for a pulse, but I could already see that his life force was gone. Crandall would never make it home to his wife and daughter. I was crying before I realized it, pushing my thoughts into his mind, searching for a spark of life. There was nothing.

Dimly, I became aware of Shadrach kneeling beside me, his hands over mine on top of Crandall's body. "He's gone, dear. He's gone."

I nodded. We'd done well. We'd stolen the plutonium and rescued the employees. Only one missing—Shadrach's son. And only this one casualty. I felt like vomiting.

Shadrach's hand touched my shoulder. "Come and help me with the guard. I think I've healed him enough that you can look into his mind. See if he knows about my son." Shadrach was pulling me to my feet as he spoke, and since there was nothing I could do to help Crandall, I went with him. Soothing feelings came from Shadrach's hands where he touched me, and some of my tiredness leaked away. At that moment, he reminded me so much of Dimitri, I wanted to fall into his arms and be comforted.

Instead, I knelt down next to the unconscious guard, who had three bullet wounds—two in his chest and one near his groin. Was this the man who had killed Crandall? His life force was burning more brightly than those of the other seven soldiers, and in his mind, I found a lake of unconsciousness and thought bubbles instead of the black emptiness of death.

There was no fast way to explore his mind. Unlike with a conscious person, I couldn't insert a thought or verbally encourage his mind to bring up what I was looking for. It was slow going. This agent was not an Iranian sympathizer, and he detested the employees and the few agents from that area of the world, but he was, as so many Emporium Unbounded were, a true believer of his importance in society and in the Utopia the Emporium pushed, like perfumed and disguised waste, in front of their devotees.

No sign yet of Shadrach's son.

Chopper sounds reverberated through the still-dark morning sky, momentarily drawing my attention. "We have visitors! Two choppers!" The worried shout came from Cort, but then he looked at his phone and relaxed. "It's Ritter and Jace. Must have caught a ride from the CIA."

I continued looking into the guard's mind. He was ordinary, as far as Unbounded went. He had two brothers and a sister who were mortal. Long dead. He didn't mourn them. They were inferior.

Ritter reached us moments later, squatting beside me, and I relaxed against the arm he slid around my back.

It felt right to have him with me. "I'm sorry," I told him in a whisper. "I was wrong about waiting."

"What?" He stared at me, obviously concerned. But I couldn't exactly explain with everyone listening.

That was when a huge pressure inside me burst, releasing like an infected tooth spilling pus, though I hadn't realized I was under so much pressure until that precise moment. I knew exactly what it was: the shiny snake had burst through the first box I'd formed. The pressure made sense to me now since the box was created from my own thoughts and was a part of me every bit as much as that snake was Delia's construct. With the release of pressure came not pain but a sweet relief that made me catch my breath.

When I didn't elaborate, Ritter said, "We have a little problem. Stella went back to the hotel after we passed off the cask, and she said that reporter's there. The one you sent to the airport. Apparently, he didn't leave but contacted the rental agency and had them activate the GPS in his car, which led him to the hotel. Says he's heard from Shadrach's son."

I was surprised that Walker had the guts to come searching for us after his Hunter contact had been killed. "Wait, how did he remember us? I took the thoughts from his mind."

"He recorded it all on his phone. Part of the fight in the alleyway, and then your conversation in the car."

I cursed under my breath. I should have caught that from his thoughts. I'd been sloppy, and I hated that. "He knows where Habid is?"

"Says he does, but he won't tell us anything unless we bring him along." A rush of breath squeezed between his lips before Ritter added, "Idiot."

"Right." Apparently the reporter had a death wish. Shaking my head, I stared back down at the unconscious guard, mentally stepping out of the way of his memory from two days ago. I was getting closer. Maybe.

In the next instant, I found what I was looking for. I saw how the guard and his buddies had raided the employee condo back in the city and brought everyone here. Everyone except the troublemaker, Habid Salemi, who had been hauled away with the plutonium by the senior guards.

I made a faint sound in the back of my throat. "Oh, no."

"What?" Ritter asked.

I took a moment to collect my thoughts. What I'd found in this guard's mind told me that our op wasn't nearly over but just beginning. I turned my head to look at Ritter, who still had his arm around me. "The cask from the boat—was there anything in it?"

"Enough weapons-grade plutonium to make a bomb." Ritter's voice was grim.

I was on to another memory now inside the guard's unconscious thoughts, and I shut my eyes to concentrate better. "Then it wasn't the only shipment. Just the first." Everyone's attention focused more intently on me.

"You mean to Iran?" Shadrach gasped in horror. "More than one shipment of plutonium to Iran?"

"I don't think so." I opened my eyes, still probing the guard's memory bubble. "According to this guy, the rumor is that the shipment we intercepted was bound for Iraq."

Ritter glanced at Cort, horror echoing on their faces, but it was Shadrach who spoke. "Makes sense. If they're going to encourage Iran to strike at Israel and US targets in Iraq, giving terrorists in Iraq the ability to fire back at Iran . . ."

He shook his head, furrows creasing his forehead. "If they succeed, this century will become the bloodiest humankind has ever known."

I agreed. With the Emporium pulling the puppet strings, no one was safe. "We have to stop them."

"You finished here?" Ritter asked me, glancing at the unconscious man.

I nodded. "He doesn't know any more."

"The CIA has agreed to transport these fellows to our plane at the airport," Ritter said, gesturing at the unconscious Emporium guards, "so we can eventually get them to Mexico. I'll send Jace with them."

I had forgotten that Jace had come with Ritter, but I could feel my brother now, off to the edge of the clearing, already hefting one of the Emporium guards.

"Mari," Ritter added in a lower voice. "I need you to shift to the plane to help Chris prepare the berths. Better go into the woods first. It's getting light, and they don't know about us." He jerked his head toward the four CIA agents who had accompanied him.

Mari grinned and started to walk toward the comparative darkness of the trees. I felt her shift before she was quite out of sight, but I doubted the CIA agents would notice.

I stared at where she'd vanished as I said to Ritter, "Now that they know we're on to them, the Emporium won't use the route they detailed in Desoto's papers to smuggle the plutonium into Iran. They'll shake things up to make sure we don't grab it like we did the other."

"Come on." Ritter pulled me to my feet, his hands gripping mine far too tightly, but I wasn't about to complain.

"Looks like we'll be taking that reporter along after all. If he knows how to find Shadrach's son, he might lead us straight to the plutonium."

I hoped he was right.

I also hoped that Walker Anderson wouldn't be one more death I would have on my conscience.

CHAPTER 15

After the Emporium guards had been loaded into the CIA choppers, the rest of us borrowed the Emporium guards' van and rode back to the hotel. Cort drove and Shadrack was in the front with him, while Ritter and I sat on the floor in the back, where the seats had been removed to fit more workers. I felt content for the moment to lie back against him with his arms around me.

When I told Ritter that I regretted making him wait, I meant that I should have married him the first moment I knew how I felt about him. But marriage to an Unbounded meant a lot longer than I could even fathom. I'd been so afraid that in a hundred years, I'd want out of the deal or that I'd regret making the commitment. Or that maybe I'd wished to have spent time with Keene, whose demands never frightened me like Ritter's. Keene asked for nothing; Ritter asked for it all.

We hit a bump in the road and Ritter's arms tighten around me, giving me strength to be honest with myself.

Sure, Ritter asked for it all, but wasn't that what I wanted? Maybe the real truth was that Ritter was so much a part of me and our lives so filled with turmoil, that I was afraid of losing him—and therefore myself.

Ritter wanted children. I'd seen him envisioning me with a belly full of his baby, but he would let me make that decision, and in the meantime, I was reasonably confident I could work out Stella's nanites. It wasn't as if we only had a few decades to decide. I had a thousand years before my fertility would begin to decline in the slightest. He could wait. We could wait—until I reached a time when having a baby would be more important than the fear of losing the child.

Yet now, with the snake having burst from the first box, I knew we didn't have much time. I would have to face Delia very soon.

I'd wasted these last weeks when we could have been together, but I was going to fix that at the first opportunity. A shiver of anticipation slid through me. Ritter's hand rubbed over my thigh, telling me that I was projecting and that it was affecting him. I didn't care.

Thoughts flew through my head. Now that the pressure inside that box was released, I felt better and stronger than I'd felt in weeks. Ritter was here. We were together. For the moment, that was enough. The snake in my head was probably feasting abundantly without Jeane around, but for once I didn't feel tired or weak. I felt exuberant. Confident. In control. It had been weeks since I'd felt this good.

The feeling wouldn't last because the snake would eventually break through the outer box, and what happened then, I didn't know. But my whole future was riding on the outcome of my confrontation with Delia Vesey. I had to beat her because if I didn't, I'd lose everything I ever cared about.

When we arrived at the hotel, Cort and Keene left for the airport, taking the Unbounded agent I'd brought back earlier. I was glad the brothers would have some time alone because I was curious about Keene's ability, and Cort, once Keene told him what was going on, should be able to understand and explain the talent, if anyone could.

In the brief moment that we were together before Keene headed for the airport, I'd felt my strength increase. Keene didn't seem to be doing it on purpose, so I took Ritter aside and made sure he told Chris to give the all unconscious Emporium soldiers another dose of knockout juice before Keene arrived, just in case they were also affected by his ability.

When we entered the hotel room, Stella looked up from her laptop, looking no worse for her desperate fight on the boat. "Good, you're all back in one piece."

I had a brief vision of Dr. Crandall, blood welling from his back. *Not all of us.* But I didn't say it aloud. My eyes wandered to Walker Anderson, who'd stood up from the chair next to Stella as we entered. "Where is Habid?" I demanded.

He glanced nervously at the queen bed closest to the door where Jeane still lay unconscious and not breathing. His jaw clenched with determination. "Not until you promise to take me along."

Anger swept through me at the request. I glanced at Ritter. *May I?* I thought at him. He inclined his head, and I moved to Walker's side and shoved him against the wall, placing one hand on his neck and the other against his stomach. "What makes you think you can force us to do anything?" I put all the fury I felt at Crandall's senseless death into the words.

"Because," choked out Walker, "you guys aren't like them."

Ritter had moved to my side. Not because he was worried about Walker striking back but to give me pointers. "Really, you should push a little lower and harder, like I told you with Jeane back home."

"Like this?" I dug my thumb deeper.

Walker's eyes grew big. "Stop," he gasped. "Can't . . . breathe."

"Hmm. It works." I smiled at Ritter, letting up slightly without releasing my hold.

"Why'd you stop?" Ritter asked, his dark eyes glittering dangerously. "What do you care if one more foolish mortal dies?" I knew his words were only to scare the reporter. I'd seen Ritter go to great lengths to protect innocent mortals— even stupid ones like Walker.

"You have a point," I said. "He seems determined to get himself killed anyway, doesn't he?" Walker's eyes widened further.

A soft gasp from the bed pulled our attention away from Walker. Jeane was, apparently, back in the world of the living. I released the reporter, ignoring him as he huddled against the wall, clutching his throat.

"Ohhh," Jeane moaned. "I sure hate this, but it's beginning to be a habit with me these days." Her hand went to the hole in her wet suit where she'd taken the bullet. "It went right through me, didn't it?"

Shadrach glided to her side, shaken out of the morose state he'd fallen into on the drive back. He put his hand in the middle of her chest, closing his eyes. "Yes, the bullet is out. If you'll lie still a moment or two, I can help direct the healing. From the rate of repairs, it looks like the curequick is doing its job."

"Sure is. I'm as high as a kite." She laughed at the cliché, batting her eyes at Shadrach. "You sure have a way with your hands."

"You need to learn to stay out of the line of fire," I said to her, bothered by the smile Shadrach gave her in return. Wasn't the guy married? "You almost cost us the plutonium."

"But we got it, right?" she asked.

"We got some of it," I corrected. With Jeane awake, the larger box that still contained the snake in my head was no longer emitting blue light. I hoped that I continued feeling great with her help.

Walker pushed himself away from the wall, his pale, narrow face unyielding. "Ha! I knew it was something big, and I guessed it was nuclear, which is why I came down here in the first place. When Habid contacted me tonight, he said something about plutonium, and I think he's near the shipment. Or *a* shipment, I guess, if you already recovered some of it."

Stella turned to him, her headset blinking. "And you didn't think to tell me he mentioned plutonium when he contacted you?"

He shrugged. "You didn't promise you'd take me with you . . . or, uh, nearly choke me to death for information." Walker looked at me and rubbed his neck, as if expecting a repeat. Both lamps and the two overhead lights had been turned on, and in the oddly bright glow, the reddish highlights in his blond hair were more apparent.

For a moment no one spoke. Reporters weren't exactly our friends at the moment, especially those who knew about Unbounded, and none of us wanted to drag him along. But we *had* to recover the rest of the plutonium.

I moved toward Walker again, this time slowly. His eyes

grew wary, but he wasn't backing down. A twinge of guilt gnawed at me as I pushed through his shield and into his mind. "Walker," I said, "where is Habid? What did he say about the plutonium? If you don't tell me, I assure you I can get that information without your help."

He hesitated only a second. "Okay, I'll tell you everything, but you still have to take me along. I've learned enough about you to know you're not the same as those other Unbounded, no matter how you threaten me. It's all going to come out someday, and you'll need someone like me to tell your side. Because no way is this going to be easy for the American people to swallow. For *any* of us normal people to swallow." His gaze flicked to Ritter as the rush of words ended. "Mortals, I mean."

I nearly rolled my eyes. Ambition wafted from him like an unmistakable stench. Strong enough to drown out his very real fear. "You need to tell us everything, Walker. Every second you wait brings us closer to eight million deaths. And more. How are you communicating with Habid?"

"So you'll take me with you?" Walker countered.

My fists clenched, but before I could respond, Stella said, "Apparently, Walker has some friends who imagine themselves spies. They've created a device that's similar to a sat phone, except that it only sends a limited burst of information—text—at regular times. It rotates broadcasting channels, very like our locator chips. Well, in a much less sophisticated way. Walker sent this device to Habid when they started their conversation because Habid kept hinting that he was afraid for his life."

Shadrach made a noise in his throat from his place seated on the bed near Jeane, his mouth tight and his dark eyes bottomless.

Walker nodded, his eyes avoiding both Shadrach and Ritter. "I was worried he'd be kidnapped or killed before he told me the information about the nuclear weapon— that's what I thought it was at that point, not plutonium to make the weapon. I knew if I didn't find out where it was going and who it was meant for, I wouldn't have anything, and he insisted on meeting before he told me any details. So I sent him my tracking device just in case something happened. The last time I talked to him, he sounded extremely spooked."

"I have no idea how Habid kept Walker's device through his capture," Stella added, one brow arching, "but I can imagine."

"It *was* waterproof." Walker grimaced slightly. "A bit big, maybe, but he could have swallowed it if he was determined. If he did swallow it, that would explain why it took him several days to send a message."

"So what did the message say?" Shadrach popped up from the bed, his skin deeply flushed. Like us, he was losing patience with the reporter. "If you don't tell me, I *will* kill you. I swear it. Habid is my son. My wife's only son."

Walker's nostrils flared. "Okay, look, he was still in Venezuela but leaving on a plane. To Morocco. He heard them say Casablanca. The next broadcast window will be tomorrow. He should be able to tell us more."

The lights on Stella's headset began winking at a higher rate, and I knew she was already on the problem of getting us to Morocco.

After a glance at me, Ritter fixed his gaze on Walker. "Go wait in the hall."

Walker blinked his confusion. "Wait a minute. I'm the only one who knows the sequence of the codes, and I'm not going to tell you." His jaw clenched as he glanced at Shadrach. "Even if you torture me."

Ritter's upper lip twitched slightly. "You have no idea what we're capable of. Wait in the hall. Now." Threat dripped from every word. Walker grabbed a jacket from the chair he'd been sitting in and obeyed. When he was gone, Ritter asked me, "You can get the codes from him?"

I nodded. "I already got the first one."

"Is that wise?" Jeane asked. "With that thing in your head?" Everyone ignored her.

"What are we going to do about our prisoners?" I'd started worrying about them the minute I knew we were heading to Morocco. The unconscious Emporium guards were probably already stowed in the bunks on the plane.

"Oh, right," Stella said with a grimace. "No way can we fly into Morocco with that kind of cargo. We'll have to put them somewhere here until we can come back for them." Left unspoken was the knowledge that if the roles had been reversed, the Emporium would probably cut our people into three parts and dump them into the ocean on the flight over.

"I'm more worried about weapons," Ritter said. "We'll probably have to leave them on the plane in Morocco, unless Ava's got something up her sleeve that I don't know about to get us past their customs inspection. Last I heard, we don't have many contacts there."

"Let me check." Stella tapped something into her computer. "You're right. We don't. At least not at the level we'd need to get past a search of the plane, but rearming there won't be a problem. And Ava says the president will be able to pull some strings to get Chris immediate clearance to land."

"The Emporium doesn't seem to have any problem getting

past Moroccan customs," I reminded them. "They're flying in with plutonium. *Flying,* which is a no-no where volatile substances are concerned, right? Who are they bribing?"

From her perch on the bed, Jeane responded. "Probably Mohammed VI, if he's taken over for his father by now. I knew Hassan II back in the day, and both of them are the kind to align themselves with whoever they view as the greatest power. Not very well liked. Hassan's own people tried to assassinate him twice." She gave a dry laugh. "Can't say I blame them, though my relationship with Hassan was considerably more . . . enjoyable."

Shadrach frowned. "Mohammed has actually seemed to bring some stability to the country, though I don't admire him at all as a person."

"Save the politics for later," I said. "What are we going to do about the reporter?"

"We should take him," Shadrach said. "This is my son we're talking about—my *mortal* son. I don't want to risk his life more than absolutely necessary."

"I also vote for taking him." Stella's laptop brought up a succession of pictures of what I assumed was Casablanca, flashing so fast across the screen I knew I'd have to channel her ability to catch any of it.

Ritter and I both stared at her.

"What?" she asked. "We're always complaining about having to save these mortals on our own, and how none of them are knowledgeable enough to risk their lives to help themselves. This guy is aware of what's at stake, and he knows what the Unbounded are and he's willing to help. He's also right about our story needing to be told. Better to have him on our side than against us."

Ritter looked at me, obviously indifferent about the

answer. "Fine, let him come," I said, "but he's on his own. I'm not taking care of him." I flashed a purposeful glance at Jeane. I was already stuck with one person who had proven only halfway effective at taking care of herself.

My insinuation didn't go unnoticed. "You'll be glad I'm around the next time you meet Delia," Jeane said.

"Unless you get yourself shot again," I muttered.

Ignoring me, Jeane shifted her position on the pillows and gave Shadrach one of her annoying smiles. "Thank you. I'm feeling much better now."

"When will we leave?" I asked.

"We should be cleared soon," Stella said. "We can't let them get too far ahead. Of all the Islamic countries to choose from, I'd say Morocco is one of those most friendly to US visitors. No doubt the reason the Emporium chose the country for their backup plan. My bet is they'll hand off the plutonium to the Iranians and get out of the way. Because I'm pretty sure once Ava and the president finish in Washington, there's going to be some kind of public backlash."

"The American people will probably forgive the Emporium in a heartbeat if they donate money or act like they're protecting the US from Iran." I sank down into the chair next to Stella, all at once feeling my efforts with Walker. "Everything is forgiven when a common enemy appears. A little spin and the Emporium might come out of this a lot better than we think. For all we know, they own half the media."

Stella's nod was short. "We'll just have to make certain they don't succeed." An odd note in her voice alerted my attention. What was up with her? I hoped it didn't have anything to do with Chris.

Before I could dwell more on this new concern, Ritter

turned on his heel and started for the door. "Shouldn't take me long to find a warehouse to stash our guests. I'll call Cort and the others to give them a heads-up so they can start unloading them."

As he spoke, Mari appeared in the room, exactly where Shadrach was standing near the bed. Shadrach gasped, and we stared as she partially materialized and then stepped away from him, becoming completely solid. Despite Shadrach's exclamation, neither seem damaged.

"That was weird," Mari said, glancing over at Shadrach who was gaping at her in shock. "Oh, don't worry. I could see the space was occupied when I was almost there, and I just had to tweak the numbers a bit. It's cool."

Shadrach still appeared disconcerted. I couldn't blame him.

"I'll take the reporter with me," Ritter said, diverting our attention from Mari and Shadrach. "Make sure he doesn't call in any stories."

"I already took his recording devices," Stella said. "But he may have previously sent files to a different location. We'll have to find out before this is over."

"We've a long way to go yet. Cort took the SUV, so I'll take the reporter's car. You guys will have to use the one Shadrach rented. Meet you there as soon as I can." Ritter walked to the door, and I went with him, sensing there was something more he wanted to say.

At the door, he hesitated, his voice lowering so only I could hear. "Don't take any chances. The Emporium will be looking for us now, and Stella—" He broke off. "Something's not right. Her fighting is off."

"I'll ask her about it."

His hand left the knob and gripped mine. "I'm still

waiting to hear what you meant back there in the clearing. About making me wait."

His touch rippled through my veins, warming me. I knew he would ask, which was why I'd said it. I didn't want to change my mind. "Later."

"I'll hold you to that."

I watched him leave, hoping there would be a later. The glow in my head had died, but that snake thing was still there. I wasn't even sure I could find Delia before it destroyed me.

Would she be involved in the exchange in Morocco? It was possible but doubtful. Iranian Islamic extremists didn't deal well with women, so if she was present, she would likely be out of sight or at another location altogether. She wouldn't even appear, unless she had a good reason.

I am a good reason. She'll come for me. After me, was more like it. Was I ready? There was only one way to find out. With her construct sucking my energy, a sliver of doubt had wormed its way into my heart.

I helped Stella pack our equipment while Jeane, Mari, and Shadrach talked quietly near the far bed. Glancing over her shoulder at them, Stella placed a small cell phone in my hand. "I found it on Jeane," she said, her voice low.

I rubbed a finger over the silver case. "She didn't have this when we arrived. Oh, it must have been at the bar earlier. She got close to this guy—assaulted him really. I thought it was odd to call attention to us like that. Now I know why. She either took it off him, or from someone else while I was taking care of him. I should have frisked her."

"You couldn't have known. Anyway, it's recently been factory reset. No way for me to tell what calls she made, if any. Not without my gear at home, and even then . . ." Stella shrugged.

Jeane was up to something—whether it was an innocent phone call or a complete betrayal—but I still had to take her with me. Right now she was the only thing standing between Delia and what might be a complete meltdown of my brain. I'd have to find a way to take her out later if she was a traitor.

"Let's get out of here," I told Stella. "The sooner we do, the better I'll feel."

CHAPTER 16

"IT'S CALLED SYNERGY," CORT SAID FROM THE KITCHEN AREA OF THE plane where we were talking privately together.

Though my energy level was still high and I'd been absorbing constantly to increase it, I was still craving the comfort only physical food could give me. One of the sweet things about being quasi-immortal was the high metabolism. I could eat as much chocolate as I wanted, and I was taking mine in the form of rich cocoa with a healthy splash of coconut flavoring and a mound of whipped cream.

"Synergy?" I looked past him at Keene, who was playing cards with Mari and Jace in the closest set of four seats. Stella and Shadrach were in the other set, where we had been sitting with them. Walker and Jeane, the outcasts, sat in the set of two seats across the aisle on the same side as the small kitchen, while Ritter and Chris were in the cockpit flying the plane. It would take nine hours, give or take, to reach our destination, depending on the air currents.

"Yes. Keene can see the patterns like me, only he can also

rearrange them, making them stronger." Cort smiled, his pride in his brother evident. "He doesn't understand them like I do, so he can't make new medicines or figure out how two things interact to make a real-world application, but he can change the actual physical makeup of things. Not just things but people. Theoretically, that would give him a huge advantage in just about every situation. " He added a packet of creamer to his cup of coffee, stirring slowly. "The problem with not understanding the meaning of the patterns makes it dangerous because he has to learn each situation through trial and error. He can't just look at it and understand so he can make it work the first time."

"Maybe that will come eventually."

Cort nodded. "I hope so. Because, if not, he'll be very limited. Possibly a detriment to all of us. He knows that, and he's working on controlling it."

"He helped me."

"I know. But it was dangerous."

"He'd never hurt me."

"Not on purpose."

"Well, he knows at least how to increase my endurance. My strength."

Cort puzzled over that for a minute before clearing his throat and saying, "That may be important soon."

I knew he referred to my upcoming confrontation with Delia. I hadn't told him or anyone about the inner box breaking. I'd tried to form yet a third box, but there seemed to be some sort of limitation in my mind, so I'd contented myself by reinforcing the second one. It was large enough that I should have room inside to contain the growing snake for a time. I'd know when the pressure began building.

"There is something I need you to do for me," I said, taking a gulp of chocolate. "It's about Ritter."

"I see what's happening with you two. We were sitting outside that factory when you ran into trouble with Walker's attackers. He didn't even call Stella to verify but took off to find you—in our only vehicle, I might add."

"Does that happen a lot among Unbounded? How did he know?"

Cort leaned against the tiny sink, as if preparing for a speech. He was an intellectual at heart, a teacher, and he enjoyed the role of mentor. "I've never seen it happen firsthand, but historically there have been mental connections between couples, usually both sensing Unbounded. I don't think Ritter felt your danger until you began using your ability in that alleyway, but there's no way you could mentally reach that far, so it's one of those unexplainable things."

I frowned, not wanting to say what I must. "Could it be related to the snake?"

He didn't dismiss the idea instantly but considered it for a long while. "Given that it connects you to Delia, I have to admit it's a possibility."

So the very thing that might be risking my life also might be forging the connection between me and Ritter. It was unsettling.

"Historically, the bond is only formed between permanent companions."

I stared at him. "What does that mean? What happens if one of us dies?"

"You survive, go on. It's not a death sentence. But those I've heard about never find another mate."

I hadn't asked for it, but would I want it gone? From the

beginning, I'd been more aware of Ritter than anyone else. I *wanted* him more than I'd wanted any man, even Keene, who had won a slice of my heart. The realization of our connection pulsed fear through my blood and filled me with worry. If something happened to me, what would it do to Ritter?

I glanced up at Cort, whose mouth was set in a grim line which told me he was just as apprehensive about it as I was. "Thanks," I said.

"You're welcome. Now what was it you wanted me to do?"

MOROCCO, THE KINGDOM OF THE WEST, WAS A STUDY OF VARIATIONS, from its beautiful sandy beaches in the north to the rugged, mountainous interior that gave way to the desolate Sahara. The contrast was emphasized by the rich and poor areas of the cities and the variety of languages spoken—Berber, Arabic, and French among them. Casablanca, Morocco's largest city, though not its capital, was more of the same. Stretches of modern buildings sat next to sections with stained, older ones. Wide streets were only minutes from narrow roads that were crowded with street vendors and their clients. Western clothes mixed in with colorful robes and head coverings.

We arrived after ten at night, having lost most of Sunday to the long flight and the time change. Another hour was spent clearing customs, our weapons safely tucked into a hidden compartment on the plane, which Chris would watch over as usual. We drove in two separate rental vehicles to Old Medina, where we were met by Basilio Chafik, who owned a block of buildings in the area. Though he was

Islamic, he didn't have a hatred toward the West. His two wives, Amina and Yalda, both of whom wore robes with head and face coverings, were polite and welcoming. It wasn't long before I realized that one of Basilio's forefathers had been Unbounded, and that he'd known Ava all his life.

Their living quarters, located above a mini mall, looked like an old apartment building, but inside was more house-like, modern, and lushly decorated. The low ceilings and narrow corridors made me feel safe and secure, a welcome illusion, at least for me. Though Amina and Yalda's robes were a boring tan and conservative gray, the furnishings were all brightly colored, and sweeping curtains draped walls, doorways, and even several of the ceilings.

"My wives will show you ladies to your quarters on the next floor," Basilio said. "The men will have rooms down here, but of course you are free to interact. My wives are traditional, but they understand you do not share our faith. They will provide you with head and face coverings, which I recommend you wear when you go out. No need to call attention to your nationality." He inclined his head toward me. "Especially you with your blond hair. The Emporium will be on high alert. For the record, it is never safe for women to walk around Old Medina at night, but then, you aren't ordinary women, are you?"

We hadn't attracted attention at the airport, but our arrival at Basilio's hadn't gone unnoticed, especially Jeane, who'd changed into a short-sleeved, tight-fitting dress on the plane that had earned her several catcalls from men in a nearby bar.

"I think we should all get some rest," Stella said. "My equipment will alert us if Habid tries to contact us with his location. I'll let you all know."

"We have made a sitting room available upstairs that is large enough to serve as a meeting room for you," Basilio said. "Will you take some refreshments there now?"

Declining politely, the rest of the women and I followed the wives up the stairs. After showing us the sitting room, Yalda led me to a small but luxurious bedroom that had long, sheer white curtains over a minuscule window, gold drapes over the bed, and an elaborate armoire in the corner. She said something in Arabic, pointing down the hallway, and I assumed she was talking about the bathroom. I was curious about her marital situation—Shadrach had told us that polygamy was no longer promoted but still accepted in Morocco as long as the women had a choice, which was still not the case in many Islamic cultures. But Yalda didn't seem the type to share her thoughts with a stranger, even if she had been able to speak English.

I hovered near the door to make sure Jeane went into the next room. I'd just settled onto the bed, fully dressed, when a tap came on the door and Stella entered at my invitation. "Basilio has assured me there is no phone available to Jeane, and I've got my phone programmed to alert me if she tries to go too far. Even so, having her here worries me." Her gaze focused on my face. "How are you feeling?"

"Good."

"No more glowing lights?"

"No. Look, now that you're here, I want to try the nanite thing again."

"Are you sure?"

I nodded. "I've worked it out in my head. I think I know what to do now."

"You realize you'll have to channel my ability every day to keep these nanites in place."

"Only for a few minutes and then they'll work for a least a day. And I won't need to do it regularly before I meet with Delia and get this *thing* taken care of." I felt a rush of anger mingled with fear. I'd never be able to live my life if I couldn't win the war I waged.

Stella moved toward me, sitting on the bed and drawing up her feet. "What's wrong? What brought this on?"

Something inside me crumpled at the sympathy in her voice, and my tears threatened to fall. "I just don't want to wait anymore."

"That, I understand completely." She squeezed my arm before going to the door. "I'll go get some nanites and come right back."

Moments later we sat on the bed, my hand gripping hers. "Okay, show me." I entered her mind as her barrier dropped. I knew how to follow her thoughts already, and how a technopath could follow the pathways in her body to find the nanites and tell them what to do. The trick was finding the right path and maintaining consistency. The neural pathways of the brain and body were much more complicated to navigate than simple thoughts.

"It's not working. I can't seem to get there," I said and pushed what I was seeing at Stella.

She laughed aloud. "You're looking at it like a physician. Just reach out to the nanite. That's what you're communicating with. Make it go where you want. You don't need to follow it."

I copied what Stella was showing me with the nanites in my own bloodstream. It was terribly complicated, but by channeling the ability, it somehow made sense, like communicating with a computer. All the pieces were intact. I could even feel the faint pulses of the tracker in my arm, which was the closest we'd come to nanite technology that could fool our bodies into not rejecting it. Stella and those like her had created the technology but found it proved useless on a larger scale, except for technopaths—and me, since I could channel her. "Okay," I said with a triumph I didn't try to hide. "I can see how to do it now."

Just as I was disconnecting from her, I saw something more inside Stella, and maybe if I admitted it to myself, I'd expected it all along: a life force so tiny that I couldn't distinguish it from hers outside her body.

"Oh, Stella," I breathed, opening my eyes. I was happy and devastated all at once. I knew what this baby meant for her.

"What?" When I didn't answer, her eyes shone brighter. "Then you can see it."

"Is it my brother's?"

She nodded, her cheeks reddening faintly. "Yes."

"How far along?"

"I don't know. The nanites told me something was different, but I wasn't even sure until just now. Of course it was only a matter of time, so I guess I did know. Mostly."

I understood then the reason she'd held back on the boat during the fighting. Whether purposefully or not, she'd been protecting her child.

"What about the kids?" I loved my friend and wanted her happiness, but I wondered what it would do to Chris and my niece and nephew.

"We haven't decided what to tell them." Stella looked away from me as she spoke. "When it eventually happened, I mean. We planned this, but he doesn't know yet that we were successful. Look, I know what you're thinking, but it's just a business arrangement. I want a child. He's a good dad."

I shook my head. "He loves you. Whatever he agreed to, however that baby got inside you, he loves you, and you don't love him. You're going to break his heart."

"No, I won't." Stella stood and looked down at me, her open palms pressed tightly against her thighs. "It's not like that."

"Yes. It is. Remember, I saw you two back at the Fortress."

She slumped to the bed, bringing her hands to her face. "Oh, Erin, am I so selfish? I wanted my husband's baby, but both Bronson and my baby are gone, and Chris is here. He knew how I felt, and I thought . . ." She closed her eyes, a stark pain written on her face that reminded me of when she'd lost her baby. So much had happened that it was hard to believe it had occurred less than six weeks ago. Tears started down her cheeks. "I don't mean to hurt him. I just want the ache to go away."

I put my arms around her and hugged her tightly. "I wish everything could have been different for you. I'm sorry."

She shook her head. "It's okay. I thought I was being responsible. I went to the lab. I manipulated his sperm. I did everything I could to increase the chance of our child being Unbounded. I know Chris is seventh generation, but I hope . . ." Her eyes unfocused for a moment and the slightest glimmer of optimism touched her beautiful face. "I know it's wrong when Chris and I aren't in a committed relationship, but somehow, I'm glad."

Glad for the child's existence, she meant, and I surprised myself by laughing. "Of course. I guess I feel that way too." Her baby was hope for the future. "But this means you can't be anywhere near that plutonium," I said. "If something happens, I'll never forgive myself."

"What will I tell the others?"

"For now we only have to tell Ritter, and he already knows something's up."

"Because of what happened on the boat." She ran a finger below an almond-shaped eye, glowing now with a subtle warmth. "I just wasn't myself."

Since she'd lost her baby while defending my niece and nephew from an Emporium attack, how could I blame her? I certainly could never repay her, and maybe Chris even owed her this. If only he hadn't also given her his heart.

"Right," I said, forcing down emotions that were too close to the surface. "Anyway, you can stay away from the main action and coordinate our efforts. With Cort and Keene here, we have enough manpower."

"Keene." Stella's smile was full this time. "When do you think he'll make the announcement about his Change? I think Mari and Chris are the only ones of us who don't know. Well, and Jeane."

We talked for a few more minutes, and Stella asked again about the snake before she left, but the box had stopped glowing the instant I dropped our connection after our nanite session. I wasn't feeling too much pressure, yet, though I could tell the effort had taken some toll on me.

When Stella was gone, I lay back on the bed, breathing deeply and absorbing nutrients. The flavor of spice touched my tongue, and I regretted turning down Basilio's refreshments. But it was too late to inconvenience the family now. We were already putting them in danger just by being here.

Closing my eyes, I investigated the box in my head. No blue lights. Yet even as I tapped the box, my ability activated and the twin lights flickered into existence. Expecting to feel nothing but a slight warmth, I reached out to one as I had so many times before. A sharp, piercing sensation filled me, as if I were being jabbed by a thousand pins. Abruptly, I felt a tug, and I was drawn into the light.

Falling.

Falling.

Or being dragged.

At the end of the fall, I caught a glimpse of Delia Vesey, or at least her mind. Her attention diverted from whoever she was with, and she turned her thoughts inward. Toward me. Chills crawled over my shoulders. I scrambled, pulling myself back along the light, exerting every bit of effort I could find. The light seemed to dig beneath my fingernails. More pinpoints of agony. I pressed on.

I came back to myself with a gasp, sitting up in the darkness, though I was sure I'd left the lamp on.

"What is it?" Ritter's voice came from beside the bed, and I pushed into his arms as he sat next to me.

"Nothing. A dream." Maybe.

"Sorry if I startled you. Shadrach's son just signaled, and Stella is deciphering the message now."

"That's good," I said, feeling unsteady. Had I really seen Delia? Had her construct grown so strong, or was she nearby?

"I came to tell you to get ready to move on the intel, but you were sleeping so soundly that I decided to leave and come back later once I knew our destination." His hand rested on my stomach, sending heat through me. The next instant he was kissing me, and I was kissing him back, my mouth opening beneath his exploring tongue.

After a long moment I rested my cheek against his, listening to his quickened breath. "When we get back, I have a surprise for you," I whispered, slipping my hands beneath his shirt and pulling him on top of me. I could feel the bond between us like a tangible thing.

"I can't wait." His lips found mine once more. I could feel exactly how he wanted to touch me, protect me, and make me laugh. His emotion filled me so full, there was no room for words. He groaned softly, lifting his lips from mine to say, "Lately, I always know what you're feeling, even when you're not sending it to me. Is this what you experience with others all the time?"

"Yeah. Kind of. With those who don't block. Though I'm trying not to use my ability at the moment." I shivered when I thought about Delia and what had just happened to me. How much time had passed since I'd touched the blue light?

His arms tightened around me. "Do you want me to return for you later?"

"No, I want to come. Let's go see what Habid has to say."

We slid from the bed, our arms still tangled together. I smiled, but before I could twist free, he stilled, his eyes catching mine in the darkness. He brushed his lips against my cheek before he found my mouth, breathing me in for a long moment. Then he pulled back to search my eyes. "I know you're afraid."

I blinked at that, but before I could deny it, he squeezed my waist. "I feel it too, whenever I think of losing you, but then I remember one very important thing." He paused as his thoughts spread through our connection, and I could see that he felt my determination every bit as much as my fear. I was scared, yes, but what we had together also made me courageous. That was what he remembered. He kissed me again, slower this time. The comfort he desperately wanted to give me ran through my body. This time when he pulled away, his touch lingered long after his lips left mine.

"You're stronger than Delia is," he said. "Don't ever forget that."

I nodded, the weight of my fear diminishing at his words. His fingers grasped tightly to mine as we headed for the door.

When we arrived in the sitting room where the others had gathered, I discovered I'd lost two hours to sleep—or to my hallucination about Delia—not just the few minutes it had seemed. I planned to ask Jeane about that the first chance I got. The light wasn't glowing now, and while I didn't feel rested, I wasn't overly tired, especially considering what we'd been through the past twenty-four hours.

The sitting room was long and narrow, and fit us all as promised, though the long couches on either side of the room almost met the two coffee tables in the middle. These were filled with platters of meats, cheeses, fruits, cakes, and other things I didn't recognize. Full cups of tea stood waiting on insulated cup holders—mint by the aroma.

"Habid is here in Casablanca," Stella announced as we entered, looking up from her laptop that she'd placed on the end of the coffee table nearest the door.

"And so is the cargo," Walker added, "and by that I assume he means the plutonium."

"Where?" I settled next to Jeane, who sat across from Stella and was wearing robes that looked anything but drab on her. The others in our party were spread out over the rest of the couches. Ritter, who had remained standing, leaned over Stella to look at her screen.

"About three to four miles southwest of here near a place called L'Oasis." Stella drew a line with her finger, and I scooted forward to peer over the laptop screen. "I was able to track the transmission, and it verifies what he said about the location."

"Is he still broadcasting?" Ritter asked, glancing at the doorway where our host Basilio had appeared, straining under the weight of a wooden crate from which jutted several assault rifles.

"No, he's stopped." It was Walker who replied. The reporter had taken on a new air of confidence since I'd seen him last. Maybe because he felt useful. "The window won't open again for another ten hours. It's not regular, and I can't change the preprogramming. But don't you think he would have indicated if he thought he was going to be moved? So that's probably where the exchange is taking place. Maybe tonight." He glanced at Basilio. "Or maybe after morning prayers."

The irony of that wasn't lost on me, but Basilio, long accustomed to a religion whose extremists fought their holy wars in the name of God, only nodded. "That will be the most likely time. Prayer will be finished just before sunrise." He waited as platters were resituated before placing the crate on one of the coffee tables.

"Then let's go now," Ritter said. "The Emporium won't have had time to do anything fancy to protect the place from Erin or Mari." He grabbed one of the machine guns, and Jace followed, making sounds of approval.

"We don't know that," Stella said. "It might be a house they've owned for years and forgotten about, or it might be something they've bought or updated recently."

"I'm betting not," Ritter countered. "We have them off-balance."

"Hopefully." Stella's frown reminded me of the baby.

"Stella should stay in the car and coordinate," I said. "With Walker."

Ritter's eyes met mine, and he nodded, though I hadn't told him yet about her condition. Walker didn't disagree, and I thought maybe he had some sense after all.

"We have to make sure my son is safe." Shadrach gazed at Ritter anxiously. "We owe him that much for locating the plutonium."

"We'll do our best, of course, but keep in mind that if your son hadn't contacted a reporter"—Ritter spat it like a dirty word, though he didn't look at Walker—"they wouldn't have moved the plutonium early, and we wouldn't be scrambling to keep up with them now."

"I wouldn't have known the plutonium was even in Venezuela without my son," Shadrach insisted. "Because of him, we recovered the other batch."

Ritter nodded. "As I said, we'll do our best." But we all knew, and Shadrach needed to accept, that the life of his son had to be weighed against the lives of eight million Israelis and a war that would take even more casualties.

How would I feel if it were someone I loved? I glanced at Ritter and knew exactly how I would feel. "We'll get him," I assured Shadrach. "We'll go in and hit them hard." I waited only a second to add, "But Jeane should stay here." If I was going to use my ability, she wouldn't be any help to me, and nulling the Emporium agents hadn't gone so well last time.

"No, I'm prepared." She pulled aside her robe to show an armored vest. She lifted her gaze to Basilio, who had averted his eyes, though less of her skin was showing now than when she'd arrived. "Thanks to our host."

Ritter and Jace crowded around Stella's laptop and began planning how to enter the building that seemed to be a house of sorts. Probably well-secured. I was going to insist that Jeane stay behind, maybe even bring up the cell phone she'd stolen and the possibility of securing her in a locked room, but at that moment, she leaned in close and said, "When are you going to tell him?"

I turned to her, seeing that her eyes were not on Ritter but on Jace. "What do you mean?" I said slowly.

"He looks just like Stefan. Or close enough."

I glanced hurriedly at Jace, but he was arguing with Ritter. Something about a roof. He always liked the idea of going in from a roof. Last time he'd been right.

I shifted my stare back to Jeane. "I don't know what you're talking about."

"I think you do."

There was no doubt in my mind that she was threatening me. "You leave him out of this," I said through clenched teeth.

She smiled. "Be glad to. You and I need each other, Erin. At least until we get rid of Delia. After that, we'll see." She gave me one of her movie-star smiles.

I didn't know what to say to that because she was right. I was going to need her if my plan to face Delia would have any chance of success, and I didn't like that one bit. "Okay," I said finally, "but you will leave my brother out of it."

I looked back at the others to find Ritter staring at me, obviously aware that something was going on, and I clamped down on my shield. Thankfully, this didn't require use of my ability.

I was going to have to be careful if I didn't want to endanger Ritter with the plan I was beginning to formulate regarding my confrontation with Delia. No matter what, I wasn't going to risk him.

CHAPTER 17

THIRTY MINUTES LATER, WE WERE HUNKERED DOWN OUTSIDE THE mansion where we hoped they were holding Habid. Though the stuccoed and tiled house was larger than its neighbors and set back from the road to make space for a massive stone archway that led to a courtyard in front of the house, there would be many casualties if something went wrong with the plutonium. I would have preferred a less inhabited location.

Cort and Jace were going in by way of the roof and then through some window, to Jace's joy, and the rest of us were scattered around the house, connected by radio. I had vetoed the traditional Muslim robes, as had Mari, and instead we were outfitted in our black metamaterial bodysuits from wrists to ankles, nearly invisible in the night.

"Erin?" Ritter said in my ear. "What you got?"

"About a dozen life forces inside. They're doubled near the entries. There are a couple upstairs. All of them are shielded." The blue lights in my mind were bright again, and I didn't dare exert too much more effort, not this far away. The pressure was beginning to build in my head, which meant the snake was pushing against the walls of the second box. "I need to get closer if I'm going to break through any shields."

"Move in."

I took the back door, channeling Ritter this time and not Jace, who was farther away. I took the first guard out with a single silenced shot, and the other with two quick punches.

Jeane stepped from the shadows. "I knew we'd make a good team."

No wonder they hadn't anticipated me. Most Emporium agents were combat Unbounded, bred to the ability because of long centuries of conflict, and I hadn't expected them to fall to me with so little effort. I found a third guard by the door, but I took him out with another silenced bullet. All Unbounded. Still, it seemed a little *too* easy. They must not have known we were coming.

Maybe we would get out of this with both Habid and the plutonium. "Back is clear," I said into my mic.

"Side clear," Keene answered, who had gone in with Mari.

"Front clear," Ritter said.

"We're on the second level," Jace said. "Three guards down. No sign of Habid."

"Check all the rooms." Shadrach's voice was tight.

I sent out my thoughts, searching for life forces. Nothing standing except what belonged to us. "I don't like this," I murmured.

"Is there a basement?" This from Stella in the car. "He has to be somewhere."

I crept along the corridor, checking each doorway as I passed. My feeling of anxiety ratcheted tighter. When Jeane bumped into me, I startled.

"Relax," she said, switching off her mic. "We've done it. All we need now is to find the plutonium."

I turned off my own mic. "Maybe. Or she could be here masking life forces. I can do it, and I know she can."

"You mean Delia?" Jeane gave a snort in the darkness. "Believe me. If she were here, you'd know."

"What do you mean?"

"The people I saw her experiment on always could tell, even if their ability wasn't sensing. Maybe that light you talked about will get brighter if she's close. Something."

My breath rushed out in a single burst. "I saw her today. She was so real. So close."

"Really?" Jeane's voice was disconcerted, but I sensed an underlying excitement. "Then maybe she's come to us."

"That's a good thing?" I asked. "Is that what you were trying to do with the cell phone? Contact her?"

"What if I was?" Jeane stepped closer. "Look, you know we have to face her. And I think seeing her like you did means you're ready."

"What it means is that she can get into my mind."

"Then you can also get into hers, and if I can null her ability, even just partially, you can win."

It *was* what I'd planned—I'd be lying to myself if I didn't admit it—but that was before I'd felt the tremendous pull of the light. Delia might be stronger than I knew.

"Look at the light now," Jeane urged. "See if she's close. Even if she's hiding her life force, you should be able to feel her."

Leaving my eyes open to watch Jeane, I pushed out my thoughts until the light glowed. Then I reached out and touched the edge, ready to pull back if I was sucked inside. The tug was there, but this time I was ready. I followed slowly, not entering the full stream, but gliding along beside it in the same direction. I mentally traced the flow outside to the border of the property before pulling away. "She's not here, either the building or the property." I could almost feel Jeane grinning, but I added quickly, "But the tugging. It's there."

"She must not be far."

"Then we have to get out of here. She won't be alone."

I turned back on my mic, but before I could alert the others, Mari's voice came through my earbud. "Found it! The guys we jumped were guarding it. Keene's running a check on it now."

"My son?" Shadrach asked.

"Sorry. I don't see him," Mari said.

I pushed out my thoughts, again risking the blue light, searching for even the faintest signs of a life force I didn't already know about. "I'm sorry, Shadrach. He's not here. I'm not getting anyone except the guards."

Mari's voice came through the radio again. "The plutonium *is* in the cask. We really got it!"

"Everybody, pull out," Ritter ordered. "We have to secure the plutonium."

"But Habid has to be here!" Desperation laced Shadrach's words.

"He's not," I said. "We'll find him the next time he transmits."

"They'll know. They'll find the transmitter. They'll look for it once they realize what's happened here." He was right, and there wasn't anything we could do about it.

"Pull out," Ritter said again through our earbuds.

"He's his mother's only son," Shadrach whispered. "She is the wife of my heart, and I've failed her."

For a moment I thought about erasing the guards' memories, filling the plutonium cask with something fake, and somehow healing them enough so they wouldn't know we'd been here. But I knew my limitations. However much it might hurt Shadrach, there was nothing we could do but leave.

Though our mission had been a success, we were a quiet group driving back to Basilio's. There, we parked in the underground garage he kept for his family, in case our vehicle had been identified. After debating awhile, we decided against taking the plutonium inside our host's living quarters and hid the cask in a storage bin he kept in the garage.

"Keene, you and Jace take the first watch, okay?" Ritter said. "We'll go upstairs and get things arranged with Ava in DC. We aren't letting this thing out of our sight until we hand it off, and that might not be for another ten or twelve hours. Keep the door locked and your mics on."

"Piece of cake." Jace sat on the hood of our rental car, his rifle ready. I smiled in spite of my own regret where Habid was concerned.

We left them and made our way up the stairs to the main apartments. Basilio answered his door with a smile and no questions. Stella, Ritter, and Cort hurried to call Ava on the computer, and Walker and Mari went to their rooms, leaving me alone in the hallway with Jeane and a morose Shadrach.

"He's just a boy." Deep furrows etched into Shadrach's brow. "He wanted to prove himself to me. I told his mother I would bring him home."

"We're not giving up," I said.

"They'll kill him." Without meeting my eyes, Shadrach stumbled down the hall and out of our sight.

He was probably right. Unless . . . "Look, Jeane, I have an idea." I glanced at the doorway to the sitting room and back at Jeane to make sure we were alone. "If Delia really is in town, and we find her, maybe we can get Habid back."

A smile crossed her face. "Let's do it."

"First thing in the morning." Because as anxious as I was to finally challenge Delia and get her snake out of my head, there was something I had to do first, something I wouldn't share with Jeane in a million years. I started toward the sitting room but hesitated, turning again toward her. "Don't tell the others."

She made a motion of sealing her lips. "Wake me up when the time comes."

"Do you really think we can do it?"

"I'm sure of it."

Maybe I was stupid to believe her. Maybe all she wanted was to get back to the Emporium herself. Or maybe she planned to sacrifice me to make her own move on Delia. It really didn't matter—I had to go through with it. I'd known from the first moment I'd met Delia that only one of us would eventually survive. Two weeks ago I was sure it would be me. Now, I wasn't as confident, but Ritter still thought I could do it, and I believed in him. I would face Delia here and now.

As if thinking of him called his attention, Ritter emerged from the sitting room. "Erin, I need to talk to you. Jeane, give us a moment." Jeane studied him with languid eyes before she turned and swayed toward her room without a word.

"What is it?" I asked Ritter, my stomach clenching. I felt the knot of torment he tried to hide from me, and I almost expected him to tell me he knew my plan. His next words shocked me.

"It's your grandmother. I'm sorry, but she's been taken by the Emporium."

For a moment, I thought he meant Ava, but Ritter had never referred to our leader—even when talking about her to me—as anything but Ava, so that meant he was talking about my actual grandmother. My gloriously independent mortal grandmother who had refused Renegade protection in order to maintain her normal life.

"No," I whispered.

Ritter reached out and took my hand, which I grabbed like a lifeline. "They're demanding the return of the plutonium," he said. "The plutonium we took in Venezuela."

"Jonny," I whispered. "He must have identified me, so they acted against her."

"We don't know how it happened." He tugged at my hand gently, and I went with him into the sitting room where Cort and Stella perched on a couch in stunned silence.

I hurried toward the computer, dropping onto the couch between Stella and Cort. Ava stared at me from the screen of Stella's laptop, her features tight and drawn. "What are we going to do?" I asked.

Ava's head swung back and forth slowly, her image distorting slightly on the screen. "Unfortunately, there's really nothing we can do. They'll find out soon enough from their own channels that we no longer have the plutonium from Venezuela. We might be able to negotiate with the shipment you just secured, but how can we do that? You know what's at stake. We're talking about millions of lives."

Only moments earlier I'd been sympathizing with Shadrach, but now it was my loved one's life on the line, and everything had changed. What did I care about eight million people I didn't know and would never meet? I loved my grandmother. We had always been close. I would give my life for hers.

"We have to do something," I said, tears burning my eyes.

Ava's chin lifted slightly. "We will. We'll make sure the Emporium doesn't succeed." Her face softened. "Look, Erin, I feel exactly the way you do. She's family. I watched her grow from a baby. But she would never want us to value her life more than so many others. Even if I believed we'd be successful in getting her back, I know what her position is on this, and I respect that. When it's all over, we can attempt a rescue, if we believe she's still alive, but there is no way we can trade nuclear war for her life."

I'd feared from the beginning that something like this might happen. That my work against the Emporium would destroy the lives of the mortals I loved. Everything inside me screamed to save my grandmother. I knew Delia well enough to know that if I didn't give her what she wanted, she'd kill my grandmother without a second thought. Tears fell down my cheeks. Next to me, Stella grabbed my hand and held it tightly, her face reflecting my pain.

For a moment I was tempted to grab the cask from Jace and Keene and contact Delia myself. My mind conjured up all sorts of scenarios where I would single-handedly best Delia and her guards, drag her back to America to save my grandmother, and somehow retain the plutonium as well.

I wasn't deluded enough to believe I could do it all. There was too much risk. I nodded at Ava. "You're right."

"I'm leaving DC on the flight with the CIA to collect the cask," Ava said, "so I'll be in Casablanca soon."

She disconnected, and I sat there for a moment staring at the black screen, still feeling as if I'd fallen from a cliff. My grandmother was dead, or as good as. The Emporium would know that we couldn't give in to their demands, and she was too old to be useful for their breeding program, which meant they wouldn't waste time ending her life.

I'm sorry, Grandma, I thought, feeling weak and useless. The irony of the timing didn't escape me. She had finally promised to go into hiding with my parents, but she'd waited too long.

I looked at Cort, who was staring at me, a question in his eyes. He leaned forward and I accepted his comforting hug. "You still want to go through with tonight?"

For a moment, I was confused, until I realized that he meant the surprise for Ritter. Taking a deep breath, I whispered, "I'll be ready in a half hour." He nodded and released me.

I stood, feeling my fate was set. While the others turned over the plutonium to the CIA, I would confront Delia, both to save myself and to avenge my grandmother's death.

But first I would do something that I should have done weeks ago, and Cort was going to help me.

CHAPTER 18

UP ON THE ROOF OF BASILIO'S BUILDING, THE STARS TWINKLED overhead, but my acrophobia was under control, locked in the box of my thought construction. Once, my heart would have raced and I would have collapsed under what felt like the weight of the entire star-encrusted sky, unable to move except maybe to crawl. But months of rooftop practice had made my presence here possible, if not quite comfortable, and it gave me a strange satisfaction to have chosen this high place for tonight.

Except for the altitude, Basilio's rooftop resembled a courtyard and even had several raised sections of flowers that I suspected his wives tended themselves. I wondered if sometimes they removed their head coverings and lifted their faces to the sun, or if they feared someone might observe them, even here.

Ritter arrived, dressed in a sleek, well-cut black suit,

though where he got it I couldn't say. It fit his wide shoulders perfectly and made my knees weak.

I was wearing my red dress, the one I'd packed without much hope of wearing on this trip. As jeans and T-shirts were my normal attire, I'd of course forgotten the shoes, but Stella proved to have a strappy black pair that were nice, if not perfect. She'd given me a lacy black scarf to drape around my bare arms, for which I was glad. The temperature was mild in Casablanca, even in January, but there was a light breeze up here on the roof.

"How did you know?" I asked Ritter.

"Cort told me the truth." Stepping closer, his arms went around me. "We've been friends a long time. He didn't want me to show up looking like a . . ."

"A soldier?"

He laughed. "Something like that."

"But that's one of the things I like most about you." Delighting in his combat abilities was somewhat morbid, as was the fact that even when he was covered in blood, I wanted him. But that was who I was now. What I had become with my Change.

He kissed me long and deep, and I lost all sense of which way was up—an unsteadiness that had nothing to do with my fear of heights. I wanted to beg him to run away with me, somewhere Delia would never find us, but I knew that wouldn't stop her plans for me. Time was running out.

"Where is Cort?" I asked.

"He's coming, but are you sure about this?" Ritter kissed me again, running his hand up my back.

"I'm sure."

"What about your parents?"

"They'll never know." My mother would still have a church wedding. The man I'd grown up thinking was my father—the man who still was my father in every true sense of the word—would still give me away.

Well, if I lived that long.

I could hide the secret from my family, but I couldn't risk leaving Ritter to mourn another fiancée. He'd watched the Emporium murder the woman he'd once loved over two centuries ago, and while I might not make it through my encounter with Delia, I would leave him knowing I had taken the plunge. I'd made the commitment.

To be honest, I was scared witless. But I was even more scared of letting him go. What happened with my grandmother proved that waiting too long could cost you everything.

Cort showed up a minute later, also wearing a suit. Stella and Jace were with him to serve as witnesses. Mari was the bridesmaid. The stars winked down as Cort spoke the words that were by now just a formality. "Do either of you have anything to add?" The way he said it told me Ritter had requested him to ask the question, and I waited for what he might have planned.

Ritter nodded and met my gaze. "Once, you told me you wanted to be loved by someone who would love you with his whole being. Erin, I do. And I will always love you that way. Regardless of what comes in the future, this moment will always be the best moment of my life."

I believed him. I couldn't speak, but I opened my mind to his and our thoughts became one. He knew about Stella and my success with the nanites, about my fears, and what he meant to me.

I held only one thing back.

He caught the tear beneath my eye with his finger, rubbing gently before kissing me deeply.

"Hey, you're jumping the gun," Cort said with a laugh. "But I now pronounce you husband and wife."

Ritter kissed me again, and when he drew away, the others descended on us with hugs and kisses and silly advice that made me feel almost normal.

Finally, they were finished, and with a quick farewell, Ritter picked me up and carried me downstairs to the bedroom. Neither of us reached for the light. He removed his jacket before slowly unzipping my dress, his finger trailing down my skin, lighting fires along the way. I unbuttoned his shirt, running my hand over his chest. I kissed him there, and he arched against me with a groan.

He laid me back on the bed, slanting his mouth over mine. My flesh sang and my heart pounded. I'd wanted him for what seemed like forever. He kissed my lips, trailing down to the hollow between my breasts, his tongue feeling rough against my skin. His finger came up and hooked the necklace there, the one he'd given me that held our engagement ring and the bands that had belonged to his mother and sister.

His emotions spilled over, mingling with mine until there seemed to be no room to contain them. It worried me to see the blue lights burning furiously, and I had the horrible thought that my unwanted visitor was feeding on our shared emotions.

Ritter's mouth found mine again as his hands went under me, tucking me against the length of his body. I pushed closer. He pulled away slightly and more of our clothing dropped to the floor. His mouth worked its way over every inch of my body, and his tongue followed, making me tremble with need. I also tasted his skin, wrapping my arms around him more tightly. I deepened our kiss, pressing him on, feeling an urgency to become part of him.

"No way am I going to hurry," he murmured against my lips. "I'm going to enjoy every second of this. I've been waiting too long."

"So have I." I hooked my legs and drew him closer.

The blue lights in my mind burst into flame.

Then I was falling away from him. Falling. Falling. Sucked into the raging torrent of blue light. I knew where it was taking me, and I wasn't about to let it happened.

I pulled back from it, fighting to return to my own mind. From somewhere far away I heard Ritter saying, "Erin? Erin?" His voice was panicked.

I wanted to call out to him, but it was all I could do to gain purchase against the tremendous flow.

Maybe I'd waited too long to excise the snake. Maybe Delia was going to win.

Out over the city my mind was dragged along the path of the light. Through streets and around buildings. To an opulent hotel with bellboys and five-star service. Dragged, fighting and pushing every bit of the way.

I could feel my nemesis on the other end of that light, knew she'd been witness to my intimacy with Ritter. She had enjoyed it, like a voyeur. Maybe some of the pleasure I had given to Ritter came from her.

Feeling sickened, I gathered all my remaining strength, still struggling against the flow, wondering how best to focus my efforts. I didn't know what would happen if she managed to pull me in. Would she be able to control me completely? Take over my mind? Could she turn me against my friends, forcing me to betray and murder them? Would I become a prisoner inside my own head?

All at once I understood the truth about what Delia had planned all along. It wasn't just about using me but *becoming* me.

True immortality.

That was what the snake meant to her. A way to extend her life. At seventeen hundred years old, her life expectancy had dwindled to only a few centuries—a few centuries as her body aged and finally gave out, just like the mortals she detested.

I was the only younger woman with a sensing ability that rivaled her own. I was her future, the vehicle from which she would control the world and usher in her Utopia. No wonder she hadn't told Stefan Carrington that I wasn't his daughter. Stefan who valued his seed above other Emporium Unbounded, at least as long as they worked for his dream. No doubt Delia planned to take over the role as Stefan's daughter, the black sheep finally come home, to eventually inherit the Triad from him and from Tihalt, the other member of their unholy alliance. Stefan hadn't reached the halfway point in his life. With Stefan's full support, instead of his ongoing rivalry, and Tihalt's eternal distraction with his science, Delia would have no opposition within the Emporium leadership. The supposed family relationship between Stefan and me might even put her in a position to murder Stefan if her plan didn't go smoothly.

Delia would become me. Would I stay in my mind as a silent observer as she lived out my life? Or would she somehow be able to murder my consciousness?

No! I screamed. I sent a flash down the remaining length of blue light.

Abruptly, the connection broke, though not before I heard Delia's laugh. *Soon,* she promised. I didn't think she understood that I'd figured out her plan, but maybe at this point her control over me was such that she didn't care if I did.

Again I heard Ritter calling to me. And shouting to the others for help. I clung to him. My mind was still full of flames. I was burning, burning.

Delia was laughing.

Then I felt Shadrach's touch and my world went blessedly dark.

CHAPTER 19

I AWOKE TO SEE FAINT TENDRILS OF LIGHT GLOWING BEHIND THE SHEER curtains over the tiny window. I was in Ritter's arms, and they tightened briefly around me as I shifted position. He was sleeping the deep sleep of a man who'd had a restless night, and as I stared at him, I remembered him calling me back. The panic in his voice.

"I'm okay," I whispered, though it was a lie.

If Delia succeeded, what would happen to me?

I lifted Ritter's arm and slipped out carefully. That he didn't stir attested to both his exhaustion and the fact that he trusted me. He didn't know Delia had been so close to success last night. Could she have filled my body at this distance? Or would she have needed to make me come to her? I simply didn't know.

Someone had put a nightgown on me, and the silk felt sensuous against my skin. Probably one of Stella's. I was just as likely to wear an old T-shirt. Maybe that would change now that I was married.

Married.

I almost lost it at the thought of our failed night and Delia's interference. We'd waited so long. *My fault.* I'd been too hung up on logistics, on the risks to my emotions.

I had to admit Delia's plan was brilliant. No one would know. If she played her game well, she might even be able to bring down much of the Renegade network before my friends understood what had happened. Or maybe they'd just think I'd turned traitor.

These thoughts only strengthened my resolve. I would face her. I might not win, but she wouldn't either. Not completely. I wouldn't let her hurt the friends that had become family. To that end, I typed out a message on my phone, scheduling it for delivery later that day.

Gathering my bodysuit, my weapons, and the tan robes and face coverings Yalda had offered me, I left the room. I didn't take my phone. Stella could track that too quickly, and if things didn't work out, I couldn't have Delia using me to hurt them. Carrying my bundle down the hall, I slipped into Jeane's room.

"Get up," I said, yanking open the curtains around her bed.

She yawned, stretching her arms out wide. "It's not even six."

"I know where Delia is." I pulled off my nightgown and began working my bodysuit over my legs and torso.

Jeane sat up. "Where?"

"At a hotel. I'll know it when I see it." I felt my arm for my locator chip and used a knife Basilio had given me to extract it before pulling on the rest of the suit.

I checked my knives and guns in each pocket. I would have rather had my own weapons instead of Basilio's, but any battle between Delia and me would be mental, so I would have to be satisfied with his offerings. I stopped adjusting my weapons to face Jeane. "You can do this, right?"

Her wide eyes stared back. "The question is, can you?"

"I don't know."

She scowled as she pushed herself from the bed. "You'd better know. I don't want to end up in a hole for another twenty years."

"It will all depend on you." I hesitated before adding. "But if I try to kill you, shoot me." I handed her a pistol.

"What?"

I brought my face close to hers. "That thing in my head isn't what any of us thought. It's not to control me. Somehow she plans to transfer herself *into* me. Permanently."

She was stunned into silence, but only for a few seconds. "That explains a lot. All her experiments with that worm of an assistant. I thought it was only for control, but if she's found a way to move her consciousness, she'd—"

"Be immortal. And I'm not too sure she can't take over from a distance. Every minute I stay here, I'm a danger to the others. So hurry!"

Jeane yanked on a pair of black pants, followed by an impractical white blouse, her protective vest, and the gray robes from the night before. "Okay, I'm ready."

"They'll follow us if they can," I said, pushing aside her robe to cut out the locator chip in her arm. She grimaced, looking away.

On the lower floor, we found Amina and Yalda already up, still fully covered except their large dark eyes. "Good morning," I said, trying to hide my anxiety. "We need a taxi."

"At the bottom of the street," Amina said in heavily

accented English. "Many wait there." She reached over and adjusted my head covering.

"Thank you."

Jeane and I hurried from the house. No one stared twice at us as we strode down the walk, except two tourists dressed in jeans and bright sweatshirts. We hailed a red *petit* taxi and slipped inside. "To the best hotel in town," I said. "Expensive. Great service. Something tall, a white building with an uneven slant to the top floor—or roof, I guess. I'll know it when I see it."

If the dark man was surprised to hear someone dressed so natively speaking in English, he didn't show it. "I know the one," he said, his English coming out with a British flare. "It is the tourist favorite. I, however, would recommend something with more of the rich flavor of Casablanca."

"We're meeting friends."

"Ah, I see. Then to the Sofitel, it is."

We didn't speak at all on the way, the taxi hurtling through the streets that seemed too busy this early in the morning. Now that we'd left successfully, I was having second thoughts. Ever since Venezuela, facing Delia alone was exactly what I intended because I wasn't willing to risk any of my friends, and learning of her real plan to take over my life had only increased my desire to protect them. If she succeeded, they would be completely at her mercy. How would they be able to kill my body, even if she inhabited it? Better that I died before that happened.

According to Keene, Morocco wasn't one of the Emporium's headquarters, and last night we had put what were probably most of Delia's accompanying soldiers out of the picture—at least until they healed. That meant I had a good chance at challenging Delia without too much interference.

She *wanted* to see me, after all. If I succeeded, my strength would hopefully be restored and getting out wouldn't be too much of a problem. There were a few gaping holes in my plan, to be sure, but what difference did that make? There was hope, and sometimes only hope had gotten me through my previous confrontations with her. I also had Ritter's trust to hold onto.

Yet going in with only Jeane for backup suddenly didn't seem like such a good idea.

Because Delia had known for months what her plan was and would be ready for me. And she would want revenge for the stolen plutonium every bit as much as I wanted it for my grandmother. Delia seemed to know me only too well. Did that mean she had planned on my rashness? Maybe she expected me to come to her without proper backup.

As I thought it through again, I could still see no other option that didn't risk my friends. If Ritter and the others weren't here, Delia couldn't use them to control my actions, as she had used my brother and his children in the past. That didn't mean I wasn't scared, because I was terrified.

The driver skidded to a stop in front of a skyscraper with a double-door entry and a mirrored section that curved around the lower part of the building and glistened in the rising sun. "Is this the hotel?"

"Yes." There was no mistaking the white tower that reached into the sky far above its neighbors. I handed him my credit card, and he swiped it on a cell phone he had on the seat.

We climbed from the little red cab, and Jeane started for the entrance. "Wait," I said. The walkway in front of the hotel was empty, though there were plenty of cars still zooming past.

"What?" She looked back at me over her shoulder, tossing her head for the invisible cameras. "Don't tell me you're having second thoughts. There's no other way to get that thing out of you except facing her. In fact, I'm pretty sure you'll have to kill her."

"I know, but we need to talk this through. This isn't her stronghold, and I'm betting that last night we pretty much demolished the entourage she always drags along with her. But she'll have others around. We have to make sure we'll be able to get out."

Her face darkened. "There's nothing really to plan. We either succeed or we don't. I can null her and her soldiers, and you can fight them or blast them with your mind or whatever. Getting out will be easy once we take care of Delia."

Jace must have been bragging to her about me. "That doesn't mean we go in completely blind." I was thinking about calling Ritter to ask for his advice. Or was I only fooling myself? Did I want Ritter to convince me to tell him where I was? I felt for my phone, forgetting that I'd left it behind. Jeane returned to my side, stepping close. Something hard jabbed into my side.

"This is for your own good," Jeane said. "Now get going, or I'll shoot."

"Really? This is what you're doing? I'd think you'd want all the advantage we can get. I'm not going to be able to fight Delia half dead from a gunshot."

"We have to get her now before she takes control of you. You're my only chance." She pushed at me, but I refused to budge.

"Only chance of what?" I asked. "Why do you want her so badly? You're safe from her with us."

She glared, her nostrils flaring and her face so tight she was shaking. "I'll never be safe as long as she lives! Never. You don't know the things she did to me. Now move!" She poked me again with the gun.

Dimitri had told me some Unbounded had damaged minds that he couldn't repair. I'd seen for myself minds damaged from Delia's experiments, and Jeane certainly seemed unbalanced since her dealings with the Triad leader. Maybe being almost dead for twenty years had something to do with it.

"Okay," I said, taking a step forward.

She followed me, but with the next step, I twisted and slammed my right hand into the gun under her robes, jamming it into her body. I followed with a left hook to her head and she staggered, the gun clattering to the ground. She groaned and brought a hand to her ear.

I scooped up the gun, stepping close to her, one hand on her back and the other digging the gun into her belly. "This isn't a game, Jeane," I said tightly. "We're either on the same team or we're not. I'm not going anywhere with you at gunpoint. I'd rather you kill me and hand me over to Delia."

She grimaced. "Fine. I just want this over."

I stepped away, concealing the gun under my robe, noting that we had attracted the attention of a small group of early-rising tourists who had congregated at the doors to the hotel. They were alternately staring at us and looking back inside the hotel doors, as if debating whether we were very close friends consoling one another or if I was threatening Jeane.

I put an arm around her. "Smile," I ordered.

She turned actress from one second to the next, leaning toward me with a little curtsey and giving a laugh that would carry all the way to the door. Feeling exposed with the many windows staring down at us, I hurried her inside. We both averted our eyes as we passed the tourists.

Inside, the motif was black and white, the white tiled floor decorated with lavish swirls of black. The life forces nearby burned brightly—so they weren't blocking. We walked up to the black reception desk. "I need a room," I said. "Do you have one available? Our luggage will be coming shortly with our husbands." What I really wanted was a reason to be in the hotel, and we might be able to use a room in case we needed someplace to hole up for a while until we could completely escape.

We were turning away toward a waiting bellhop when a group of blocking life forces entered the hotel. I didn't need to turn to know who they were. Jeane swore under her breath. "So much for low-key," she muttered.

Ritter's face was drawn in a scowl, his black eyes molten fury, and his dark hair uncombed. He wore a set of off-white robes, but I knew he only did it to hide the assault rifle and other assorted weapons. There was something intrinsically sexy about him despite—or maybe because of—the robes, and my heart did some kind of ridiculous happy dance. *Mine.* The thought wasn't new to me, but it was the first time it was really true.

With him were Cort, Mari, and Keene, none looking too happy. In fact, Keene's glower matched Ritter's almost perfectly. Everyone except Ritter was wearing a jacket, and each carried a duffel bag that was probably full of weapons.

I headed to a set of couches by a black pillar, and they followed. "How did you find me, Your Deathliness?" I said in a low voice to Ritter, letting him know by the nickname that I wasn't backing down from what I'd done.

He sat down next to me. "Why did you come here alone?"

"This is *my* fight."

He scooted closer, squishing into me. "It's all of ours."

"You don't understand."

Ritter leaned close, his anger growing. "It's *you* who doesn't understand. We stick together. No one sacrifices themselves for the others."

"I've seen you put yourself into much more danger." Like entering an Emporium headquarters to rescue me. "Anyway, all bets are off now. Delia can control me."

"I don't believe it," he growled. Any closer and he'd be on top of me, and despite all the robes between us, I felt naked under his glare. "My bet is on you."

"I'm not willing to risk that you might be wrong."

"After last night on the roof, it isn't just *your* choice."

"That's exactly why it *is* my choice."

Keene heaved an exaggerated sigh. "Look, you two. You can indulge in a lover's spat about this another time. Because right now that bellhop looks ready to call the police."

He and Cort were standing in front of us, trying to block the bellhop's view, but the man did appear nervous at Ritter's obvious aggression. Ritter eased back from me, making a motion with his head at Mari, who walked over to smooth things over with the bellhop.

I asked Ritter again, "How did you find me?"

His voice lowered. "You think I don't know what last night was all about? It was goodbye. Or at least until you passed out." He glanced around. "This hotel is just like you showed me. I knew you were headed here the second I realized you were gone. Luckily, I had Stella tag you again after that episode last night."

I clenched my teeth. Of course. We'd been together, and he'd felt it when I was pulled into the blue light. He had come at least part of the way with me—I'd felt him, clung to him—and he was worried enough about what he'd seen to take precautions.

"Did you ever think," he added, his voice growing rough and unsteady, "that maybe our being together is the reason you got back at all?"

I hadn't. I only knew that Delia would murder him if given the chance, and I'd do anything to save him. "I have to face her."

"I know, and this is as good a place as any. But I go with you."

"I'm going too." This from Keene.

Ritter shook his head. "No. You guys stay here and guard our exit. Make sure Delia doesn't have backup. Protect Mari in case Erin needs to use her ability to shift out."

"I'm going," Keene insisted. "You stay. You're no good to her. I am."

"Oh, so you're finally going to admit what you are?" Ritter sneered. "Not like we don't already know."

Keene glanced back at Mari and the bellhop, and I knew that she still didn't know about Keene's Change. Not yet. "I can make Erin stronger in ways you can't," Keene said, not backing down. "I don't care what your ego says. She needs me more than she needs you."

"From what your brother says, you might just as easily blow everyone up." Ritter's voice was mocking, but I sensed he was masking worry that Keene might be right—that Keene could help me more in this situation than Ritter himself.

Keene inclined his head. "Maybe," he conceded. "And maybe Erin would rather blow up than become Delia."

That told me Stella had gotten into my phone and found

my message. At least now they knew what we were really up against. I didn't know whether to weep with pride or scream in frustration that both Ritter and Keene were willing to risk their lives for me.

Silence fell between the glaring men. Much as I didn't want to admit it, Keene was right. He was more useful in this situation. As far as I knew, Delia could only force people to fight for her, not channel their abilities directly. That meant I wouldn't need to channel Ritter because physically I should be more than her match, so Keene or Mari would be more help to me than Ritter if I had to shift or if I needed more strength.

At the same time I knew Ritter wouldn't abandon me.

"I say we all go," Cort said. "Stella's coordinating with Ava, who is apparently on her way with Dimitri and more CIA. We only have to hold out for a few hours."

I opened my mouth to reply when my brain suddenly flashed blue as the connection between Delia and her creature inside my mind flared to life. I wasn't even using my ability.

Or was I?

I became keenly aware of each person's thoughts around me. Ritter was angry, desperate, hurt, and protective; Keene was willing to sacrifice his freedom to save me; Cort was determined and infinitely curious at the new patterns he saw in the atoms making up my brain; Mari was afraid Delia would capture her, but just as afraid she'd fail me; and the bellhop was hoping he'd finish with us quickly so he could grab breakfast. All but Jeane, who was completely dark.

I extended a shield around the others, hoping that if Delia was aware of my arrival, she wouldn't be able to sense their life forces. Unfortunately, I wasn't altogether sure it worked because the two blue lights still seeped through the shield, perhaps even brighter with my effort. The pressure in my mind built to a painful level.

"We have to do this now." I hoped my fear didn't show in my voice. I didn't know what would happen if the snake burst from the second box before the battle. "She might know we're here. Or that we're close."

"Let's go," Ritter said.

Fortunately, Mari had finally convinced the bellhop that we didn't need his services, the handful of American dollars she shoved at him doing more than any of her persuasions.

"Thank you for not bringing Jace," I said to Ritter as we made our way to the elevator.

"He's guarding the plutonium. Stella doesn't want to get too close."

"You could have left it with Shadrach."

"Maybe. He seems distraught."

Distraught? Every now and then, Ritter's manner of speaking reminded me of how very long he'd lived. Regardless, I knew he'd left Jace behind for me. My brother had always been a little rash—a trait that apparently ran in our family, at least in those who had the active Unbounded gene—and I was worried that he didn't understand well enough what was at stake. That once he met his birth father, something would change. Stefan Carrington's charisma was overwhelming.

"So are we going to knock on her door?" Jeane asked as the elevator door closed.

Mari held up a key card. "No, we're just going to walk inside. The bellhop was nice enough to donate this to our cause. Unknowingly, of course." She grinned, making the death grip on my heart lessen marginally.

We left the elevator several floors before the penthouse and took the stairs from there, pausing in the stairwell after we crept up the last flight. I pushed my thoughts through the shield bubble I'd created around us, searching for life forces. "Two just in the hall," I whispered.

"That's all?" Ritter asked.

I bit back a sharp retort because I knew he wasn't over being mad at me. And I couldn't blame him—I'd also be angry if our roles were reversed. I had to admit that I felt better with him here, even if my concern for him and the others had replaced my original fears about going in alone. I had to remind myself that this wasn't an Emporium stronghold, and it was doubtful they had as many people in place in Casablanca's city government as they did in Washington DC. Morocco wasn't exactly a stepladder to world control.

Ritter nodded at Cort, who came to stand near him. Cort reached for the stairwell door and, on Ritter's signal, opened it with a fluid motion. Ritter moved so fast, he almost vanished from sight. He cut down the two men guarding the hallway with a few punches. Neither Cort nor Keene had time to let off a silenced shot.

Jeane stepped past me, her eyes holding mine with a hint of satisfaction that told me she'd used her ability on the men so they couldn't instinctively react to Ritter's accelerated attack.

Ritter and Cort hurried forward and fanned out on either side of the penthouse door. With a soft sound resembling an intake of breath, Mari appeared next to Cort. Jeane followed more sedately, stepping delicately over the fallen men. On her heels, Keene paused to send two silenced shots into one of the downed guards. I did the same to the other man. We couldn't have them reviving and coming after us. I just hoped no hotel employees found reason to come here before we were safely gone.

The blue light was flickering now and growing, like a flame receiving more oxygen. Delia had to be close.

While Ritter glanced at his phone, which contained the blueprints of the hotel Stella had sent him, I concentrated on what was inside the penthouse. No life forced glowed in the larger room on the other side of the door, but there was a faint life force in one of the back bedrooms. I pointed and held up one finger. Ritter met my eyes, and I saw the worry there plainly. Exactly my reaction. Delia couldn't possibly be there alone, could she? So either she was shielding her own life force and the one I was picking up was a guard, or she wasn't here.

I felt nearly panicked at this thought. Last night I almost hadn't made it back to my body. What if that was her plan all along? Maybe Delia didn't need to confront me to win. The pressure in my mind was great, but I resisted the urge to touch the box or the streams of blue light, worried that I'd no longer be in control.

Mari pushed in the key card and pulled it out again, stepping back. Ritter slowly eased the door open and slipped inside with Cort. We all followed carefully, guns drawn. Only Jeane had no weapon. Her eyes glistened brightly, reminiscent of the blue lights in my head.

Ritter and Cort were already heading down the hall, checking each room thoroughly, one by one. I started after them. The life force I felt was dim. So dim, the person could be dying. I pushed out tentatively . . . searching. There, I had it. A surge of elation ran through me as I examined the barely conscious thoughts. It was Habid, Shadrach's son! I made my way to the door at the end of the hallway, turned the knob, and pushed it open. The room was dark and nothing appeared to be inside. The fading life force beckoned me to the closet.

The instant I walked into the dark room, I knew it was a mistake. Immediately, half a dozen life forces blinked into existence. I could feel a similar thing happening in the other penthouse rooms as at least two sensing Unbounded uncovered the shields they'd used to hide their comrades' presence. Soldiers burst from closets, bathrooms, and from behind beds. Each carried an assault rifle.

CHAPTER 20

THE LIGHTS FLICKERED ON IN THE ROOM TO REVEAL DELIA VESEY, sitting on a leather chair near a black desk. Standing at her side was her assistant, a sensing Emporium agent. I recognized that slight figure, the tight blond curls, and the crunched facial features only too well after the incident in New York. He was Lew Roberts, and like my would-be brother, Jonny, he looked seventeen or eighteen because of his forced early Change, but he was also over a hundred. Two soldiers stood on each side of the door, four in all, their rifles aimed at my head. One snatched the gun from my hand.

"Hello, Erin," Delia said, arising. "I wouldn't move if I were you."

I was thinking of doing just that, but the blue lights in my mind emitted a blinding flash, as if welcoming the woman. I clamped down on my thoughts. I wouldn't let her in. Not like this.

As Delia came toward me, her assistant flicked open the

heavy curtains to provide more light, revealing an impressive panoramic view of Casablanca, the Hassan II Mosque towering over the other buildings in the distance. It was impressive and foreign, and for an instant, I felt dwarfed at its majesty.

If judged only by looks alone, Delia's thin lips would have precluded her from true beauty, but her regal face, the intent expression in her brown eyes, and her confident carriage made her striking. She wore a tan pantsuit, with a sheer, flowing duster that fluttered as she walked. The early morning light was kind, and her wrinkles and graying hair seemed muted. She appeared to be only in her sixties, but I knew better.

Lew Roberts trailed his mentor like the lapdog he was. I hated the disgusting man, though less than I should, given that he'd been a part of an attempt to use me as an incubator for his genetically enhanced sperm. He was only Delia's pawn.

One of the guards took a knife and cut off my robes and head coverings, and then he and another man thoroughly checked me for weapons. As they took my pistols, knives, and even a bit of rope, I tried to reach my friends outside the room, but my thoughts couldn't find them.

Was Jeane using her ability out there and was that what was preventing me? Was she helping Ritter and the others? Except for the block, I felt normal, and Delia and her assistant didn't seem to notice anything odd, so whatever Jeane was doing, it wasn't targeted inside this room.

A deep shout came from somewhere in the penthouse, and I felt sick not knowing what was happening. This was why I'd wanted to come alone. Because Delia and I would still have to battle, but now she had more ammunition against me. I was worried more about my friends than defeating her.

Pushing past my fear, I reached out to both Delia and Lew. Lew's shield was a tremendous whorling black mass that seemed to have a life of its own. It was the kind of mental shield I was helping our Renegades develop, one I would have trouble getting through, even at full power. Delia's barrier, however, was different this time. I couldn't see past the granite wall, but the blue lights in my mind reached out to her and disappeared inside her shield like an umbilical. I suspected if I touched the blue, I could ride it and delve inside her mind, but since that's what her thought construct was apparently designed to do, I wasn't sure that was the way to fight her. Then again, there didn't seem to be any other way. I wasn't getting through those four armed guards, even if Jeane managed to null their abilities.

From the closet came a brief flicker of the faint life force there. *Habid.* I couldn't help him now, but I would certainly try to get us both out of here. I reached out to him and thought, *Hang on. We're coming.* Hope could do marvelous things, though where I was concerned, it seemed to bring pain just as often. Like thinking about my poor grandmother.

But I was still alive. So that was something.

We heard sounds in the hallway and turned as Ritter and Cort were shoved into the room. Ritter hadn't been captured easily and was bleeding from a split lip and a cut on his head, and through the half-torn robe, I could see at least one bullet wound in his right shoulder, the arm hanging uselessly at his side. The earbud he'd been wearing earlier to connect with Stella was missing. Two guards, a man and a woman, held pistols at his head, each of them sporting numerous wounds. In stark contrast, Cort and his two male captors seemed unhurt.

Keene was pushed into the room next by none other than Edgel, a tall, broad man with a large flat nose, close-cropped hair, and glorious black skin. Only months earlier, Edgel had worked for Keene, who had been under his father's control. It seemed a lifetime ago. There had been respect and loyalty between them, but subsequent run-ins had shown us that Edgel's loyalty to the Emporium ran far deeper than any friendship he'd felt for Keene. I knew Edgel blamed us for the death of his mortal daughter, her existence the only secret he'd ever kept from the Emporium, and the revenge he sought against us made him that much more dangerous.

Jeane came in after Keene, her face frozen in shock, though the male guard with her seemed less fierce than the others. The additional Emporium agents brought the total in the room to ten, all Unbounded, plus Delia and Lew. Not overwhelming odds if they hadn't surprised us.

My fault, I thought. *I'm the one who was in a hurry to get here.* Yet what other choice could I have made? Tomorrow, it might have been Delia who woke up in Ritter's arms. The idea of her touching his body, even with my hand, made me furious.

Mari was nowhere to be seen, so apparently she'd shifted somewhere when the unveiling had begun. But she wouldn't go far. She knew that as long as I could reach her, I could shift out. I wouldn't abandon the others, of course, but shifting to another location could be helpful. However, I didn't search for her now, not wanting to call Delia's attention to her. As long as that blue light was between us, I couldn't trust myself.

"Ah, welcome," Delia said to Ritter and the others,

"though I must say, I'm a little surprised. I didn't think Erin would risk her friends like this. She's already recently lost her dear grandmother."

Bile rose in my throat. "Let them go," I snarled.

She laughed. "Oh, no. I'm sure Tihalt will be happy to have his sons back." She gave Cort a mirthless grin and then laughed again as her eyes fixed on Keene. I knew she was noticing his Change. "It's never too late," she said. "Your father will be pleased."

Keene spat on the carpet, but that only seemed to increase Delia's amusement. Her eyes wandered over to settle on Jeane. "Thank you, dear, for bringing her."

Jeane's gaze didn't change, but Delia's face suddenly darkened. With an abrupt, angry motion, she signaled Lew, who lunged toward Jeane. Flicking out a knife, he grabbed her around the neck, holding the blade to her throat. Beads of blood appeared on her pale flesh. She grimaced with pain, her head arching back into her captor's chest, their eyes meeting.

"Don't try that again." Lew's nostrils flared slightly as he spoke, his voice high and nasal. They knew each other; I could see it in both their eyes. There was history here. I wondered if Jeane had spurned him at one time. I wouldn't be surprised, and if so, I knew he would take great pleasure in hurting her now.

"You belong to me," Delia told her. "You always have. You live only because you are useful. Don't waste that or maybe I'll find you need another decade or two of rest."

"Rest!" Jeane's eyes blazed with hatred.

"You'll be rewarded soon." Delia's comment came out more patronizing than soothing, but I doubted it was on purpose.

Again, Jeane's eyes rolled up to meet Lew's. Met and held for at least two seconds, and then both looked away. *History,* I thought. Knowing Lew's cruelty, I wondered if Jeane wasn't better off rotting in the bomb shelter where we'd found her.

"You can let her go, Lew," Delia said. "For now."

Delia swiveled her head back to the rest of us, clapping her hands together as if closing a book. "So, this is the group that caused me havoc in Venezuela and again here last night. Well, that's over now." She drew in a deep breath, looking at Edgel. "If you'll please go collect our package. It should be here by now." Edgel nodded and moved out of the room, taking one of the guards near Cort with him. I hoped they wouldn't run into Mari, wherever she was hiding.

The tension was so high in the room, I could have felt it through all the mental shield construction in the world. Ritter, Cort, and Keene were alert, and I knew they were ready to act. Jeane also met my gaze, her eyes moving back and forth between me and the guards, her face determined. So, maybe she was nulling at least some of their abilities. If they weren't sensing Unbounded, they shouldn't notice until it was too late. I was reasonably confident Delia and Lew wouldn't realize what Jeane was doing, either, unless they were actually inside their guards' minds, which wasn't necessary at the moment. Of course, that still left Delia and Lew to deal with, and that would fall to me.

I wished I knew more about the snake she'd planted in my head. Or the piece of her thoughts—whatever it was. What was it doing? Well, beside connecting us and draining my strength. And how could I get rid of it? If I asked, she wouldn't answer outright, and I wondered if I'd have no choice but to ride the stream of blue light and find the answer inside her mind. Though I'd been in her consciousness before, something in me recoiled at the idea now. Before it had been my choice; with the blue lights, all control was hers. I didn't want to fall into any trap she'd created for me.

"This thing in my head," I said. "What is it?"

Delia's dark eyes glittered with an emotion I couldn't define. She stepped close to me, bringing up her hand to my cheek, but stopped just short of touching my skin. Even so, I almost felt her physical caress. "Ah, Erin," she said softly, "this would have been so much simpler if you had been willing to work with me. But don't worry. The gift I gave you is only something to help you become more powerful." Her grin sent fingers of icy dread through my stomach. "And we all know that power is everything."

Edgel was coming back now, and to my surprise, he was pushing a luggage cart with a white-covered mound that looked all too familiar. Delia strode over, her sheer duster flowing like a bridal veil. She threw off the sheet, revealing the cask we'd stolen last night—or one very like it.

"You have more?" Fury pulsed through me.

"Oh, no." Delia glided back to me. "This is the same cask you stole from me last night. We had no idea Habid was signaling you or that you knew how to track us to that house." She didn't look toward the closet where the man still lay dying, and it was all I could do not to look in that direction myself. "But one of your friends was kind enough to return it."

My head whipped toward Jeane. "No," she said. "Like I'd want her to have a nuclear weapon. She's crazy. Besides, I've been with you."

Delia laughed. "No, it wasn't our dear Jeane." Her voice implied that it should have been.

In horror, I followed Delia's gaze to the doorway behind us where the guard who'd left with Edgel had reappeared with Shadrach Azima. Ritter's face became a mass of fury. Cort's expression was pained, and Keene shook his head in disgust.

Shadrach avoided us all, having eyes only for Delia. "You said you had my son. That you would give him to me if I returned this."

"Shadrach! What are you doing?" This from Cort. "You can't trust her."

The healer's gaze didn't waver. "My son. Please."

"Eight million lives," Cort said. "That's just the beginning."

"She took my grandmother," I told Shadrach. "Don't you think I'd do anything to get her back? How is Habid going to feel knowing he was responsible for the end of the world?" With a sick feeling, I remembered that Jace had been watching the plutonium. Had Shadrach done something to my brother?

"My son," Shadrach repeated, his eyes not leaving Delia's face.

Motioning Shadrach into the room, Delia looked at Lew, who hurried over to the cask, a device in his hands. Opening the cask with a code, he checked it with his machine. "Intact."

Delia waved a thin hand toward the closet. "He's in there."

With a hoarse sob, Shadrach stumbled across the room like a drunken man intent on his fix. I was angry with him beyond speech, yet I was glad his son would get help because I knew how it felt to lose someone you cared so much about. Shadrach might be able to save Habid's life. Perhaps. That didn't excuse what Shadrach had done. He would be the catalyst for the eventual collapse of the world and enslavement of the mortal population.

This confrontation might become the final lost battle.

Shadrach ripped open the door. As he did, a sword that was fastened to the door by a metal bar also moved forward, severing Habid's head as he sat tied to a chair. The head clunked to the ground.

"Noooooo!" His father screamed in horror, collapsing near his son, grabbing the bleeding head, trying to reattach it.

Too late. There was no longer a hint of even a faint life force in Habid's body. Several seconds later, Shadrach came to the same conclusion. With a roar of anguish, he launched himself in Delia's direction. A whoosh from Edgel's silenced gun took him in the head, spattering his brain over the wall. He dropped to the carpet. Not permanently dead like his mortal son, but I looked away, sickened.

I thought of my grandmother, and I knew for sure she was dead.

Keene stepped forward, holding out an open hand toward the plutonium cask. "Stop. I won't let you have this. I'll blow it up here."

"I don't think—" Delia's retort was cut off as the internal monitors on the cask burst into frantic beeping.

"Keene!" Cort said, as the beeping became a wailing siren. "You can't control it! You don't know how far to go!"

"How far?" Keene's voice was so tight it hurt my ears. "As far as I need to. If I take out the building—the city, even— it won't be as big as Israel. Three million instead of eight. And no war. Not even Delia Vesey could come back from this. No focus points will remain attached. It's an acceptable exchange."

"Or you might just blow up the entire continent!" Cort stepped toward his brother, practically yelling to be heard over the screeching alarm.

"Shoot him," Delia ordered.

Cort raised his arms in front of Keene. "No! He has to stop the reaction or it's going to blow!"

Understanding dawned on Delia as she realized Keene had an ability that could take it all away from her: the trillions of dollars, the political control, her eternal life.

"Erin," Keene said. "Leave."

He meant for me to shift and take Mari away, wherever she was. Ritter's eyes met mine with a sharp nod. I shook my head. "I'm not leaving."

Sorrow flashed so fast across Keene's face that I wasn't sure I'd seen correctly. "Then we all die."

But it wasn't the only way. I had to reach Delia—now. Inside my mind, I went toward the nearest stream of blue light. Immediately, it sucked at me, pulling me in. For a brief, blinding moment of agony, there was a rip in my consciousness.

In the next second I was in Delia's mind, past her shield, seeing through her eyes. I looked for her thought stream. Surely if I pushed hard enough, I could control her. I could make her do what I wanted. Or I could channel her own ability, becoming even more powerful. I would win this thing yet.

"Wait!" Delia held up her hand before I could do anything. "Stand down everyone! You can leave. All of you! Safe passage. You can even take the cask."

Keene frowned, his eyes disbelieving. I felt exactly the same way.

"I mean it!" Delia's voice was practically a shriek.

"What about that thing inside Erin?" Ritter shoved past the two guards targeting him. "What about her?"

I tried to speak from my own body, but nothing came out of my mouth. That was when I realized the blue lights had become a two-way street. Not only was the energy seeping from my body on one path, but now, once it arrived in Delia's mind, it was being returned to me on the second path, laden with energy that flowed directly from her thought stream. Two blue lights. Two paths for different purposes.

What is that all about? Mentally, I stepped closer and shoved my hands into the energy stream that was returning to my mind, gasping as Delia's memories poured through me. Days, months, years. People she had known. Plans she had enacted. Men she had loved and betrayed. Women she had used and thrown away. Women like Jeane, who I saw had been forced to kill her ex-president lover. Like my grandmother who had refused to be used as a bargaining chip and had been killed while attempting a daring escape from her Emporium guards. All things Delia were speeding along the light, transferring at an astonishing velocity. An entire download of seventeen hundred years of knowledge and experience.

No wonder Delia's snake—no, her thought construction—had grown so big in my mind. It wasn't just feeding off me, it was transferring everything Delia would need to keep her who she was while becoming me. She would have it all—my youth and memories combined with her vast experience. And when she had finished with me, she would breed herself another body to use when mine aged. Immoral immortality.

Usually, when in someone's head, I could still see through my eyes and use my body. This time was different.

Delia had blocked me completely, severing me from the portion of myself that remained behind. Desperately, I clawed my way through the thoughts, trying to follow the light as it left Delia's mind, fighting to get back to myself.

I saw it now. Everything had played into Delia's plan. She hadn't been able to predict that Keene would act as he had, or that his doing so would force me to confront her in the only way I knew how, but she had jumped at the opportunity.

Come and fight me! I screamed.

But Delia Vesey was no longer in residence. I would be left here, a shadow version of myself. With only the immediate knowledge and memories I'd brought with me. The rest of my mind, myself, the person I was, would stay in my body to be overrun or stamped out by Delia.

I tried to dive into the energy stream that ran between us so I could return with it to my own body, but it kept ejecting me, so I backtracked to the thinner stream of blue light where it entered her brain and began to inch along, struggling to get out of Delia's head, my progress painfully slow.

"I think she means it," someone said. "Let's go." My voice, but not really me. I couldn't even see my body through Delia's eyes because my effort to return was taking all my concentration.

"What about that thing?" Ritter insisted.

"I think I've figured it out," Delia said, imbuing my voice with confidence.

The wailing in the room lessened to beeping as Keene altered his meddling with the plutonium.

No! I shouted, still blind and mute. *She's not me. No!*

"Okay," Cort said. "I say we leave. Grab that thing, Keene."

Ritter! I anguished.

With a frantic push, I mentally reached the edge of my own body. As I fought to enter, I could see that the larger box containing the snake had burst, filling the space I usually occupied until it was all Delia. The barrier she'd created prevented me from reentering my mind. She was me now. She was in control.

I couldn't give up.

I was still me—at least part of me. Maybe from Delia's body I could channel someone else and get them to stop her.

But who? I could only channel one person at a time. If I chose Ritter, I could turn Delia's aged body into a fighting machine and retract her order to let everyone go. But then we'd still be at a standoff, and every moment I could feel Delia strengthening the shield around my mind to keep me out permanently, no matter how strong I might become in her body. Though I doubted she would allow me to live at all. She had a plan for everything.

If I chose Keene, I could blow up the place. Or just as likely cause my own body to fall apart—which brought us right back to where I'd begun. Jeane, of course, was useless since I couldn't channel her.

Cort. That might be it. Not only could he see the patterns in atoms, including energy, but he could understand how they worked. Maybe using his ability, I could study what Delia had created and mentally target her weakness.

I reached out to him, feeling my consciousness sucked back into Delia's body. *Cort.* His shield was tight, but I could get through it, right? What was it I normally used to help me? I felt as if I'd left some vital piece of information back in my body, a memory I was accustomed to leaving behind and retrieving when needed. Well, there was nothing to do but use every bit of energy I could access in Delia's mind to carve a tiny hole in Cort's shield.

There, somehow I did it. I felt Delia's knees buckle. Or my knees, since I was every bit as much her as she was me.

"Delia!" I was vaguely aware of the shout coming from Edgel. I felt hands supporting me.

Cort, it's me. I—

Pain sliced through my shoulder, and I blinked open Delia's eyes to see Jeane standing over me with a knife she'd gotten from somewhere. "Stop," I made Delia's voice say. "It's me. Don't—"

Edgel thrust her away, pushing her toward Lew. "Watch her." Funny how he would save me now. *If only he knew.*

"Let's go! She said we could go." My voice again, but Delia didn't quite sound like me anymore.

I was weakening fast. I had to focus and stop wasting energy trying to communicate with Cort and get to work. Holding onto his ability, I began looking at the streams still stretching between me and Delia. The flow was ebbing now. I didn't have much time. I'd channeled Cort's ability before, and while it was miraculous, science had never really been an interest for me. Now my life depended on him.

Maybe I should have chosen Ritter or Keene.

Reaching for my eroding confidence, I forced my way back along the blue light, holding onto my connection with Cort. But everywhere I looked with his ability, I saw no weakness I could pry or push at. Nothing to use against her. The one good thing about the ebbing flow and being cut off from myself was that Delia could no longer feed on me, and the energy I gathered from her body now was mine. I made it back along the path, but I couldn't enter my own head. There was too much Delia, and the barrier she'd created, though mostly transparent to me, appeared impenetrable. I might already be too late.

Then I saw it lying among the coils and layers of Delia's presence. My small thought construct, the box that held my fear of heights. That was the answer—an answer that had come from within me, not from Cort. All I had to do was to release it. If I could get to it.

I reached for it, straining, but the barrier was too strong. No way to get in, but maybe I didn't need to, not completely. I only needed to dissolve the box. I shoved as hard as I could against Delia's thought barrier, trying to push it over slightly. Trying to pull the box closer. Nothing.

Delia! I screamed.

I could feel her mental laughter. I saw the image she flashed to me: her hand in Ritter's. She would kill him and the others at the first opportunity. I had no doubt.

No!

At that moment, I saw what Cort's ability permitted me to notice—a tiny weakness. A flaw in Delia's newly created shield that would allow me to reach my box. I slammed at it with all my might. Once, and then again, and a third time until my entire being vibrated with the force. There, just enough of a crack to pull the box toward me. My thought construct, my creation. It would obey my command. All I had to do was to touch it. It slammed up against the shield and my consciousness grazed the surface.

It fell apart.

The contents of the box came tumbling out, but she had no idea what it meant. She exulted in it. Her greedy hands wrapped around my greatest fear and it slid through her fingers like gold in a treasure box. *It's all mine now, what-ever it is. Whatever you were hiding in there. Be a graceful loser, Erin.* With another laugh, she sealed the crack I'd made in her shield.

Time for the next step in my plan. Still channeling Cort, I let myself slip back into Delia's body and looked at the plutonium cask through her eyes, but the atoms told me Cort had been right. Messing with that was far too dangerous. But there was a natural gas line I might be able to use instead.

Reaching for Keene, I shoved up against his shield. It was tighter than ever, and I didn't know if I could break through another shield. I'd have to ask him verbally. I'd have to use Delia's mouth. I pulled in all my strength, concentrating it in one place, forcing her mouth open.

"Keene," I said in a voice I didn't recognize as either Delia's or mine, "I need your help."

He looked at me as if I'd lost my mind.

Jeane broke away from Lew, and this time she carried a sword. "I hate you," she screamed. "You killed him. You locked me up. Burn in hell, witch!"

The sword was coming at my throat. Too fast for me to defend myself.

Then Ritter was there blocking the sword with a chair he held in his left hand. "Stop!" he roared. "It's not Delia."

Everyone froze.

"Help her, Keene," Ritter ordered.

"No!" protested Delia from my body. "It's a trap. Let's get out of here."

Ritter grabbed my hand—my old lady hand. "This is Erin." He turned to glare at Delia in my body. "What have you done?"

She grabbed a gun from one of her stunned soldiers, turning it in Ritter's direction, but Ritter was ready for her. He pushed her back hard. Even one-handed, I knew he could beat her—but only until she got through his shield. Then she would control him.

Edgel and the other Emporium guards stood uncertainly, hands on their weapons, not knowing who to attack. They'd figure it out before too long. I had to work fast.

Keene dropped his shield. *Do this,* I pushed into his mind, guiding him to the gas line, showing him what to do. What atoms to accelerate and which to combine. *Upward and out, exactly like this. No variation. And give me more strength, like you did in Venezuela. Hurry!*

"Hit the floor!" I screamed.

I sent the thought to Mari as well, finding her in the stairwell. I saw in her unblocked mind that she'd shifted to Basilio's when Shadrach arrived, to alert Stella and check on Jace—who apparently was okay after being drugged by Shadrach—but she was back, wondering if she should try to help us now or wait for them.

I thrust out a mental shield around my friends, leaving only a slice of window that Keene could work through. My heart—no, Delia's heart—pounded furiously.

A tremendous explosion ripped through the penthouse. Metal screeched and debris went flying. A few Emporium soldiers who hadn't obeyed my command went flying too.

All at once the room was bared to the open sky.

Delia began screaming.

CHAPTER 21

ALONG WITH THE SHIELD I'D THROWN AROUND MY FRIENDS AND my own body, I'd protected the plutonium cask as well, but I really had no way of knowing if it would be enough until the roof and most of the outer penthouse walls had disappeared in the explosion. For a moment, during the blast itself, it was all I could do to keep my mind linked with Keene's and Cort's.

It was over. The natural gas line was ruptured, but the plutonium was untouched, our ears undamaged, the floor intact, and the city below us safe.

Thanks, I said, dropping contact with the brothers. I'd need all my strength for the next battle.

Ritter was already in motion. He heaved one guard off the building and dived for another. I noticed he was using his wounded arm again, so he must have partially healed and was pushing past the pain. Mari had appeared and was battling another man by the door. She flashed around him appearing and disappearing.

I sought out Jeane, who lay near me, sprawled over Delia's assistant. "Do your job!" I yelled at her.

She hesitated only a second before staring at Mari's opponent, who abruptly crumpled under the knife Mari slipped between his ribs. Ritter punched his opponent unconscious as Keene and Cort joined the fray.

Leaving them to take care of the others, I focused on Delia, who was still whimpering, clutching her hands over her head. "It's so big," she moaned. "The sky. It's falling. Crushing. Ohhh!" She wasn't laughing at what I had hidden in that box now.

I didn't bother standing but pushed my thoughts outward. Her shield was completely gone, and I slipped inside easily. The second I was there, Delia's fear—no, my fear—attacked with full vengeance, but I shoved it back with the determination I'd learned from my long practices on so many rooftops and faced the cowering woman—or the mental rendering of her in my mind.

At once, the image of my machete was in my hand. *My machete,* I thought. *That's what I forgot earlier.* I went after her, flashing light.

Lew! Delia cried out, desperately reaching for her assistant. I knew that I might not be strong enough against the two of them, but I was going to try.

Lew didn't answer Delia's call. I swung again. The impact sent a wave of light pulsing along every nerve.

Delia screamed once more, but this time it was only in my mind. I was back in charge of my physical body. I pushed harder, shoving her into the glistening black snake that latched onto her like a giant, groping child. Bringing my hands together, I formed a similar thread—black with a shiny, silver interior, throwing everything I had into it.

My construct burst into life, swelling as large as Delia's creation. It plowed into her—biting, twisting, devouring.

Delia tried to run, to leave my head, but I blocked her. *No escape,* I said. *This is your final battle.*

Swinging the machete, I cut into her consciousness, sinking the blade deep. She threw something at me, a small thought that latched on like a leech, reminding me of the snake she'd first put in my head. I pulled it from me and threw it back at her. I slashed again. Harder. Light filled my mind.

Her dying scream shook to the depths of my core.

She was gone. Even now her construct faded away and vanished completely. Nothing remained. I was alone in my own body.

I lifted my head, jumped up in time to see Ritter take out the last guard. The view out over the city was astounding, and I expected a wave of nausea, but it didn't come. I wasn't driven to my knees or biting my lip to keep from crying out. I was just there. No fear. No snake. No boxes.

I laughed. It was glorious up here. Though I'd forced myself to many rooftops over the past months since my Change, I'd never been able to see the beauty of the view. I wanted to step closer to the edge and hold out my arms to embrace it all. I bit my lip, but this time it was only to keep back tears of elation.

Ritter caught me to him. *Yes, it's me,* I told him. But he already knew.

A sound made us turn. Behind us we saw Jeane. She had a sword again in her hand, and this time no one stopped her as she sliced through Delia's neck and torso, severing all three focus points.

I believed Delia's mind was already gone—and

permanently so—but killing her body would give us all peace in the months to come.

Jeane turned to Lew, Delia's assistant, and hugged him. Their lips met in a torrid display.

Ritter mumbled a curse under his breath. I knew exactly what he felt. Yes, there was definitely history behind that kiss.

Cort pushed up from where he'd been kneeling next to the body of a fallen guard. Shaking plaster from his hair, he picked his way toward us through the pieces of concrete from the demolished walls. "Stella just got through to me. She and Jace are downstairs with a vehicle. Stella says to get down fast while everyone's still in a panic. They're evacuating the hotel. She's spread a rumor over the Internet about a gas leak, but bloggers are claiming an airplane hit the building and it's about to collapse."

"Let's go," Ritter said, his hand wrapping around mine.

"What about Shadrach?" I asked. But the closet area where he'd been lying was completely gone, shattered into a million pieces.

A police chopper chose that moment to zoom by, directing us to evacuate if we could. Asking if there were wounded. A stupid question when there were at least eight prone guards lying among the rubble as well as Delia's mutilated corpse.

A news crew was close on the police chopper's tail, and I was stunned to see Walker Anderson peering down at me from a window. He was grinning. We averted our faces as the police ordered the news chopper away.

"Uh, we have a problem." Keene pointed at Lew and Jeane, both of whom had picked up assault rifles and were pointing them at us.

Ritter rolled his eyes, but Jeane's next words stopped him. "I'm nulling all your abilities." Even as she spoke, my senses went dark. Behind me, Mari gasped as she apparently tried to shift and failed.

"Lew can get inside your minds now," Jeane continued. "Your shields won't be strong enough to keep him out. If you try to fight back, you'll be in more pain than you can imagine. Even if some of you manage to escape, you won't all get away. And we'll make sure to kill any wounded you leave behind. Permanently."

"You can't be serious," Cort said.

Heat flushed Ritter's face. "You *want* to stay with the Emporium?"

Jeane rolled her neck and gave a little laugh. "Of course. It was only Delia I wanted to get rid of."

"We can't let you stay with them." Ritter's grim expression was frightening. "You'd use your ability against us."

"Well, I don't see that you have a choice." Jeaned looked at her companion. "Right, Lew?"

I met Lew's eyes with a sneer. "You're just changing one master for another, aren't you?" He didn't reply.

"Shut up," Jeane said.

I really should have killed her.

Jeane gave me her stupid movie-star grin. "Better give up now, Erin, or you'll have more than your grandmother to mourn. I promise, I'll see that the Emporium treats you as well as you treated me."

Her comment about my grandmother hit me like a sword to the stomach, twisting in deep. No way was it going to end like this. We'd all rather die than end up as Emporium prisoners, even without Delia ruling the Triad. Reaching deep, I stretched my arms toward the floor, absorbing nutrients as fast as possible. Jeane's ability was just like any other, and now, without Delia draining me, I might be able to block her. *I am strong enough.* I had to be. I waited, gathering everything I could absorb. I might not have more than one chance.

"Let's go," Jeane said, motioning in the direction of the hallway with her rifle.

Concentrating on Jeane's deadening influence, I brought up my arms, using the physical gesture to focus my thoughts. And shoved back. Hard.

Abruptly, my senses jumped into life again. I extended my shield around Ritter and the others. I couldn't break through Lew's impressive mind shield, but I could stop him from hurting my friends' minds and maybe deflect a few bullets. My shield might even eliminate Jeane's effect on them. Maybe.

I grinned at Jeane. "I don't think so." To Ritter, I added under my breath. "Get him." Even with Jeane blocking Ritter's ability, I'd bet on him any day against that scrawny pinhead.

Ritter didn't hesitate. He launched himself at Lew even as I went for Jeane. They fired, but we'd taken them completely by surprise, and the bullets went astray. Or maybe they were just inept, having depended all their very long lives on others to protect them.

I landed on Jeane and knocked her to the ground. Ripping the gun from her, I tossed it aside. She was kicking and punching and yelling obscenities. "Nighty night," I said. I put my hand on her throat in exactly the right spot, just as Ritter had taught me.

"What do you know?" I said, as her body went limp a few minutes later, "it really works." I glanced around and saw that Ritter had also made short work of Lew, who lay unconscious on the ground.

Rising, I started to pick Jeane up, to carry her out and down to our waiting car.

The next second, the *rat-a-tat-tat* of machine gun fire made me duck. Ritter came toward me at full speed, grabbing me with his good arm and hurrying me out of the way as bullets sprayed into the rubble-strewn carpet behind us. From the corner of my eye, I caught a glimpse of yet another chopper, this time stamped with what looked like Morocco's royal seal. Either Jeane hadn't been lying about her connection with the ruling family or the Emporium did have some very high connections here.

We caught up with Keene and Cort in the gaping doorway. As the chopper angled for a better position, we helped the brothers get the plutonium past the rubble in the penthouse to the outer hallway, which still had its ceiling. I was relieved to be hidden from the royal chopper, until more bullets sprayed above us, some ripping through the roof.

We ran for the stairs, where Mari had shifted and was waiting. When we made it to the main floor, we found more pandemonium. People ran in all directions, some lugging suitcases, others with children in their arms. There were no hotel employees in sight and no police officers or rescue workers. Apparently, fear of the building's possible collapse outweighed the importance of their duty.

Jace appeared out of the crowd. "This way." He pushed a luggage cart toward us, where we deposited the cask, and soon we were running through a hallway to a deserted kitchen and down a ramp where Stella waited nearby with the SUV.

There was a crowd even here, milling around a body lying in some rubble. I hoped it was one of the Emporium guards that had fallen during the blast or the ensuing battle and not some innocent bystander hit by tumbling debris. Regardless, I didn't know how the Emporium, the Renegades, or the US government would be able to cover up what had happened here.

HOURS LATER, AFTER WE'D SAFELY HANDED OFF THE PLUTONIUM TO CIA agents, our group gathered in the sitting room in another of Basilio's properties and stared with concern at a television and three different laptops. We watched as continuous news coverage spread out over the world. Walker Anderson, who had fled after Mari had come to warn Stella and Jace, was the center of attention. He had video of Desoto's guard in Texas coming back to life, of Delia's body and blurry figures on top of the ruined hotel. He had Stella's decoder, which was being examined by some of the most brilliant minds in the mortal world. With this "proof" came his story of a race of long-lived people and the strange powers they held.

"They won't believe him," Mari said, obviously afraid of what it would do to us if they did.

Stella shook her head. "They *will* believe him because there are several similar reports from people who found remains of the Emporium guards that fell off the roof. Dead, but not quite. The ones we left on the rooftop—and Jeane— are conveniently missing, but apparently the others were left behind."

She blinked behind the eyepiece of her neural headset, and the display on one of the laptops changed. "This report says the Moroccan government has several of the guards under constant surveillance, and while they are definitely dead, their tissue is regenerating. We have doctors claiming that it might be the beginning of a cure for all ailments, and conspiracy theorists saying it's either an alien invasion or a zombie virus."

We all groaned. I didn't know whether to run in fear of how the mortals would react or hope that somehow it would be all right.

"Ava's on the phone with the president now," Dimitri said. "I think at this point it's more of a what-to-say situation than how to cover it up."

"Then this is it." I was glad to be wedged in on the love seat between Ritter and Dimitri, the two most important men in my life besides the man who'd raised me. It was hard to believe this was really happening, and it must be stranger to them, especially to Dimitri, who had kept the Unbounded secret for a millennia. "The mortals will hate us once it gets out about the plutonium." So far, Walker was the only one talking about that, but the employees we'd saved in Venezuela were bound to confirm at least the existence of the plutonium.

"We need damage control," Cort said from his seat next to Stella on the couch opposite us. Beside Cort, Keene nodded silently. He'd been quiet since learning that two passersby had been killed by debris from the hotel explosion, and nothing we said seemed to shake him out of it.

Mari settled somewhat awkwardly on the armrest next to Dimitri, chewing on a fingernail. "Will we have to stay in hiding?"

"From the Emporium, at least. If they take over." Jace stood by the television near the heavily curtained window. Every so often, he'd peek out, as if expecting reporters or police at Basilio's main residence across the street, but it was already one in the afternoon—seven hours after we'd gone to the hotel—and no one had come. It appeared that Walker had chosen not to name us.

"Taking over won't be as easy without the money," Dimitri said.

Ava swept into the room wearing an off-white suit, exuding her usual confidence, her hair swept up in an elaborate twist at the back of her head. "President Mann is going to make an announcement. Now that we've recovered the plutonium and averted the war, he and his staff feel—and I agree—that the best thing we can do is to confirm the existence of Unbounded." She raised a finger and added, "With some . . . well, variations. Obviously, he won't be detailing our long war with the Emporium."

"But isn't that what the Emporium wanted?" Mari asked. "To tell the world about Unbounded? Does this mean they're going to be able to take over the government?"

Ava shook her head. "Remember the documents you got from Desoto's? Well, the president is about to make some very prominent arrests—mostly those people the Emporium has put in place to further their agenda. If there has ever been a time when we have the upper hand, that time is now."

Ritter chuckled, the first sign of levity I'd seen from him since the battle. "You're saying they won't have sufficient people left in high places to be able to take control."

Ava shared his grin. "That's exactly what I'm hoping."

"He's on now," Stella said. The laptop facing us on the coffee table turned to an image of President Mann. Seconds later the local television station switched to the same image.

"That was fast," Jace said, coming to sit on the floor near the love seat. "It's just after eight in the morning there, right? Kind of early for this sort of thing."

"No one in the White House went to bed last night." Ava

remained standing, but she moved closer to the couch to get a better view of the two laptops facing Stella.

On the screen, the camera closed in on the press secretary as he stepped to the podium on a stage. His eyes were bloodshot, and his hair wasn't quite in place. By the looks of things, he'd had a rough night. "The president is here to address the events that occurred in Morocco last night while most of America was sleeping. He will not take questions at this time. Afterward, I will read a statement. Again, questions will not be permitted. However, we will hold another press conference tomorrow and will be answering questions then. Mr. President." With apparent relief, the press secretary stepped back from the podium as the president came forward.

As usual, President Vincent Mann was a compelling figure. His dark head was balding, but he exuded strength, confidence, and vitality. The American people had grown to love him these past weeks since he'd taken over for President Stevens after his illness, and everyone was sure he'd win the next election. I hadn't been a fan at all until I'd met his son, Patrick, but I knew now that Vincent Mann was sincere in his duties and obligations. He wasn't perfect, but he was on our side.

"I am here," President Mann began, "to both confirm and correct some allegations that have been made regarding the events in Morocco. First, I want to confirm that we have found a gene in some people that allows them to live extended lives. Even up to two thousand years."

The room around him went crazy. Reporters blurted questions, cameras flashed, and people waved their recorders. President Mann waited until the hubbub died.

"You all know the story that came to light several weeks

ago when I became President of the United States. How we discovered that our biological son had been mixed up at birth and adopted by others, and how the son we loved and raised as our own nearly died in a skydiving accident a few months ago. I have appreciated your support through his recovery and through our reunion with our biological son. But there is more to the story. Patrick, the son we raised, is one of these long-lived people. The Unboundaried, or Unbounded, as they call themselves. Because of this, his life was threatened, and he has since been living in Europe for his safety. However, he'll be here with me tomorrow to answer your questions."

"The face of the Unbounded," I whispered. If anyone could do it, it would be Patrick Mann. He was a technopath like Stella and would have access to all the media references in the world. He could instantly scan psychology posts and review how people reacted to crises in history. He'd know how to calm fears.

"This is all new to Patrick as well. As you can imagine, he was just as surprised as the rest of us when he realized that he was different, but after learning about it these past weeks, I am confident that this evolution, or whatever it is, will be something we as a people will successfully face together. Many changes will be in store, but we will remain united. These people have talents, dreams, and a love of family as any of us do, and I believe they will be—and have already been—a boon to our society."

He paused for the applause, but the room was silent. Then murmuring voices rose in fear, followed by a raised shout. "What about the plutonium? Were these Unbounded really going to sell it to Iran to start a war?"

The gathered crowd all reacted at once, hollering and

waving to get his attention. President Mann held up a hand for silence. "No questions, please. Save them for tomorrow, when we will all know better what questions to ask. However, the plutonium rumor is the second item on today's very short list, so I will speak to that." A welcome murmur ran through the reporters.

"Some time ago," Mann continued, "we had some reports about weapons-grade plutonium being illegally produced and sold. Last night we seized two shipments, one in Venezuela and one in Morocco. Naturally, we couldn't announce any of this until we had successfully completed the operation. We are currently working to dismantle the factory with the Venezuelan government and clean the surrounding area, which has been contaminated. We have also offered Morocco our help in bringing to justice those who have brought chaos to Casablanca. Having experienced similar terrorist attacks, we understand their outrage."

Mann's voice grew quiet as he looked down, sorrow filling his face. "Greed—plain and simple—was the reason for this brazen, immoral attack on world peace, and we have issued twenty-seven arrest warrants for those involved. We are confident that the documents we possess will result in charges of treason. More arrests are pending. I am saddened to say that eighteen of those people serve in our government."

Another murmur broke out and more hands rose. Mann ignored the hands, staring gravely over the crowd. "While it's true at least one of those being charged is Unbounded, most are like us. That's right, our own people betrayed us." His voice grew in volume. "There were also several Unbounded who were responsible for capturing the pluto-nium and bringing it to safety, and we are all deeply in their debt. To them, I say, thank you. Thank you for risking your lives. That's all for today. We will be spending time in the next days, weeks, and months with world leaders to decide where to go from here." He paused, but not long enough for the questions to come. "Greed is a terrible thing, my friends. But we are one nation"—he held up a finger over his head—"one nation, however diverse our people. This is a new era, to be sure, and we will face it with courage and justice for all. Thank you."

Ignoring the flurry of comments and questions that predictably followed his words, he turned and left the stage, replaced by the press secretary, who began discussing possible medical advancements that might come through studying Unbounded.

Jace made a face. "They're going to have us under a microscope."

"Not us," Ava said. "Patrick Mann. Be glad he's willing. The rest of us are going to lie low until they get some legislation through. There's going to be widespread panic, no matter how beautiful the president's speech."

"It was beautiful," Dimitri put in. He gave her a steady look. "I hope he thanked you for writing it."

Ava lifted one shoulder in a half shrug. "He did."

"Any word about Shadrach?" Keene asked.

Stella's face grew somber. "They found him. He's in the hospital, and I'd like Dimitri to take a look at him. At any rate, he'll have to face justice for his actions."

I could still see Habid's falling head as the closet door swung open. If Shadrach hadn't betrayed us, would I have opened the door and killed Habid? Or would I have seen the plan in Delia's mind and saved him? In the end, it really didn't matter because he would have died in the explosion.

"I understand why he did it," I said. "I don't agree, but I understand why."

"We all know why he did it." Ava gave me a wistful smile, and her surface thoughts told me she was thinking of our own situation with my grandmother. I'd told Ava about her bravery. It made me feel better about her death somehow. I was proud of her. We both were.

"Oh, no, look at this." Stella switched all the laptops to another station, where a group of Hunters were beginning their own press conference. Their timing made me wonder if they'd hoped to beat the president to the announcement. I knew the Hunters' comments would be full of hate and prejudice, but they would stop short of admitting how many Unbounded they had murdered during their fifty-odd years of hunting.

Ava sighed. "We already know what they're going to say. Start posting about witch hunts and race persecution, linking them with current ideals held by the Hunters. That'll help mitigate their comments."

"On it." Stella's headset began blinking. "I'll have our allies do the same."

Ava folded her arms and stared down at us. "I think just maybe, with a lot of damage control, we'll be okay." Her sense of relief was palpable. Finally the mortals knew. Eventually, they'd understand the stakes and support our cause.

"You know," Jace said, "if we survive this, we might just become in high demand. Employers won't have to waste so much time training and finding new employees or have to pay medical or dental insurance. Different abilities will be sought for different reasons. People will be willing to pay." He brightened. "I might even be able to get a date."

"I think maybe we'd better leave the whole ability thing

out of it," I said. As it was, I was unsure how we could avoid an eventual caste system from forming, especially if people learned the truth about some of our gifts.

"Agreed," Ritter said.

Stella looked up from her laptop. "That's what I'm hearing from everyone. We already have enough challenges ahead. Walker has made some statements about abilities, but he doesn't really know enough to make trouble—and I doubt any of us will fill him in. It will all become apparent eventually, but meanwhile we don't need people scanning the sky for Superman."

I glanced at Keene, because I'd been wondering if changing atoms could make levitation possible for him. He met my gaze, but when he spoke it wasn't about abilities. "I think," he said, "that it's time to go home."

EVERYONE DID GO HOME. EXCEPT RITTER AND ME, WHO UPON OUR arrival in San Diego at midnight, drove to the tallest hotel in the city and rented a corner room with a double balcony. We had an impressive view of the city lights from one balcony and a fabulous, dizzying view of the ocean from the other. I couldn't get enough of it. I felt free, as if I were flying. Stella's nanites were at work, there was no Delia between Ritter and me, and I felt ready for anything.

I did experience an occasional flash that I knew came from Delia's memories, but I was sure that was because of what I'd seen in her energy stream rather than any psychic residue. Memories, just like those I'd gathered from other people. They might become useful one day.

Ritter approached me where I stood at the balcony

railing, the slight breeze from the ocean whipping my sheer nightgown around my thighs. It was a little cold, but it was so breathtakingly beautiful that I didn't want to go inside. He wrapped his warm arms around me and kissed my neck. I rotated toward him, loving the shudders he sent up my skin and throughout my body. As I kissed him deeply, he responded, dropping his mind shield. Everything we had become to each other was apparent in his touch, in his thoughts. Together we rode a wave of emotion.

Abruptly, he stopped kissing me and pushed his face into my neck. "I thought I was going to have to kill you," he said, his voice low and tortured. "Permanently."

"I know." I lifted his head so I could see his eyes. "I would have rather you do that than let her control my body."

He nodded. "That's why I would have done it."

We were silent a moment, until I said, "What now? The world has gone crazy." We weren't in hiding anymore, but every sign told us that it was going to be rough for a while—a long while.

Ritter's fingers trailed over my back. "Now we pick up the pieces."

"We're getting pretty good at that."

"Right now, I only want to be good at one thing." He lowered his mouth to mine. "I'm going to make love to you all night. All week. Maybe every day for the rest of my life."

I wrapped my arms around him. "I know."

THE END

OUTTAKE

RITTER'S PHILOSOPHY

Ritter was never without at least a dozen weapons, except during training, and he insisted we all remain constantly ready with our own weapons. If he had his way, he'd arm teachers, mothers, fathers, and every other responsible citizen in the entire nation, and train them. That way, the next time a drugged-up youth appeared in a school to shoot innocent kids or opened fire in a mall, the victims would be able to defend themselves. That went double for any attack by the Emporium. He believed—and I agreed—that a nation who allowed itself to be disarmed by its leaders was asking for domination.

TEYLA BRANTON GREW UP AVIDLY READING SCIENCE FICTION AND
fantasy and watching Star Trek reruns with her large family.
They lived on a little farm where she loved to visit the soli-
tary cow and collect (and juggle) the eggs, usually making it
back to the house with most of them intact. On that same
farm she once owned thirty-three gerbils and eighteen cats,
not a good mix, as it turns out. Teyla always had her nose
in a book and daydreamed about someday creating her own
worlds.

Teyla is now married, mostly grown up, and has seven
kids, including a one-year-old, so life at her house can be
very interesting (and loud), but writing keeps her sane.
She thrives on the energy and daily amusement offered by
her children, the semi-ordered chaos giving her a constant
source of writing material. Grabbing any snatch of free time
from her hectic life, Teyla writes novels, often with a child
on her lap. She warns her children that if they don't behave,
they just might find themselves in her next book! She's been
known to wear pajamas all day when working on a deadline,

and is often distracted enough to burn dinner. (Okay, pretty much 90% of the time.) A sign on her office door reads: DANGER. WRITER AT WORK. ENTER AT YOUR OWN RISK.

She loves writing fiction and traveling, and she hopes to write and travel a lot more. She also loves shooting guns, martial arts, and belly dancing. She has worked in the publishing business for over twenty years. Teyla also writes romance and suspense under the name Rachel Branton. For more information, please visit http://www.TeylaBranton.com.

CPSIA information can be obtained at www.ICGtesting.com
Printed in the USA
LVOW05s2135011014

406884LV00012B/268/P

9 781939 203472